Gibraltar

Gibraltar

The Conquest of Iberia

Shariq Ali Khan

authorHOUSE®

AuthorHouse™
1663 Liberty Drive
Bloomington, IN 47403
www.authorhouse.com
Phone: 1-800-839-8640

Published by AuthorHouse   02/27/2013

ISBN: 978-1-4817-8564-8 (sc)
ISBN: 978-1-4817-8565-5 (e)

This book is printed on acid-free paper.

Contents

Dedicated to those
Whom I share my heritage with

A note from the author:

The story in this book is based on historic events that are well known. Intricate details however are ambiguous and much of the knowledge about the exact development is hypothetical. Historians will always debate these issues as they are subject to much controversy even among experts. Therefore elaborate description and occurrence of persons, places, buildings, landscapes and also partly the events are derived from the author's imagination to fill the gaps and make the narrative livelier. In all cases however these fictive elements suit the bigger picture. The author has conducted extensive research into this period of history before and while writing this book. The full truth will only be known on one final day! We can only try our best to document it . . .

Foreword

Dear Reader,

Before I leave you to travel into a completely different era and float through the stream of time experiencing an adventure as I wish it to be, let me briefly explain why I have chosen to write this book and how I have written it. The idea came about when my brother and I were looking for Muslim role-models other than the most obvious ones, the Prophet Mohammed (peace be upon him[1], pbuh) and his Companions. Most definitely Tariq Ibn Ziyad fits the picture very well. With the permission of the Almighty, he managed to do something very unique. He conquered land that previously belonged to another civilisation and was welcomed by the natives with open arms. Not only that, but he freed them from tyranny and oppression on their own request within a very short period of time, while the presence of his army, the conquerors and descendents, lasted for many centuries. It was perhaps the most fruitful, productive and constructive period of history mankind has ever witnessed.

Surely this man must have been very different from us today. It takes not only courage, determination, strength and passion but also wisdom, patience, knowledge and leadership to do what he did. As a matter of fact it has been argued by immanent historians and military experts that Tariq Ibn Ziyad must have been the most brilliant strategist and military leader ever. Not even Alexander the Great, Napoleon Bonaparte, Hannibal or Cesar could outdo his achievement of conquering Gothic

---

[1]   Muslim attribute for Prophets to send blessings on them and indicate one's peace with their teachings.

Hispania, the whole Iberian Peninsula with 5000-7000 odd men within a handful of years. I must vehemently disagree. In my opinion he was not the best, but only second to our Prophet Mohammed (pbuh). And both didn't just use military tactics. Both worked with emotion and reason, hearts and minds, people and power and under guidance of Allah, the Almighty, of course!

What Tariq Ibn Ziyad did was certainly outstanding though. At the same time he could never have done it alone. There are definite gaps in the knowledge about that period of time and the events surrounding this conquest. I have spent many months researching, studying and comparing the sources and filled in the gaps in the most logical and plausible manner I could. Quite naturally there are elements of fiction in my story, more or less similar to Homer, Shakespeare or Goethe, although I definitely don't want to put myself into the same category as them!

Apart from that I feel that a story like this cannot be the mere result of my own writing. At a very early stage it took over. It overwhelmed me. It developed a self-dynamics and came to life. I lived for it and I thought, breathed and spoke for it. Night and day. It demanded a lot of sacrifice! I definitely do not believe it is revealed, but it is most certainly inspired by sources unseen. I pray the good ones under guidance of the Almighty, not the bad ones under guidance of the Evil one, whom He created to test us. The nature of the story would not allow it to be a mere product of my imagination alone. Nothing is. Everything is under some sort of guidance, good or bad.

By no means do I claim to grasp the absolute truth! Art is not meant to be that way. Any work of art can be looked at like a statue. You take the raw material and mould it into shape and the approximate outline is ready very quickly. After that a lot of time and effort is spent on completing the intricate details, sand-papering the surfaces, hammering and slicing into the gaps. The longer you take for that, the better it gets, to a certain extent, after which you start distorting it and over-producing, so that the quality would rather diminish than improve. Knowing when to stop is an intricate art in itself and requires a lot of experience, for the perfectionist can be the biggest enemy of his own work. I have tried to stop at the right moment.

This story is naturally polarised. Tariq is its hero and Roderick is its villain. The evil reign and tragic end of Roderick the Terrible can be compared to Hitler, although the Hispanic Visigoths might no longer have been real Germans (neither was Hitler), but rather a mixed tribe, perhaps with predominantly Germanic or Scandinavian features amongst the gentry and monarchy.

German-Muslim relations are slightly different from Anglo-Islamic relations. During a later epoch Frederic Barabarossa who intended to approach Jerusalem during the 3rd Crusade is said to have drowned in a shallow stream between Italy and Syria and the whole German army went home. That is in slight contrast to what Richard the Lionheart did, although the confrontation between Richard and Saladdin is said to be one of mutual respect more than anything else. Centuries later after that the Ottoman occupation of Vienna represented another brief clash of civilisations, after which all German rulers were in coalition with Muslims in one way or the other, while Anglicans ruled imperialistically over large parts of Muslim land. The French did so in North Africa of course, disturbed only briefly by Mountbatten and Rommel.

A few things I actually find quite fascinating about the Goths. First of all their origins[2], which are shrouded in mystery. Some say they crossed from Scandinavia like Vikings, or from the Baltic Islands to the Baltics, or even the Ukraine, Poland and then Eastern Germany and so on. Others insist they are originally Germans, collated Germanic tribes. There is wild and far-reaching speculation about their actual ancestry.

Another very important aspect is their primary choice of religion. After leaving paganism (as it is understood today) they didn't follow Catholicism or mainstream Christianity as it was at that time from the beginning on. They were initially Arianic, following Arius of Alexandria's teachings of one God and Jesus (pbuh) being his Messenger rather than heir or son or his equal. Hence it might be argued from an Islamic perspective that their initial success over Trinitarian Rome was actually

---

2   Where Did the Goths Come From, Michael Kulikowski Explains That Our Main Source Shouldn't Be Trusted, http://ancienthistory.about.com/od/jordanes/a/GothOrigins.htm

based on a non-Trinitarian, more blessed approach. Moreover, since their rise occurred during the 3rd-4th century AD, one could say from an Islamic perspective that they were actually the bearers of truth in an age when Rome had deviated from true Nazarene Christianity, which was like Islam. Had it not been for them upholding true Monotheism (besides the rare Jews), Mohammed (pbuh) might have been sent earlier to re-deliver the message of the unity of Allah. Later on however towards the end of the 7th century the Goths were rapidly converting to Catholicism, perhaps a reason for their downfall as they gradually succumbed to average Trinitarian Christianity.

This might be mere speculation, but interesting nevertheless. Last but not least, the Goths were for many centuries the dominating civilisation in Europe and like their origins are dubious, so is their downfall. For a very long time they might have been just and prosperous. After that they merely sunk into the pits and dark dungeons of history, assimilated by Franks, Arabs, Romans and Vikings. In any case the Goths were very strange and mysterious people, which is the reason why even today there is a dark youth-culture based around their name, even a whole music-genre and fashion style, "Goth", the "Goths" or "Gothic". Of course Gothic architecture has survived in medieval buildings and churches as well as a romanticist late 19th century revival of such.

I believe in the collective memory of a people. The Muslim Conquest of Iberia has left its marks in the European psyche with clear contributions to the sciences such as Mathematics, Medicine, Chemistry, Astronomy, etc. Technologies such as windmills and watermills thrived and spread across Europe through the Moors. It also had its repercussion in constitutions such as the Magna Charta, the basic constitutional laws of European constitutions, even the USA and the morality and attitude of people and nations. The Koran contributed at least equally as much as the Bible to European civilisation, this can be proven as I believe. Naturally of course much of the morality of these two books is the same.

There is this peculiar relationship and unnecessary conflict between two forces that we call the West and the East. Germans called it "das Abendland und das Morgenland," others call it Greco-Roman-Occident and Islamic-Orient or yet others Judeo-Christian and Muslim. The relationship between these two is at the centre of focus now more than ever before. Therefore I see this story in a particularly modern context. It is extremely relevant to the current political climate.

Why did I write a lengthy Prologue and choose to put it at the end? It is because I wanted to describe the historic context in precision and the developments immediately preceding the Conquest of Iberia and how it came about. It is decisively relevant. Also the choice of this topic is significant. I put the Prologue at the end because I did not want to scare off any reader who might not be interested in factual history. So anyone who is interested in it should read the Prologue first before he reads the book. But I wished to describe what is commonly viewed in the "West" as "Spreading Islam by the sword", explain it more intricately and intensely. I was once a pacifist, but I find that particular form of Pacifism to be quite alien to the truth by now.

As for the early Middle Ages, there was a lot of blatant violence in those times. It was just a question of "why, for which cause and how". This is why I am not ashamed to say, that this is a war novel. At the same time it is philosophical, historical and theological, dealing with comparative theology in particular. An action-packed treaty, if you wish, of early Islamic morality and success, eagerly overcoming the post-9/11 passivity of Muslims suffering under an artificial stereo-typical label.

There's a time and a place for everything. We all want justice and freedom. And for that we're allowed to fight, we are expected to fight. May it be with words or with weapons. My choice is quite obvious; I write. Just to prevent misunderstandings let me say, if it comes to violence inevitably I believe in the battlefield though, not in the suicide-belt. I support the man-to-man combat and not the pushing of buttons from the air or afar, hence killing honour, depriving people of a fair chance. I am not a radical, fanatic or extremist, so I would never kill anyone for my opinion outside the battlefield. I am a fundamentalist though as I believe in the fundaments of Islam and I believe that Islam is fundamentally and absolutely the truth in its core, mal-practiced by many albeit. And it is the original form of all religions!

With this statement allow me to release you into a time long gone, a lesson to be learnt, whose morality is that if we were still the same as back then, we would be better, more pleasing to other people. We would also be more pleasing to the One who sent us, who didn't want Islam to dominate all the while so there would still be a choice against it. What would be the point in the individual seeking and searching for the truth, if Muslims were omnipotent in worldly terms? This is why we are "like scum on the oceans blown apart by the tide"[3]. Muslims have gotten their priorities entirely wrong by now and need vehement rectification. Their moral expectations are far beyond their actual standards and practice. They are more repelling to seekers of truth than attractive. They are not worse than others though, I wouldn't go that far. The majority are harmless farmers and some are very noble people.

Islamic dogma however being the unequivocal and eternal truth is there to be grasped by each-and-everyone who can, as is Muslim history.

I hope you enjoy this piece of history.

Yours truly,

Shariq Ali Khan
February 2013

---

[3] Remark of the Prophet Mohammed (peace be upon him) when asked about the Muslims of the later Ages, he said they would be weak, not because of their rare numbers but because they would be…

The Start

"And why should you not fight in the cause of Allah and of those who, being weak, are ill-treated (and oppressed)?—Men, women, and children, whose cry is: "Our Lord! Rescue us from this town, whose people are oppressors; and raise for us from your people one who will protect us; and raise for us from your people one who will help us!"
Surah 4 (Women) Verse 75

Sparkling jewels like rubies and coral surfacing the waters spread by waves across the ocean perpetually pounding the coast. At the feet of the cliffs ships lay one after another as far as vision could reach; lofty sails ready to take the load across the Straight under clear blue skies, deep as the eyes of the people of the North, where across the narrow passage of the seas rose cliffs shrouded in a cloud of mystery. In fact they were always like that. The land of the Vandals had never lain bare its secrets easily. It needed to be conquered, accessed. It needed to be eased of its burden eternally: The darkness.

A tall impressive man signalled for prayer-time. He came from across the desert with the tribes of the Fulani in East Africa, and the Mandinka from Timbuktu in Mali, master seamen who were one day soon to cross the Atlantic and find new land beyond the seas, centuries later during the Inquisition to be condemned as captains of the fleet of Columbus carrying him to the Americas. Imam Bilal Al-Din, engulfed in white garment with his head wrapped in a bright light blue turban found the highest point and lifted his shining black-blue hand, swiftly waving it to and fro high towards the sky, towering above the cliffs where the armies had assembled. Immediately his signal was followed in the most harmonious and enchanting, yet confident and commanding manner by the mesmerising and irresistible call to prayer.

Warriors, rushing by from all sides, dismounting their horses, laying down their weapons, started to take off their hard armour, to reveal their soft cloaks and replaced the helmets with turbans that were hanging down in long red rich brocade. White and red, that was the colour of battle. White being the garment of burial, red, the blood from the wound gushing forth from a fresh cut, ready to fight, eager to win, keen to die in the cause of Allah.

"Straighten your lines and close your gaps", the Muslim warriors understood precisely what that meant, shoulder to shoulder, foot to foot, feet as far apart as shoulders were wide, precise formation as in battle, symbolising strength, discipline, control, order and unity in faith. Even an inch of gap was a gift to Satan, a symbol of repulsion from each other, a sign of discord. There was no gap that day. Sadly it has grown ever since. The Jews and Christians stood behind them, raising their hands, kneeling, sitting, whichever way their subsequent faith commanded them, with scrolls, the People of the Book.

What made this scene unique though was that all faiths joined in a special Council prayer, the Istikhara, after the noon prayer. A bright smile on the faces in light of the enormous task facing the army made the whole scene too bizarre for a battle, while the lines to the side grew longer and longer, everyone keen to be in the front lines. Pure bliss lighted up their faces, kindled by the bright shine from the aura of the Prophet (pbuh) that was still immanent and omnipresent in those times. It was the smile of joy of the warrior who fights for truth and justice. It has eversince faded gradually throughout the centuries, turned into bitterness in the face of defeat, a defeat caused by deviation. But that very day, in this very manner over 5000 men stood in prayer. Passing by the lines one could see the soldiers glowing, waxed together at four points, arms tied tightly, perfect posture, proud stance, yet lowly spirit, the mode of victory! Bilal spoke and the men behind him repeated his words as they had done throughout the prayer to carry his words through the lines:

"O Allah we seek your council by your knowledge and by your Power. We seek strength and ask you from your immense favour. For verily you are able while we are not, and verily you know while we know not, as you are the Knower of the unseen. O Allah, if you know this affair of crossing this sea and conquering the land of the Vandals to be good for us in relation to our religion, our life and end, then decree and facilitate it for us and bless us with it. And if you know this affair to be ill for us in relation to our religion, our life and end, then remove it from us and remove us from it. And decree for us what is good, and whatever it may be make us satisfied with such."

With these words that he had spoken into the palms of his raised hands in front of his face, the Imam Bilal blew the words into his hands, stroke his palms over his face and chest and wiped the vapour of his breath over his head, because in the vapour is water and on water lies the Throne of Allah. Life He created out of water and through water he reigns, chooses to reign, over the people, Hydrogen existing in abundance over all spheres of the universe.

And so he concluded "Allah, the Greatest" and raised his hands once again over his ears to tie them tightly over his chest and conducted the Guidance prayer, after which he concluded: "Alif Lam Mim, Ya Allah, Ya Ali, Ya Hei, Ya Qaijoum, Ya Ahad, Ya Samad, Ya Baqi, Ya Badi ....", from the Koran's mystical letters. Afterwards he counted the 99 names of Allah to remind the congregation and himself of his divine characteristics. O Allah, o Living One, o Self Subsisting One, o Unique One, o Eternal One, o Enduring One, o Remaining One . . .

All of a sudden a fair man stood up from the congregation and stepped hastily at first, then running stride, to the front of the lines, climbed up to the highest point overviewing the Sea and the Straight with the distant dark cliffs behind his back on the other side, that would one day be known by his name, the sun being in his face during these midday hours. His dark red eye brows and his shining light-brown beard waving in the wind like his cloak and his turban with the white flags on top of the spears behind him in the mild summer breeze, his hazel eyes staring across the lines, serious, determined and committed, yet soft and compassionate towards his men:

"O men of Allah. A letter was sent to me from the Sultan, our ruler Alwalid, son of Abdulmalik. I cannot resist his command, his command is my will. People call me his slave. Let me tell you how I came to live in his palace. When I was a young boy, 5 years of age, my elderly parents embraced Islam and the village expelled them, being of pagan Berber origin, they worshipped the sun and the ocean and the mountains. We walked for days and days and then were taken as slaves by Bedouins who gave us food, drink and clothes and took us East to a big city."

The scenes of his childhood passed by him again, pale but beautiful moments of the past.

"I had never seen so many people. The market was crowded when we were marched up and the Sultan's people surrounded the slave traders, restricting them from using their whips on us by holding sticks between them and us, ensuring that none of us was hurt. The Sultan Abdulmalik came and asked my father where we came from. My father spoke no Arabic and the Sultan ordered translators. He heard our story and offered us freedom after serving him in the palace. There we lived among his family and staff for many years learning Islam, languages, science and arts until my parents passed away in his arms and received a burial in his family cemetery. Still, those were the happiest moments of my life.

I was in the same group as the sons of the Sultan, eating, sleeping and living with them, being treated the same way, if not better. We never lacked anything and the Sultan made sure every week that we got to speak to him our minds. Never did we have any complaints. Never did he ask us for anything we did not do with pleasure. Never did he not call me 'my small brother from the hills'. Never did he not embrace me. Never did he not teach me a new verse from the Koran or a story from the Prophet (pbuh), his own great-Uncle. Not a single time did he not smile when we met him once a week, unless he was out travelling, building mosques such as you have seen, the reconstruction of the temple of Solomon in Jerusalem, Dome of the Rock, the University of Cairo, Al Azhar. He also went away to invite distant tribes of the deserts, the mountains and the seas to join us in Islam, this beautiful new life".

A glistening tear escaped his eyes, he just wiped it aside.

"Now the same Sultan's son Alwalid has asked me for a favour for the first time in my life. I would call it not a favour but a pleasure to me. He is like my Brother. He is to go East and North towards Sindh and Azerbaijan. He has told me I am free to take the West and the lands across the sea. By Allah, I would not follow him for one second longer, if I was not certain, that he is submitted to our eternal Creator and Sustainer. You have heard how excellently he recites and quotes from the Koran and how precisely he implements it and acts according to it. I am confirmed in my position again and again. He has this special urge for justice and truth that none of us could match. And I believe this is the reason why he was chosen as our leader. I do not believe anyone should be ruler merely for his lineage. I believe each leader has to prove himself, and that is the hard task, the special duty of and burden on the one who inherits the throne! Believe me; he has proven himself again and again and many of you, who have prayed behind him and served under him, have witnessed it. He has just commissioned a new mosque in Damascus as well.

O men of Allah, the land has dried out. Not even your grandfathers remember a time when you had crops from the plains South of these mountains, unless beyond the big desert. We have been pressed to the ocean for food. O men of Allah, as the Northern-Christians among you will witness, (a senior monk Julian-Urban of Ceuta at the back of the lines looked up and then down in sadness) the lands where they were sent from, have been conquered by wild hoards of the North. They came centuries ago from the lands afar you may never have heard of, the Northway, Dansk and Sverge, crossed into Poland and Germany and now they rule Hispania, Gaulle, Rome and the Balkans. There were many just kings among them but now they have deviated. They are tall, fearsome and strong people, hard but stiff as steel. "Their hearts are hard," and here he quoted the Koran, *"Even harder than rocks, for among rocks there are some from which rivers gush forth; others there are which when split asunder send forth water; and others which sink for fear of Allah."*
Surah 2 (the Heifer) Verse 74.

O men of Allah, your Christian Brothers fled from the lands across the sea and asked the Sultan for help and he sent them to me for in battle I was the best, the Sultan said. And I ask you to challenge me here and now, if you don't think I deserve this title and he can take over leadership, if he is victorious. The Sultan wants to make sure that they get a good service by us, as we have been sent for the service to mankind, like our dear Prophet Mohammed (pbuh) was sent as a Mercy to creation.

Can we resist this call to duty?"

The crowd screamed with a deafening noise a clear and uniform "No, never!"

"O men of Allah, how strong is your faith? Have you ever seen the tears of a mother crying for her child when it is torn away into slavery? Have you seen the blood of the father, whose crops were burnt and the animals all slaughtered for booty? Have you suffered like the child who was misused and beaten to death? Because this is what the Visigoths did to your Christian and Jewish Brothers and Sisters across the sea.

Are you ready to cross it?"

The men jumped in excitement and shouted a clear-cut "Yes"

"Are you willing to seize it?"

The men embraced each other and some punched each other's shoulders in jest and amused, in their innocent youth.

Are you able to win it?" He smiled with his eyes across the lines when he ended his vehement words.

The men went crazy and screamed "Allah, the Greatest" 3 times. Steadily the anticipated dynamics of the crowd started to take over, from word straight to action. They reached for their armoury and weapons, and stormed to the horses, down the steep cliffs towards the coastline and into the futuristic boats some of which were like cones at the front, armoured with steel and had small shafts for arrows to pass through. The Middle of these 30metre vessels was low nearing the waterline for descending and ascending and the back reached far up from the water level with the captain's deck and the rudder at the back. Sails were set but only rudders were meant to be used towards the end, they were not meant to sail far anymore, they were not meant to last.

These ships were built across the kingdoms, sailed by during the past weeks, assembled for training and bonding. Along the clear bright coastline which was covered with these vessels one after the other, 100s of vessels were lined up towards the horizon. The men stormed in and packed in weapons and horses, tents, food and clothing. Action, restless movement, as commanders were watching eagerly and pushing and pulling the warriors to the right places in the lines of duty, giving clear short instructions, the men therewhile laughing and cheering, happy not stressed like they would have been expected to be.

This was a different breed of men altogether, almost as if the commanders were the servants and the men only there for enjoyment not minding anyone's force but taking it lightly. These were happy people and nobody could steal this eternal happiness from them, it was God-given, in life and death, no difference! A shattering noise dominated the place, the shattering of steel. Across the coast-line and seen from a bird's-eye view down the hills along the horizon across the sea to the cliffs lay the land of the North, the land of the Vandals, Al-Andalus, unknown, yet irresistible, strange yet attractive, far away, yet so close, near to fortune, uncertain yet confident to be taken, to be conquered, to be freed, to become home. The crowd was in practice for battle . . .

"We sent a foretime our apostles with Clear Signs and sent down with them the Book and the Balance (of Right and Wrong), that men may stand forth in justice; and We sent down Iron, in which is (material for) mighty war, as well as many benefits for mankind, that Allah may test who it is that will help, Unseen, Him and His apostles: For Allah is Full of Strength, Exalted in Might (and able to enforce His Will)".
Surah 5 (Iron) Verse 25.

The entire beach was engulfed in a heavy warm-up session while a section of the army was appointed to armour the horses and the ships. Heavy steel plates were carried along that were custom-made in long pointed triangular modules to fit their purpose. The steel was stainless, it was not quite shining but matt, not reflecting the sun, and the alloy contained many different types of crystal powders and metals reaching from chromium all the way through to Nickel and Zinc from the mines of Sub-Saharan Africa, carried along the caravan routes via Timbuktu and along the West-Coast. It was the basis of all the armour apart from the body armour, which consisted of flexible chains.

Now the horses were lined up. They came from all sides down alongside the cliffs where they had made their way from across the Empire. Stallions bred for generations for speed, stamina and strength, with not a bone of fear in their tall, toned, trained bodies. There were numerous horses of all colours. They were calmed down and then held firmly in place by another man, while a third began strapping the armour over the horses' head. These magnificent creatures did not make a move of resistance, not a sound of fear. They stood firm as they were plated with armour, light as it was, still strong enough to engulf the Beasts with a pointed cone that made them look like steel-monsters of another Age, surreal and formidable as they began to stare into the distance through the eye-pouches left open in the right place, gazing at the horizon across the water into the darkness of the cliffs of Al-Andalus. As if fixated by magic that was in the steel, they were transformed into battle-tanks of their time. Not one move where before perhaps there was a step or two to the front and back, which was already considered to be perfect discipline, now the horses were like statues, one with their armour, their armour alive and stronger than its mere strength. Because now it had found its purpose. This was the moment the smiths had whispered their prayers for as they cast the steel into its formidable shape during the months of preparation.

The groups of three men that were busy with each horse now took a step or two back in amazement, mouths and eyes wide open, they did not recognise these gentle creatures anymore, which they had raised and trained with their own hands. The planning of the master-smiths from the silk-route was so extraordinary, that it did its job instantly without any trial or error! The smiths were all learned in the Word of Allah, the mystical formula of life and materials, the Creator of the Universe who taught speech made the metal soft for them and gave the knowledge of the Unseen. Each breath and move of the smiths was complemented by appropriate verses from the Koran.

Nevertheless, this was new to everyone. As valuable as they had known these new alloy-types to be, never did they even imagine such awe and perfection. Sounds of delight and wonderment could be heard across the lines.

It was now the turn of the men to get ready. One helped the other as shields and helmets of equally cone-shaped elements were mounted and assembled at the same point. They had to put on chain-suits and over it was lain strong plated armour, as if glued to the body, it resembled each man's size and shape, perfectly suited. Pointed helmets and shields were assembled like that of the horses' armour. Amazing swords that were produced for them were then taken up. They were long, bowed, sharp and strong. Some were straight, long and split to make a quick end in horse-to-horse battle, almost like two-edged, flat spears, others short and triangular in their cross section with all three sides sharp like razors. Yet others were the Chinese-type Taoist blades that run like water and a piece of cloth dropped on them is cut apart by its own weight in the wind, it drops to the ground in two pieces. They were engraved with Verses from the Koran to enhance their spirituality and beauty. The sword was the second warrior, the companion of each man, it needed to be treated with respect and most importantly, it needed to be used reluctantly. It had a soul and a conscience breathed into it by the angels under guidance from the Almighty who had sent them as He sends to the one who mentions His Name. And in His Name were all swords made, his very words were written on these surfaces. Each blade was holy.

Last but not least, some of the remaining long and wide vessels, tailor-built for carrying the horses, heavy armour and soldiers across the waters were being hammered upon by the master-smiths. Long cone-shaped fronts started to emerge out of the waters. Steel-caps that would ram any vessel to the ground instantly, but this was not a sea-to-sea combat. Nevertheless these heavy weights were to have their exact purpose in the battle to come.

Now the army was assembled, line by line, soldier by soldier they stepped up in ranks on to the ships. Horses first in perfect stride as if in drill for years and years. Same for the men, who wore their armour with pride just like the horses, who had been transformed into battle-machines. On to the vessels as Tariq and Imam Bilal walked up and down the lines to monitor the scene and make sure not one man was left behind and all was in order as the sun moved slowly down from its Zenith. They did not have any complaints, the drill was perfect. All synchronously, as if by timing the vessels set of, being pushed by a line of soldiers off the sandy beach, vessels that could dock on land and sand likewise, a clever construction. With this they set off, with this they set sail and rowed at the same time, horses tame and calm, a calm that was cold, collected and calculated, they were saving their energy for later. They were on sea, the point of no return as the winds picked up and the currents took possession of the vessels, 4 factors of direction to steer: The stream of the ocean hitting the boats, the strong wind taking the sails, the men and their rudders and the steering at the back of the ships. All 4 factors resulting in the final direction and speed they were going to take while essentially keeping distance from each other and speed steady to avoid collision and delay because they had to hit the opposite shore synchronously by command.

The Reason

"Those who believe fight in the cause of Allah, and those who reject Faith fight in the cause of Evil: So fight against the friends of Satan: feeble indeed is the cunning of Satan.

Have you not turned your vision to those who were told to hold back their hands (from fight) but establish regular prayers and spend in regular charity? When (at length) the order for fighting was issued to them, behold! A section of them feared men as—or even more than—they should have feared Allah. They said: "Our Lord! Why have You ordered us to fight? Would Thou not Grant us respite to our (natural) term, near (enough)?" Say: "Short is the enjoyment of this world: the Hereafter is the best for those who do right: Never will ye be dealt with unjustly in the very least!"

Surah 4 (Women), Verses 76/77

A dark terrible cloud had covered the sky for many years. Dark as night, nights were more pleasant. Smoke tainted the little daylight that was left. Dozens of smoke columns rose straight up while even the wind had given up its resistance. All the way to the horizon cottages burnt, farmland was set ablaze shortly before the harvest. The craze was written in his face. Roderick the Terrible followed his armour and wolf-hide covered hoards as they burnt down the village, house by house, eagerly watching each house burn down to the ground with his eyes straying from horseback to the monastery on top of the hill. The monastery was fortified so it would require some siege, some patience and therewhile some additional booty. Slaves, women and children were welcome entertainment while all the cattle were slaughtered and grilled on site. All the men and old women were killed immediately by bloody eagle or just by slitting the throat or piercing the chest. They lay bleeding in the mud. The children were inspected closely and so were the women.

"Line them all up; I want to see them all for myself!" Roderick howled like a wolf.

Roderick's men rushed by from every side leading the women and children from each household by a long rope, tied foot to foot, hand to hand, tightly. Roderick looked at them with his piercing blue eyes and his mud-spotted pale face from top to bottom, descending from his short, cold-blooded horse and pointed them out to their future owners. These miserable figures bowed and kneeled. He pulled each ones face to stare them in the eyes.

"You my friend Pelayo get 5 women and 5 children for your booty. Happy?"

"Definitely, Roderick, as long as I am the first and the best". Pelayo laughed vehemently.

"You are. You killed most of them".

"It is too easy, they have no power. Wittiza has left his people to fend for themselves. He was not very wise; he is of the lowest of our tribe. Any Visigoth King should know better than that in these times."

"Yes, we warned him often enough, now it is time to just take and stop talking".

"He was too weak, too soft; he left them to live and didn't take anything. Look how spoilt and rich they are. He even fell for their religion, worshipping some virgin and her son on the cross. Ah, these Christians and these other Believers! We Goths are born to be Pagans! Look at him. Now he is running back towards the North to tell Grandfather Siegfried about it."

"Don't worry, we got him! But what was Grandfather Siegfried going to do for him? He may be the great-great-grandson of Alaric, the conqueror of Rome, but what did he conquer himself? He only sat on inheritance and he thinks the same of us. He still thinks we are babies."

Both burst out laughing and rolling on the ground while the wine took their senses and they went on celebrating into the night in their hide-covered tents and lined up the women that had been ascribed to them inside their tents. A festive plate of pork, human flesh, bear and wolf-meats was served along with grapes by the newly taken slaves, trembling under the weight of their ill-fortune. The children hid in the corners of the tents trying to make themselves invisible while their mothers were abused and misused. In a mystical way not only the behaviour but also the faces of these Vandal started to resemble the faces of the animals they ate, actually worse, the demons of the forests and the underworld invoked all the while with the cups full to the brim with blood and wine, spilling over, gushing down the throats, were taking over their souls. Thus they ate, drank, copulated, laughed and howled deep into the night, up to the following morning, dawn being the permanent state of the day as brightness and sunlight had vanished away.

"We are out of wine" Roderick shouted out into the night storming out of his tent and throwing his horn towards the ground. "Tomorrow we will take the monastery!" Most of his people were asleep. He hit on deaf ears, apart from the monks behind the old walls inside the monastery on top of the hill. They were awake all night murmuring prayers and trembling, shaken by the noise of the barbaric hoards.

As daylight broke they lined up on horseback, spear to spear, shield to shield, hundreds of men at the feet of the shallow hillside, scaring the living daylight out of the monks who hastily gathered all the wine to push it through the gate, hoping this would be sacrifice enough for the devil. They locked the gate firmly and watched in horror from the wall as the Goths shattered the pots and began burning the gate with arrows of fire. The small monastery lay in flames within minutes and the gates fell down in ashes, burnt to charcoal in front of their very eyes. The monks offered no resistance and kneeled at the chapel while the Goths dismantled the gold and silver, jewels and crucifixes, and began melting them in a furnace they had piled up from the pots and coals. After that they started killing the monks one by one who just lay prostrate murmuring the prayers. The chapel lay in ruins, towards the afternoon the monastery was no more.

Suddenly out of the flames from one of the upper chambers rode a tall figure, Charles of Montril, the abbot who swung the sword and killed quite a few Goths before escaping through the gate that was only a hole in the wall by now and rode off towards the sea. Roderick shouted and screamed to his men:

"Hold him, catch him, I want him, he is the one who shot father!"

But his men were too busy plundering and guarding the slaves to care about anyone escaping, so Roderick rode off himself. It was quite an unequal chase, Charles with a fresh and focussed mind and a strong stallion, Roderick drunk and tired. After the cliff he noticed that he was too drunk and busy, so he shot a few arrows, but then he gave up and turned around with a sigh of almost relief escaping his breath.

"I will get you one day, Charles! I thirst for your blood, I hunger for your liver, I will dress with your scalp!" He whispered by now and murmured into his crusty beard.

Many years ago when Roderick was a child, he had seen the Gaulle monks unite with the Jews in a rebellion against his father when he ruled all of South-Gaulle. Charles of Montril had collected a small force to strike the Gothic armies wherever they marched and during one of the raids he had shot Roderick's father in the knees, a wound that never healed and eventually crippled him over the years and caused him to lay in bed during the last 10 years of his life, dying a slow painful death, while he commanded his sons to split the kingdom and ruled it remotely through his sons Roderick and Wittiza. Even before his death these two had such big differences in the way they should rule that they split the kingdom in two, hence adapting Germanic rather than Roman law, which grants the firstborn to take the whole property. Both were half-brothers from different mothers. The memory of these years was very much alive in Roderick's drunken brain and was buzzing in his mind while he was riding back slowly and angrily to the village.

Back at the monastery the remaining monks of higher rank were tied to the pillars and their chests cut open at the sternum, the sternum split, the lungs pulled out and nailed to the back of the pillars so they could still breathe, just about. Bloody Eagle. Their lungs palpitated like pigeons blowing their bellows, bloody red and like a frog's throat as if a red balloon was perpetually blown up and collapsed repeatedly. For hours and hours into the night they stood with sunken heads, begging the soldiers to strike them with a blow of mercy into oblivion, but they did not so. Instead they screamed out the same question repeatedly:

"Where is the treasure?" The Goths marched to and fro in anger, hitting the gasping men whose blood was flowing down slowly along their bodies and tainted the brown garments dark-red to black. They were trembling like the leaves in a forest canopy in an autumn storm that are about to fall, yellow and red.

Each monastery in the West was granted a box of gold from the pope every year to strengthen the Western outposts, gold that came from the East that had been collected as absolution payment from rich people for forgiveness of their sins throughout the Empire and it was still filling the Vatican's chambers. It arrived in Venice by sea and was guarded to the Vatican. Using this the monasteries paid the workers and converts to Catholicism for their services, bought and traded. The Ostrigoths had signed a truce with the pope to let this gold get through to him in exchange for the land. But the annual boxes had stopped arriving long ago. The pope was busy paying mercenaries to defend him against the

Gothic invasion, which was by now more an occupation, if not a clear-cut rule similar to the one in Hispania.

"If you tell us we will let you live".

What a life would that be? One monk after the other stopped breathing.

"Oh, these Gaulles and Romans". Said Roderick with the anger of a wolf in frenzy. "I hate them. I don't even like their meat. What good are your gods? Our gods are much better than your Father, Son and Holy Ghost! Your God was born of a virgin and died on the cross. Now you can follow him . . . I think there will be no treasure here."

And with that he commanded his troops to march off towards the South because he had heard rumours of a crossing of Moors and it was getting dark and they had consumed all the food and burnt the rest. They tied the slaves together, women and children and dragged them behind their horses, who gave off whining sobs in the face of the terror these gentle creatures could not bear.

The Arrival

"Therefore, when ye meet the Unbelievers (in fight), smite at their necks; At length, when ye have thoroughly subdued them, bind a bond firmly (on them): thereafter (is the time for) either generosity or ransom: Until the war lays down its burdens. Thus (are ye commanded): but if it had been Allah's Will, He could certainly have exacted retribution from them (Himself); but (He lets you fight) in order to test you, some with others. But those who are slain in the Way of Allah,—He will never let their deeds be lost."
Surah 47 (Mohammed) Verse 4

Roderick and Pelayo took their horses up to the highest cliff and from there they watched out to the sea. They had been called by their spies and pirates who were roaming the coasts. Their eyes were fixated as if death was approaching from the ocean, a high wave, a blazing fire or a hoard of devils to drag them down into hell. They pulled their horses away and rode down the dunes and off into the distance.

The waves shattered the coastline as the ships approached the sandy beeches and with a hissing sound hit the shore. The sails had been pulled down and packed before they arrived into an arrow's distance off the coast. These were strange vessels in deed. Long extended canoes with steelcaps at the front and extremely wide with flat sealevel centres. Purpose-built for a one-off operation. They were all brand new shining with steel surroundings, the steelcaps at the front had window-like gaps in them for arrows to be shot through. They also covered these canoe-shaped ships from the frontal view entirely so that no arrow could effectively reach the vessel from the front. All rowing in a row they stretched along the coastline and approached it almost instantly as a military formation.

Shortly before they could hit the shore an immense noise had filled the coastline, dragon-flags appeared across the sand. There they came. Hoards of Goths stormed by over the dunes and took position. There were thousands of them. They set alight their long arrows by holding them against the flaming torches held by Gaulle footsoldiers and shot them at the vessels. Almost all arrows passed their target hitting only the frontal steelcap of the vessel and sunk with a hissing sound into the sea, quenched by the waves. Those few that hit the deck were immediately extinguished by bucket-loads of sea-water, close to reach from the centre of the ships. The Muslim captains and warriors kept calm, determined and held position straight towards the shore.

Immediately upon hitting the shore the warriors pushed bags of materials tied into the sails off the deck and jumped on the horses to ride them into the shallow waves and ducking below the hail shower of arrows they span their huge shields that were integrated into the bows and rode off towards the lines of the Goths while firing the arrows through the gaps in their shields. They left the vessels to fend for themselves, which steadily succumbed to the waves tumbling to and fro and swallowing the shower of burning arrows were set ablaze, but not with one warrior inside, not with any supplies or materials left on them, sails neatly packed in sacks dropped into the tide. The gaps in between the ships were filled with huge sacks of goods sinking to the shallow ground underneath the water. The sacks were soaked with water and did not burn from the arrows of fire.

The burning arrows were in vain against the shields that were hooked to the bows and in a slim slit the arrows fitted through and the warriors could point precisely at their target. It was a practical thing in deed that these clever people brought along. Hardly an arrow from the Goths hit the warriors from the sea. Meanwhile their own arrows that were not set on fire before shooting hit nearly every target aimed at. The horses of the Muslims were shielded too with those steel fronts, much similar to the vessels but much smaller and they just warded off the arrows as if they had been matches, sticks. The shields of the warriors spun before the bows were of steel too. So no burning occurred there at all. Not even a spark.

"Thou shall not kill with fire" said the Prophet, pbuh ... so only the Lord of fire will kill with hellfire, abundantly fuelled with men and stones, flesh and bones, prepared for those who reject faith! And the men of Allah adhered to that.

The armour of the Muslim warriors sparkled in the sunlight as it was meticulously harmonic. Pointed steel shields, pointed steel helmets, pointed horse-shields all together forming one large funnel pointing to the front. The sun was in the face of the Vandals and reflected off the sea in the sparkle of the early afternoon. The lines of steel and coastal waves melted together in a dance of light, brighter than the fire from the arrows of the Goths. Blinding their sight, it was as though a wall of steel was approaching them, all sorts of mirages started appearing and the angels did the rest, groups of rhinoceros, swarms of hornets with immense spikes, ready to sting any living being, scaring the hell out of the Vandal hoards. As soon as the Muslim warriors had formed it was pretty clear to anyone that they were not going to disintegrate and the burning arrows were of no use whatsoever. When they came 10 horse-lengths near the Goths turned around in panic forced by their horses and footsoldiers and the gentry rode over them, stumping many of them to the ground along with plenty of the swordsmen and archers, crushing their unarmoured bodies and heads, their only defence being their heavy spears and their hide-coverings. They were squashed in their own blood. The footsoldiers threw away their bows and arrows, fended off the horses of the gentry with spears and fled in panic leaving their dead fellowmen to burn in their own flamed arrows that were dipped in pig-fat and the riders took off in fright towards the hills as fast as they could.

The Muslim warriors followed them and so they didn't get far, the Arab horses being branded for speed and stamina, although somewhat bogged down by the weight of their armour, still were formidable already in those days. The Gothic cold-bloods were short and stump, bred to pull wagons of beer and met, which was the beer that they brew out of honey and that befogged their minds into the next day. So this first line army of many thousand men that Roderick had hastily assembled was soon history. He, with his cousin Pelayo and a good chunk of the gentry, headed for the Sierra Nevada, where they had occupied a fort for the South, the old Phoenician fortress of Grenada, the former seat of Wittiza. They had watched the slaughtering of their hoards from the heights in silence and shock.

As the last fighting Goth threw away his spear, the swords of the Muslims had hardly left their shafts, the steel armour was laid to rest and the spears collected from the horrified Goths, who knelt and held their hands over their heads, ready to be slain, but nothing . . . Tariq shouted out in Latin:

"You are safe in the hands of the men of Allah. Fear not. Resist not. Not a hair will be torn off your heads." They were steadily chained together at the feet leaving them generous space to move and the chains in groups of 5 were tied in circles and placed in the sand, their wounds washed and attended to, their faces being in the same state of shock at the loss of the battle, expecting to be slaughtered, taken by surprise.

One could see white tents with thick white silk and linen being built up centrally and systematically within regular distance of each other where some of the severely wounded captives were carried into; hardly any of the invaders were wounded that day. These captives had certain types of wounds from arrows in the limbs, where the Muslims were commanded to aim at, cuts to the legs which were the prior target of close range combat, since killing was only the last resort in primary battle. Only during secondary battle, meaning, if an army stubbornly regrouped, killing by hitting the necks and aiming at the torso was the instruction the men of Allah were expected to follow.

In this case it was a primary combat and most of the arrow-wounds were non-lethal, although bleeding was abundant and the medics were trained to deal with that, tying off the limbs to reduce blood flow and unfortunately a few inevitable amputations with immediate substitution by wooden poles that were screwed to the bones and the remaining skin was knitted around the artificial limbs. This was also the case with many of the bruises that occurred from the trampling by the horses. Amputation was the last resort but not to be avoided in case of endangered lives. Therefore many of the captives were sedated with Opium and Morpheme from the plains of the Sindh and the mountains of Afghanistan. With their native doctors they would not have stood a chance and many thought they were to be tortured, as they expected death by a blow to the head or a spear through the heart, which would have been the case, had they stayed with their own people. There were dozens of cases of amputations and a few very unfortunately bled to death but the majority of the wounded captives were released with bandages dipped in the all-healing black-seed oil and carried back to the groups of captives placed next to fires at the campsites.

While the Muslims pulled the bags out of the water, dismantled the valuable steel caps of the ships piling them along the beech for the blacksmiths to produce more armour, swords and arrowheads, saved what they could from the valuable wood, now charcoal vessels and built up their tents for the night, a group of spies was appointed to explore the surroundings and a command of guards to keep the watch.

"I seek refuge with Allah from Satan the accursed.
In the Name of Allah, Most Gracious, Most Merciful"

With these prayers the master-smiths, impressive elderly men with gowns of heavy rich brocade and tall turbans above waving long manes and beards tied behind the neck, cast their heavenly spell and called by the angels for assistance to commence subsequent prayers and recitations from the Koran while the cast-iron was positioned close to the furnaces as the steel was molten inside a huge pile of coal. 3 men were stepping repeatedly one after another positioned around the oven on to the bellows, three of which pointed towards the pile of coals that was surrounded by a steel frame with gaps at the bottom. One could see the coals glowing red as blood and the evening-wind contributed to the breath of the fire. A funnel shaped pipe with a wide top reached through the coals and on top of it pieces of cut steel from the vessels were placed, where they melted and flowed through the pipe that reached through the pile of coals, into a mould that was placed next to the pile and gave the armour, swords, arrowheads and spear-heads their basic shapes.

After that the blacksmiths took that raw shape with an iron grip and two hammerers pounded one after the other and repeatedly onto the sword that was placed on top of a massive iron base, while another man spread a chromium powder into the semi-molten steel and poured other types of liquids and steels in between, the master-smiths turned and twisted the sword with masterly precision, focussing their eyes entirely on the shape. It was rounded from top to bottom and maintained a rod-shape at the bottom while towards the top a slim blade emerged that grew in width towards the other end. Therefore the base was a massive grip and further up it grew in flatness, width and sharpness. Hence the base was for beating and defence and the top for cutting and piercing, whilst the warrior could choose the level of cut by regulating the height he would hit the opponent with. At the very tip the sword was split and the overall shape was that of a crescent.

The whole process took around 1 hour for each sword and the arrowheads and spearheads and the shields were taken care of by assistant blacksmiths surrounding the furnace sitting and kneeling in the sand. Such furnaces were piled up along the beach as far as the eye could see. These people meant business as the sparks flew high into the evening-sky merging with the bright stars and flowing into the milky-way and the rounded clear moon. A sky manifested itself for the first time in this land after many years of darkness and cloud-cover. The angels lifted the curse of darkness over Iberia like a blanket that was being pulled off a bed.

Tariq attended to his men. He took position on a small dune: Immediately all the active shattering and murmuring stopped and the men turned with full attention and discipline to their leader:

"Oh men of Allah, whither would you flee? Behind you is the sea, before you, the enemy. You have no hope of return as all your ships are burnt. You have left now only Allah to provide you the hope of your courage and your constancy. Remember that in this country you are more unfortunate than the orphan seated at the table of the avaricious master. Your enemy is before you, protected by an innumerable army; he has men in abundance, but you, as your only aid, have your own swords, and, as your only chance for life, such chance as you can snatch from the hands of your foe. If the absolute want to which you are reduced is prolonged ever so little, if you delay to seize immediate success, your good fortune will vanish, and your enemies, whom your very presence has filled with fear, will take courage. Put far from you the disgrace from which you flee in dreams, and attack this monarch who has left his strongly fortified country to meet you. Here is a splendid opportunity to defeat him, if you will consent to expose yourselves freely to death. Do not believe that I desire to incite you to face dangers which I shall refuse to share with you. In the attack I myself will be in the fore, where the chance of life is always least.

Remember that if you suffer a few moments in patience, you will afterward enjoy supreme delight. Do not imagine that your fate can be separated from mine, and rest assured that if you fall, I shall perish with you, or avenge you. You have heard that in this country there are a large number of ravishingly beautiful Gaulle maidens; they are innocent and untouched, unspoilt by riches. The Commander of True Believers, Alwalid ibn Abdulmalik, has chosen you for this quest from among all his warriors; and he promises that you shall become his comrades and shall hold the rank of kings in this country. Such is his confidence in your intrepidity. The one fruit which he desires to obtain from your bravery is that the word of Allah shall be exalted in this country, and that the true religion shall be established here. The spoils will belong to you.

Remember that I place myself in the front of this glorious charge which I exhort you to make. At the moment when the two armies meet hand to hand, you will see me, never doubt it, seeking out this Roderick, tyrant of his people, challenging him to combat, if Allah is willing. If I perish after this, I will have had at least the satisfaction of delivering you, and you will easily find among you an experienced hero, to whom you can confidently give the task of directing you. But should I fall before I reach to Roderick, redouble your ardour, force yourselves to the attack and achieve the conquest of this country, in depriving him of life. With him dead, his soldiers will no longer defy you."

With a deafening "Allah, the Greatest", the crowd dispersed. Silently the men had gathered around the General and now they congregated to conduct the evening and night prayer that were conducted together during journeys. The sun was about to disappear behind the dunes and the firewood was gathered and piled in regular distances along the shore to warm small groups of men with one tent per 15 men and one group of captives next to them. Immediately after the prayer the captives were given water to drink and a rich diet of fish that were caught during the crossing of the straight and vegetables were prepared to be grilled on top of the open fire which was sufficient for all, even the captives.

Now that they had eaten, the somewhat stunned captives were attended to spiritually. The warriors took off their armour and their white garments, washed in the seawater had to dry so they gathered clothed in one layer of gown close to the fire with the captives. They took copies of a book and ordered translators into Latin to be placed near each group of captives. Then hymns in regular chanting voice which were interrupted at regular intervals for translation were read out to the captives as to entertain them and soothe them. You could see the level of astonishment growing in the firelit faces of the captives as the darkness spread and the night took over. And what a clear night it was. It was almost brighter than the day, the mood lit up the faces and the garments. The Gaulles and Goths were amazed. They had never seen the stars in such bright light, the moon and the milky-way with Sirius crowning the night sky. Europe had been enveloped in a cloud of smoke since the time of their grandfathers. Their ancestors told them legends of a golden horse riding across the skies to damn the world into darkness, devoured by a howling

Beast; this is how they interpreted a comet that had struck Germany and a volcanic eruption at that time. They stared in awe at the skies above them. The feeling that Change had come to Europe was strong. The Dark Ages had finally ended in Iberia.

Then the reciters who had stood up for recitation, sat down next to the captives and started conversations asking them about their religion and explaining to them the position of Islam from the Koran, that there was no God but Allah, and the life of the Prophet (pbuh) and how merciful he was towards the captives, which is why they were following his example. You could see the captives nodding willingly and comfortably while the translators repeated in Latin and Gaulle.

Some Muslims packed out strange geometrical circular instruments and pointed towards the stars, so-called Astrolabes:

"He Who created the seven heavens one above another: No want of proportion wilt thou see in the Creation of ((Allah)) Most Gracious. So turn thy vision again: seest thou any flaw?
Again turn thy vision a second time: (thy) vision will come back to thee dull and discomfited, in a state worn out.
And we have, (from of old), adorned the lowest Heaven with Lamps, and We have made such (Lamps) (as) missiles to drive away the Evil Ones, and have prepared for them the Penalty of the Blazing Fire."
Surah 67. (The Sovereignty, Control), Verses 3-5

A man could be seen overviewing the work of the soldiers turned preachers. It was Imam Bilal Al-Din. He had instructed the actions and was now watching keenly and focussing standing at certain points between the groups as to overhear many groups at once and you could see him approaching one group after the other and listening into the conversations and making suggestions to his men as how to best answer certain questions raised by the captives.

"Ya-Sheikh, you are doing well, mashallah, as Allah wished it" Tariq surprised him from the side as Imam Bilal turned to him with a happy smile.

"Likewise, my General, likewise. Alhamdulillah, all Praise be to Allah, this is a great day!"

"It is also our great honour that the Sultan has granted us by the permission of Allah, and may many more victories follow. Remember all the happy years we lived in the palace and learned and travelled. We grew up alongside in the chambers and gardens of the palace. Now it is our time to pay back, spread what he gave us. It will be a hard time that we have before us, it will be tough and not for the faint hearted."

"Yes, in deed, never underestimate the enemy, the Forces of Satan. Let us pray, make Duah, for success in this Life and the Hereafter and continued victory":

With that the Imam raised his hands to heaven and Tariq followed and they said a few verses from the Koran:

"When comes the Help of Allah and Victory, and Thou dost see, the People enter Allah's religion in crowds. Celebrate the Praises of Thy Lord and turn to him in Repentance, for He is to you oft forgiving in Grace and Mercy
Surah 110 (Help)

And then they prayed to Allah, the Almighty, to give them continued strength and victory:

"O Allah the Almighy, Allah the Eternal, Allah the Victory-giver, Allah . . . . ."

The captives meanwhile had forgotten all about their plight and were busy and engaged in debates, keenly discussing theology with their newly found friends and after the Muslims had done their night prayer together with the evening prayer as customary away from home, they still continued to talk deep into the night.

Suddenly a man was brought along by the spies and guardsmen who were placed along the dunes. He had been watching the scene all day since he had hidden behind the dunes. The guards were pulling this tall fellow to and fro, while he did not offer any resistance. Tall and strong with a beautiful horse.

"Who are you?" Tariq asked him in Latin.

"Charles of Montril".

"I know you. You look familiar. Are you not the Abbot who came to Damascus with a delegation a few years ago from Cyprus?"

"Yes, I have been there"

"We come in Peace. On your request."

"I know and I have seen."

"Join us."

"I have my duty and loyalty to Rome."

"Your delegation reached us. There are your men." Tariq pointed to the Christian camp and Charles was taken there. "Untie him, offer him hospitality".

Charles was left to roam the camp freely and join the dinner assembly with his Christian brothers, they embraced each other and kneeled and thanked God. They crossed themselves with their fingers and sat and spoke of their experiences during the past few weeks and how the Muslims had been helpful.

"How did they treat you?" Charles asked Julian-Urban of Ceuta, who had accompanied the Muslims since he was sent as a delegate by the abbot and the pope.

"Perfect gentlemen, they are men of God, they are like us morally, even better warriors, and always forthcoming, even scary as they strive their utmost to overtake us in all aspects of our own religion, a tribe of monks, would they only believe in Our Lord Jesus Christ as the Son and the

Trinity and hold the celibate. They know the Bible better than our common folk and they quote it and compare it to their book which they say is more concise and precise as it came to one man during his life and not over centuries or millennia since Moses' times. But in principle their values are like ours, you know, you were in Damascus, they honour Jesus and Mary, they are the offspring of Abraham via Ishmael, some of them are converted Israelites and even recently converted Christians, they are taking Africa by storm and without much violence." Julian was shaking at the idea of these words that uttered from his own mouth.

"Yes I know, I have seen Damascus, it is amazing just like Rome, if not better today, and Cairo and the new Alexandria, or Baghdad in the land of Abraham, but we must still be loyal to the pope. He needs us in these times. The Goths have taken all of Italy and surrounded the Vatican. Help has come from as far as Byzantine, even San Marino and Cyprus, Greece and Romania, Poland and Ukraine. All Eastern-Empires are sending their mercenary delegations to fight and they are dying like flies at the swords of these Goths. We have to ask the Moors for help for Rome." Charles was weary not to offend the guards who were still surrounding him. They were all literate in Latin and Greek, some of them even understood Gaulle because Berber and Gaulle were related like German and English in those days, only a small stretch of water separating them, even though they may have had slightly separate origins, in those times all languages were naturally closer.

"I am not sure, if they will do that. They will be busy here for a few years, they have their hands full with Roderick, and he is powerful, now that he has pushed out Wittiza. Maybe the Sultan wants to help the pope. Rumour speaks he is to join us here. Perhaps we can ask him to go to Rome instead." Julian was careful to whisper the important words.

On the next morning the captives were lined up to witness the burial of the fallen of the other side. They were carried beyond the dunes as the sand at the beach would only expose the corpses after the tide. They needed more solid ground, either mother soil or bedrock. After the mainly Christian ritual burials, most fallen were Arianic Goths and did not carry the cross, so the burial was surprisingly simple, the odd Catholic Gaulle had fallen too, they lined up the captives and Imam Bilal spoke:

"O followers of Christ (pbuh). Christ is also our Prophet. After Christ came another Prophet, the Comforter, who was announced by Christ in the Gospel of John (Chapter 14, verse 16, Chapter 15 verse 26 and Chapter 16, Verse 7 to Verse 14). Christ was sent only to the Children of the House of Israel as he emphasized himself. We follow the Way of the last Messenger since he was sent as a Mercy to mankind, a Mercy you have seen from us. Has any of you got any complaints as to how he was treated by us?"

Silence marked the faces of the captives; they stared in a state of wonder. Some of the monks who had accompanied the Muslims across the water were not so delighted at this sight and grouped up pointing and posing with their bibles under their arms, planning and plotting. Charles and Julian tried to keep them calm.

The Imam continued:

"Last night we explained to you all that there is to know for a man of Allah. We want to reach our hands out to you. We have come here in peace and justice is our mission. Roderick has left the land in ruins. The angels covered the skies with smoke since the rule of his grandfathers. This was not a blessing for the people. They have lifted this veil for us. We offer you freedom, if you join Islam and join us in fight. We offer you truth, if you vow an oath of allegiance. We offer you salvation, if you confess, no God, apart from Allah, Mohammed Messenger of Allah!"

The men were lined up and each of them was offered to be baptised into Islam and unchained immediately, if he did so. Some of the captives were reluctant and stayed in chains but the majority was unchained that very hour and offered a bath, new clothes, armour, sworn in by putting their hands on the Koran and confessing . . . :

"No God apart from Allah, Mohammed Messenger of Allah!"

. . . and handed a sword, shield and bow and arrow. They remained footsoldiers, but they had the freshest of shining armours, swords, shields and speers and a tailor made cloak and turban, which they happily accepted and wore with much pride and joy. It felt good.

"Allah the Greatest!" The crowd shouted, the newly formed ranks somewhat echoing behind the frontal horsemen, who were born Muslims, but the freshly converted Gaulles and Goths were nevertheless determined to embrace this new, strong way of life. The others in chains, a minority now, sinking their heads towards the ground and turning their heads in shame from the delight the others felt were attended to by the monks who had come over with the Conquerors. You could see the rabbis looking in vain for their likes. Roderick had made a short process of the Jews after a revolt in Toledo (Tulaytulah).

Charles and Julian were whispering words of weariness to each other and their shrinking assembly of monks and priests. But they smiled in agreement superficially to the Imam and Tariq.

So you could see a line of newly formed Muslims marching behind the men who had crossed the sea and sat mostly on horseback. And off they went inland, their heads disappearing beyond the dunes and the captives who remained chained were very few. So were the monks. Perhaps a hundred or so out of 1000. Around 900 joined Islam that glorious, sunny and windy day. A wind of change blew across the land. It was the magic of the desert. Eternal sunshine that was to last many centuries had entered Iberia and the birds sang in joy and Praise of the Almighty.

There they marched through fertile fields and lush forests, all day, looking around in delight at this green land, lead by a troop of their newly won Brothers in Islam. Straight to Grenada, a Phoenician fort that had until recently been the capital of Wittiza's kingdom, who had fled to the North calling the Sultan for help after Roderick had attacked him with an attempt of fratricide. Screaming out to the locals words of reassuring safety and insurance of security, like Mohammed (pbuh) marched back into Mecca to forgive his enemies 100 years before, they arrived at the feet of the cliffs and the city walls rose high. There they set camp. There they lay siege.

The Night set over the land, dawn was unusually long this far North as they directed their instruments, Astrolabes towards the skies to measure latitude and longitude and determined prayer times and direction. Positioning, they constantly were able to retrace their routes, recalculate prayer times, with the help of the stars and the horizon. The sun and the moon also served their purpose and during hazy days the maps they drew along the way. These people were used to navigating the desert and the seas alike for centuries and now the additional knowledge they gained from the immense progress and contact with other civilisations such as Greek books from Alexandria, Chinese and Indian travellers to Damascus and Babylonian, Zoroastrian and Assyrian converts allowed them to conquer places afar. These were the fine men of the Empire, not just outcasts. They had been carefully chosen for this mission, this charitable gift from the Muslims called Peace and Justice for Iberia.

The Conquest

"And fight them on until there is no more Tumult or oppression, and there prevail justice and faith in Allah. But if they cease, Let there be no hostility except to those who practise oppression."
Surah 2 (The Heifer), Verse 193

Towards the evening all troops had arrived at the dark-grey fortified city of Granada or Garnata, as the Arabs called it, and people, seeing the warriors marching and riding in, had been commanded towards the gate of the city by the Goths in haste. The gate was locked leaving out quite a few of the villagers and their livestock. They panicked at the arrival of the exotic looking riders with their bright white banners and shining armour. But they were merely sent back by the Muslims into the fields and farmhouses to attend their daily routines. This was much to their surprise and new to them. They had expected to be robbed at the very best.

One could see the walls of the fortified city rising as high as the slopes of the Sierra Nevada Mountains. The ground was lush green on this summer day, the springs and rivers freshly filled with the melting water from the constantly snow-covered hilltops. The Muslims stared at this scenery in bliss; some of them had seen a similar sight back home in the Atlas Mountains surrounded by desert, but only in winter, never so late the year. Water everywhere, animals grazing, who were left to roam freely, because they did not need to be lead to the water, the water coming to them, not to be fed with hay, the grass growing right under their feet. Low Celtic walls separated the lush green fields, the farm houses were abandoned though as most of the people had fled into the fortified city on instruction of Roderick.

The great dark city walls rose high into the grey sky alongside a steep mountain slope and the palace inside the walls was built against the slopes. This being the scenery that was entirely new to the Muslim warriors, Tariq prepared a letter for Roderick. He wrote in Latin on clean white garment spread out on a wooden plate with a feather dipped into black ink fresh from the bladders of a squid he pulled from an urn they had slung down along the vessel while rowing across the Straight, the squid loved to hide in there.

"In the Name of Allah the Gracious, the Merciful. Greetings to whose fathers were in union with us and who has lost his way. I am Tariq ibn Ziyad, delegate of the Sultan of Damascus to Iberia and in command of the delegate army of the Amir of Africa. Your father and their fathers were close allies and friends, commemorate the union. Your people have asked us for help against your

34

*cruel reign. Fear the judgement of the Almighty and lay down your arms. We
give you one night. We come in peace.
If however you wish to engage in warfare I challenge you to a one-to-one
battle to spare many innocent lives of your men and the men of Allah. You
can also choose your 3 best men and we will send our three best men. This
is our tradition according to the first battle of Islam at Badr close to Medina
that you know as Madyan from the Bible, where Moses (pbuh) dwelt before.
We spare the lives of our men and step forward as leaders. If you have any
honour, you will abide by it.
Let me remind you before that, that I prefer peace and you are free to remain
loyal to your religion and tribe, if you surrender. And you are also welcome to
join us in Islam, it will be better for you to declare the Confession to the Truth:
No God apart from Allah, Mohammed Messenger of Allah!"*

This piece of cloth was wrapped around an arrow, knitted together
tightly and a rider sent towards the city walls, who, under a hail shower
of burning arrows, as he rode into an arrow's distance, shielded them
off and managed, riding in a steep curve briefly along the walls, at the
nearest point to the city gate, to send off that message over the wall, right
past the heads of the astonished Goths.

On the other side it knocked down a few barrels of wine that were piled
up in the yard between palace and walls. It was pulled out and taken
to Roderick, who, at the mere sight of the arrow, frowned, as he was
leaning back on the throne covered with hide and sunken in a deep
hang-over, quenched with wine and a plate of meats. He unfolded the
cloth clinging to the arrow and tore the knitting apart. Then he tested
the sharpness of the arrowhead with his fingers, staring at it relentlessly.
It was cone-shaped and massive. Not like the Gothic arrowheads flat
and flimsy. A shiver passed through his body. He had never seen such
arrows, neither had any of his commanders. The Damascene delegations
that came during his childhood never brought along much armour and
weapons. With a frown and reluctantly he attended to the letter and
read it out to his congregation of knights. They looked at each other.
Silence. Then they burst out into drunken laughter as the wine befogged
their senses towards the evening and the letter was cast into the fireplace,
as if a piece of danger could be burnt away, hastily, carelessly.

Night set in across the land, the men had set camp and prayed for the evening and then for the night together since this was the decree on journeys away from home and in many small congregations after another as commonplace during battles. They went to bed early leaving only a few guards to surround the camp and the usual spies to roam the surrounding hills.

That night in the Christian camp someone slept very shallow. There was a noisy rumbling and the guards checked what was happening. It was Julian-Urban, twisting and tumbling around from side to side. Many a monk thought it was because they had joined the non-Christian forces and this was the punishment, the bad-conscience, a bad Omen becoming real. Julian-Urban never agreed with that and they were wondering what he had to say now. They woke him and asked him as to his dream. He stared at one distant point pulling his blanket up to his neck, trembling and shivering, the sweat running from his tonsure, the bold spot monks used to shave into their hair. He was a small man but had an impressive long face with a pointed nose and wide open eyes, his mother having been a Christian Arab, thus he whispered loud:

"I saw as if it was real, the dragon stretching his neck to the sky, 4 heads, 5 heads, then more. There was only one knight to fight him and all the others stood at distance. I heard at the horizon a call coming from behind a cloud, a bloody cross asking for help, running bloody as the knight was violently bitten by the Beast, one head after the other hit him and he fell, stood up again and again to fight. I was one of those knights standing by, unable to do anything. All of a sudden I saw our Lord Jesus Christ behind the bloody cross at the horizon, all across, pointing his finger to the sky and another finger at us. We were in this congregation, the knights standing by and letting that brave warrior fight alone, our Lord being unpleased with us. We have to pray for them and help them, we can no longer be passive and selfish. It is our Land they are freeing for us from the Vandals."

Charles of Montril and the other monks stared silently at each other and with a bad conscience towards Julian. They lay back and tried to sleep again.

Morning came early this far North at this time of the year, so they were woken by the usual chant of the call to prayer and hastily stood up, the perpetual scene of soldiers assembling for prayer with the newly converts in their midst, washing in the springs and lining up hastily with the Imam leading became routine and a guideline in their lives, the familiar rope to hold on to in order to follow the straight and narrow in these unfamiliar territories. The prayer was completed. The direction towards Mecca had been facing away from the fortifications. So the guards prayed in a second congregation while Tariq prepared to address the men:

"Yesterday we had an excellent start. We can be grateful for that. However, you should not expect that to be repeated today, this is not sea to land combat; we have lain down the heaviest of armour. This is a siege that requires a very different approach.

It is time now to act and for many of you to meet our Maker. We have not heard back from them so rest assured, they are cowards, but still they will take many of your lives. Prepare to fight, fight to win and win to die. And you know death is the biggest honour as you witness the truth and you will not need await Judgement Day, you shall enter through the gates of the gardens beneath which rivers flow and be appointed to the ranks of the righteous immediately. I envy you, if I don't follow you. If I follow you, I pity those who stay behind. Most of all though I would like to lead you. Those who live will witness the death of their brothers and long for the same. Don't forget, winning is the goal but it can only be achieved by loosing your fear of death.

They too are brave. They too fight for a cause. They too long for death. But their means is to defend king and country, while you fight for the Almighty. Tell me, which is better? Believe me, most of them are probably fighting for their lives.

They think us as fanatics because we die for the Unseen and they think of themselves as better as they fight for the seen. This, because they lack the certainty of the Hereafter. This, because their evil acts have deluded them away from the Truth and they love this life over the afterlife. This, because they are hypocrites . . ."

The crowd had been silent but was getting very excited now, they screamed and shouted out of one mouth:

"Allah, the Greatest, No God apart from Allah, Mohammed Messenger of Allah!"

A black powder was poured into a number of huge pots; the pots were then covered with wax, carefully carried to the city walls, covered by steel shields under a hail-shower of arrows. There the pots were stacked along the heavy wooden gate of the city wall. The burrow along the walls was filled with water and the men who brought the pots, covering themselves and each other with the steel shields from the heavy fire of burning arrows, had to walk across the burrow on top of wooden poles they brought along. From the top the Goths stared down along the walls with a fright that was almost like carelessness. Could it get much worse than under Roderick?

Each pot of powder had a string that was pointing out of the wax top which was now set alight by a man who, under the cover of his shield had resisted a heavy hail shower of burning arrows, one of which now conveniently served as a lighter. 3 other men were covering the pots and themselves with the shields, which they now abandoned almost instantly and ran, still under the shower of arrows, that were shot down parallel along the walls, with a hasty pace, back to the lines behind a shallow river. Most arrows were quenched silently inside the river. The arrows followed them along their path though. And by now arrows were shot in full fashion towards the lines of the Muslim army. Some arrows had to be wiped off with the steel shields because tar was covering their tips and formed a sticky layer. The men on horses watched the wooden door in suspense while reluctantly waving off the few arrows reaching them. Then all of a sudden:

"Baaaaang"

. . . the word "grenade" named after the European location it was first heard at, Granada, burst into existence that very day, tore its way into the vocabulary of the European languages within the twinkling of an eye, violently, yet without any immediate casualty, burnt itself into their conscience. Nevertheless it would turn out to have many casualties in the centuries to come, because this black powder was guided through barrels of steel, Muslims were not allowed to kill with fire, fire lacking the honour, what honour is there in killing? What is honour-killing? Surely a concept entirely alien to Islam. What can Muslims expect who practice it?

So this mighty mixture of sulphur, charcoal and potassium nitrate was not directly used for killing, but only for opening the gate that day. Some of the men of Roderick fell from the walls, screaming and drowning in the burrow's water. The gate was no more. It was shattered into millions of pieces and showered down in burning fragments into the burrow and silently with a trace of smoke, disappeared into the water. Shshsh . . . .

"Allah, the Greatest", the crowd shouted and stormed off towards the gate, again under a heavy shower of arrows, the footsoldiers carrying long planks of wood or just freshly cut trees to lay a bridge for the riders across the burrow stormed ahead. As soon as they approached the door, heavy oil and tar was poured down along the wall, much of which just glid along the huge shields, but unfortunately some of it reached and scorched the bodies of the men who fell in pain into the water screaming again and again:

"Allah, the Greatest! No God but Allah!"

Many were martyred in this way, directly to bliss, no transitional realm of the grave, no passing period, no judgement, no punishment. Just pure felicity they were longing for! Their bodies were piling up in the burrow and blood filled the pond. Some bodies floated alongside the walls together with the Goths who had fallen down from the walls, others were swimming to safety and a battle took place even outside the walls with some of the Goths who had fallen from the walls.

Most of them however stormed into the city. The city was densely packed with cattle and men and women who were cuddling up against the walls, the inner palace was built against the hillside, the fort only needed a long bowed wall to close it in, most of it was secured by the steep cliff behind it. Thus the armies met in battle at full scale. Any control was lost, any tactic, armour, shield too little to work, futile to protect, only the mere and shear ability of a man to fight, brute force, speed and power, technique of the sword taking over the decision of each man to man battle. Down from horseback, the warriors shot their arrows into the Gothic footsoldiers who rushed by from the walls and out of the palace. They were sent in as fodder for the Muslim swords and arrows, the Muslims also busy warding off the arrows from the Gothic guards lined up along the inner side of walls. Some warriors jumped down from the horses and engaged in a combat. Steel rattling, the superior stainless alloys of the Muslim long bowed swords uncut, itself cutting severely into the hides and armour of the Goths, while the heavy iron straight stiff rusty swords of the Goths split at each stroke, splintering, shattering and dropping to the ground. It was a slaughter. Within minutes the Goths lay pale with their alabaster faces blood covered and heads and limbs tumbling.

Quite a few Muslims were wounded and martyred too, not so much from cuts but from crushed bones, because the heavy iron swords of the Goths were not really capable of cutting but they much rather broke their way through joints and tendons. Any description was too weak, any words too little for this chaotic violent tumbling in the yards around the palace in the fortified enclave, red, muddy, murky. Tariq could be seen from horseback guiding his troops from side to side, himself engaged in heave battle and shooting arrows towards the palace, while burning arrows struck his horse and it plummeted down to the ground into the blood covered mud. The Goths took this chance to separate the leader from his men. They knew that was their only chance. The storm of his horsemen passed by him towards the palace as he had commanded them. He pushed himself away from underneath and pulled his leg from beneath his beloved stallion that was fatally wounded and stroke it along the back and the mane . . . then he hit the head with the words:

"In the Name of Allah, Allah, the Greatest"

With this he ended the life of the horse, sparing him a torturous end, perhaps even a stampede by the Goths. As dozens of tall figures surrounded him he stood, took posture, breathing in, unpacked his spear in one hand and sword in the other, shield over spear, swinging them around his aura in a traditional Chinese form he had learned from the tradesmen of the silk-route at the palace in Damascus.

And thus came the spots of light from the sky . . .
" *. . . with wings in pairs, 2, 3 or 4" Surah 35 (the Angels) Verse 1*

. . . and therewith was sent an atmospheric storm . . .

" *. . . a rain-laden cloud from the sky: In it are zones of darkness, and thunder and lightning: They press their fingers in their ears to keep out the stunning thunder-clap, the while they are in terror of death . . ." Surah 1 (the Heifer) Verse 19*

. . . and therewith he attracted, collated the supportive Jinn-Power of battle, dominance of the warrior underlined, so fast, so easy, so relaxed, focussed entirely on prayers whispered in the wind, breath cast in and out accelerating the forces that condensed in his immediate vicinity to amplify his breath and his moves synchronously:

"Audhobillahe Menasshaitanirrageem. Bismillahir Rahman Nirraheem. Alif, Laam Meem, Alif Laam Raa, Alif Laam Meem Saad, Kah Ha Ya Ayn Saad, Ha-Meem, Ha Meem Ayn Seen Qaf, Ta-Ha, Ya-Sin, Qaf, Nun, Saad".

He spoke with his breath in and out; loud and clear, speaking apparently while breathing in as well as breathing out, the mystical alphabets of the Quran, the eternal formula of life, the divine secrets of the universe unlocked, unleashed. The Goths would try to mimic these words and his magic for many generations to come and into Germany his magic would be repeated with the words, Abrakadabra Simsalabim. This is how the magical formula was derived from a shortened version of "Audhobillahe Menasshaitanirrageem. Bismillahir Rahman Nirraheem", which actually means "I seek refuge with Allah from Satan, the cursed being, in the Name of Allah, the Most Forgiving, the Most Merciful". Of course those who use this formula in magic shows until today are oblivious to the origins, leave alone the meanings of these words they so stylishly copy and shorten.

The deep psychological impact of these prayers, that were seen by the locals as magic was inevitable because that very day, at that very moment the Goths had to take a few steps back since all they could see was Tariq's body transformed into a centrifugal ball of light attracting bolts of lightning and shooting out rays of electric charge and thunder, like a mirage, while behind them the Muslim warriors turned back to defend Tariq, he shouted out:

"If you dare turn around for me, I will kill you with my own arrows. Push ahead!" He pulled his bow. "My command to you is clear! Storm the palace"

And immediately they retrieved back to battle against the palace-guards. All Gothic soldiers outside the palace were dead by now apart from those surrounding Tariq and those guarding the crowds alongside the inner walls, and those would rather be dead than facing these fierce moves from this fearsome warrior, 2/3rd of their own size, yet his long bowed strange sword so much in line with his moves, his spear following his swinging hands and arms with the ease of a machine that has been well-oiled, his eyes moving along with his form, ready to apply these skills. Ready for years.

The tales of old Greco-Germanic gods were revived in the minds of the Goths, super-powers of Hercules and Thor, now they could see it manifest, the monks had read it in the "Ring of the Nibelungen" or Homer's "War of Troy" and the "Odyssey", it was merely a human pure-at heart, righteous, a so-called Mumin, amplified through prayer and meditation by attracting angels and Jinn, what they would have called ferries and elves in the days before the Romans came.

As the Christian congregation stepped through the gate, Julian-Urban's dream became reality right there in front of him, but he could not act, his congregation of clerics forbade him to, holding their crosses and crossing themselves, whispering prayers on their knees. He stood and stared.

"No," screamed the Imam Bilal, "Never, I would rather die by your arrow than abandon you", and he stormed with his horse through the Gothic lines, but they struck his horse with their swords and he fell to their feet, fighting, they, hitting his armour and punching him back to the ground, while Tariq was engaged in intense meditation pointing his weapons to those who did not dare attack him.

An old Germanic witch, the likes not seen since Druidian times or those used for fortune telling during the great migration of the Vandals, clothed in dark grey hide and grey hair full of beads emerged out of the crowd and approached Bilal all of a sudden:

"The darkest of darkness shall afall you, you Black faced demon, you shall rot in the deepest of dungeons and the predators shall feed on you." With these words spoken in chanting "Althochdeutsch" or ancient Germanic she pointed her long fingernails towards him and started waving them and with a smile that turned into a mad loud laughter she tried to charm him by turning into a young damsel sparsely dressed. Bilal could not believe his own eyes.

But he knew fairly well the power of such black-magic since he had seen it in his childhood in Mali and it was the force of evil that was much wider and evenly spread across the cultures than the force of good, as different as they might be. He knew very well not to underestimate such bewildering spells and, bedazzled as he was, replied immediately without any delay in the most Islamic manner. He reached deep into his pocket and took out a sack full of gold coins that he threw towards the poor people who stood at the edge of the walls saying "In the Name of Allah". This charity would open the ears of the divine and witnesses were the angels as was Allah, whose pleasure he was seeking with his action. Then he opened the palm of the very right hand he had given the charity with and held it in front of the face of the witch reciting:

"I seek refuge with Allah from Satan the accursed.
In the Name of Allah, Most Gracious, Most Merciful.
Say, I seek refuge with the Lord of the Dawn
From the mischief of created things
From the mischief of darkness as it overspreads
From the mischief of those who practice secret arts
And from the mischief of the envious one as he practices envy"
Surah 113 (Dawn)

Immediately the witch stepped back and sunk into the ground, the darkness she had emerged from, Roderick's earth-demons crumbled right there, all Black-Magic annulled, evil-spirits were defeated at once and posed no more treat to the invasion henceforth. The people stood there staring again in amazement at one scene after the other, but much more was about to come. It was a great moment in history and it would leave its marks on the population for centuries because it was a reminder of the miracles that were promised and foretold by the monks, a sign from God. A long-lasting spell was lifted from the people of Iberia and there was a chance that nobody but a few selected actually had seen this witch. She was acting in the realm of the Jinn, the spirits made of fire free of smoke, no ash-residues when burnt, not like us or any biological life on earth for that matter, as we are all, humans, animals and plants, carbon-based and leave ash behind when consumed by fire.

Tariq meanwhile took a deep breath with another strong formula from the Koran and as if by magic without any acceleration, just with immediate speed, swung towards their lines hitting three of them at once with the spear to the left and 3 others to the right with his swinging sword that was moving much to fast for anyone to see. They, lifting their heavy swords and wooden shields, shattered, broken, in a state of limbo, not able to do much but hold their lines and fall one by one, some 25 Gothic guards. He made short process of these tall figures and they dropped whilst a ray of sunshine hit Tariq's helmet breaking through the clouds, the short thunderstorm that had set in so speedily, left with the same haste, clouds dissolved into thin air, darkness was no more. Only a rainbow at its full splendour. A sight so amazing all the Goths and Gaulles who had surrendered fell to their knees, a marvel they had not yet seen during their lives, only tales of the ancients as they cried. A fresh breeze swung in from the ocean in the distance and a full sunny day manifested itself, while Tariq pulled up the Imam from beneath the horse and they ran to the front to join their troops who were storming the palace.

Meanwhile the peasants had watched in wonder these new knights from the South. They had not seen anything like this before and a few monks cheered on and clapped, praising God and crossing themselves, pointing towards the sky and thanking their Lord for this new king he had sent.

Tariq, whilst storming arm in arm with the Imam to the front pointed and smiled at them and screamed out in Latin:

"You are safe, your women are safe, and your children are safe, your animals are safe, your crops are safe, by Allah, your land is safe! You have nothing to fear, I personally guarantee your safety in the Name of Allah as I will report to him on the Last day!"

The people rejoiced and cheered, delighted, the children jumped and played around whilst their lines were cleared from the Gothic guards who now stormed towards the palace to defend it. Some of them threw down their swords and clapped along, turning to the crowds and cheering.

"What is your name, o Sire?" Asked one monk in Latin.

"They call him Tariq Ibn Ziyad" said the Imam Bilal and we are Muslims, we have come to free you from tyranny and suppression, in the Name of Allah."

The people looked at each other, asking the monks to explain, but they were silent. Meanwhile the palace at the back of the fort towards the hillside became the host of an intense battle. Showers of arrows were exchanged and many good men lay on the ground, the steel shields covering them, yet the wounds in their legs bleeding and the muddy ground soaked, too soaked, too soft to allow them to stand up. Horses tumbling to the ground. People shouting and praising Allah, while at the foot of the peasants lay the henchmen of Roderick, dead. Once so tall, so fearsome, so superior, now reduced to pale bleeding corpses, engulfed in wolf-hide swung over their armour, as they were clothed.

Bright daylight intensified the scene. Daylight as these people had never seen before. The clouds that had been covering the skies for decades moved and succumbed to bright sunshine. People's faces lit up, they were staring up towards the sun, holding their hands in front of their blinded eyes in a state of shock, yet opening eyes and mouths far and wide at the sight of this alien celestial body they only knew as a spot of bronze clouds, merely a silver lining surrounded by deep grey clouds. Now it had finally broken through, this legend that their grandfathers had told them about, that their great grandfathers had merely known. The sun! And the blue skies! Therein was the cure for many of the diseases that they were suffering from.

Many ran out to the fields through the gate and ran across, chasing the animals along, back home, next the soaked grass dried out and was no longer covered by a layer of mist, the cattle also gazed up and one could hear them mooing and calling across the valley. Free at last. Happy for the first time since Wittiza had been expelled. At ease with themselves finally. Some of the footsoldiers who had converted to Islam in the morning embraced their families and told them all about the new invaders in haste. The people gathered cattle and sheep to guide them to the palace awaiting, anticipating the victory of the men. There they sat in front of the city walls and milked the cows and the sheep to collect the milk in buckets, awaiting the victorious soldiers, some of the young girls preparing themselves for them packed out their nicest garments to show their most beautiful sides, these red-haired and blond ladies with blue and green eyes, so new to the Muslims, so alien and yet so fascinatingly attractive, so familiar, as a smile of joy is always the key to the heart. Eyes met eyes.

The palace was still on fire when the warriors started to return with the booty in hand, golden crosses and jewels that had been plundered by the Goths and brought here during the last few years since Roderick had taken Wittiza's land by force, seized power from his half-brother. Silver platters were carried along, but most of all, golden coins and crucifixes. They had wrapped clothes to collect them. In the background they were still engaged in battle.

Inside the palace Roderick had prepared for the flight. He climbed behind a stone-altar in the central chamber, the only one still in the hands of the Goths and his servants pushed it back into place, speaking their oath to him: "My soul for you, O Roderick". The door lead to an underground tunnel and a way out of the fort along the hillside. There he ran in haste, accompanied by Pelayo and the others who had waited for him. A dozen people or so, his closest brethren. They had parked their horses at the other end of the tunnel. Just as they had plundered, so they too were plundered now. They were not able to comprehend it, only seek the distance.

One by one many large chambers were conquered by heavy battle, sword to sword, man to man, these tall Goths were strong people, but their armour was inferior and broke, did not withstand the forceful blows of stainless Arab and African metal-alloys. Chinese welding techniques had provided them with durable swords and shields that were sharper and stayed sharp for longer. Cut by cut the Goths surrendered. Kneeled and put their half cut, broken swords to the ground, holding their hands over their heads, the Palace guards. Pale corpses covered in wolf-hide and blood lay scattered along the hallways and in the mighty chambers, grey walls dimmed the light that now broke through the clouds, the windows were covered with thin hide and cloth rather than glass, these people had forgotten the technology for that including all the finesse of old Roman craftsmanship. Their art was that of destruction, not construction. Now they succumbed to their lack of respect for the fine things in life.

So for the rest of the day the front yard of the palace was cleared of the corpses and the wounded of both sides were carried into the palace side by side without a difference, the unwounded captives were chained together as generously as possible, leaving them space to walk. Tariq and Imam Bilal went through the chambers monitoring the situation and attending to the wounds of the injured of both sides alike, with boiled water, distilled wine or vinegar and bandages. The martyred Muslims, a few hundred, were buried outside along the slopes with short standing funeral prayers conducted one by one and the Goths inside a single large pit numbering around 2000. Inside the palace the wounded were carried across to the main chamber, where cloth was piled up to lay them down and give them medical care, water and food ... Then the court-yard was cleared and cleaned to house the cavalry, the horses, the tents and the arsenals. All this had been trained for in precision, military drill in battle, victory and in ransom. Midday.

Along the walls the spectators watched in anticipation the soldiers conducting the combined noon and afternoon prayers, another thing the villagers hadn't seen before. Then for all the rest of the afternoon followed the packing and building up of tents and finally as night fell in, evening and night prayers were conducted underneath a canopy of tents. After the prayers the camp was finally set up and the men were resting while the villagers brought their gifts for the liberators, buckets of milk, animals and plates of berries and mushrooms from the forests and moors, milk and cheese, the Iberian climate was like that of Scandinavia at that time, game and wild boars, the latter was rejected, still the rest accepted as generous gifts for the hungry warriors, served by young maids from every household. Vegetables and fruit were absent because the lack of sunshine didn't allow any such growth. Many of the women stayed in the fortified enclave and seemed to be reluctant to leave. The Imam called his newly converted comrades in Latin and had them translate his words to the locals:

"We come in Peace and respect the dignity of women. What is the reason why you are reluctant to leave?" The translators repeated in Gaulle, and then explained the response back to the Imam.

The maids, partly young and some of them of ripe age with children around them replied shyly looking at each other for help and support with their hands and knuckles risen up against their chests as to protect their dignity, covered in clothes and hides which lay bare some parts of their stomachs and legs. The Imam reached out to the bags and pulled out the sails, cut them with his sword into suitable pieces and handed them to the women for covering. They smiled back in happiness and raised their sweet voices like mermaids with flutes in the wind, a strange language with many new sounds like kisses to the ear, mesmerising to the listener.

"Iman Bilal, these our sisters lost their families and their homes were burnt. They came here from surrounding villages and have nothing left. Some are widows, others orphans, partly former wives with children, partly virgins, if they were not raped. They have just come down from the hills where they were in hiding from the Goths in the forests. They have nowhere to go. They need protection; the households of the village are full." Said a tall and strong man among them, Fredric, now called Alfred, a recent convert to Islam, His red-blonde hair fell down along his turban, which was as new to him as his white gown and his awkward sword. His piercing blue eyes stared at the Imam with tears full, at the brink of flowing.

"Marry these women, preference is given to the local men, choose from them now and I will do the ceremonies, we shall commence with land allocation and animals and building of houses and farms tomorrow." Short and sharp as a military command, Bilal had waited for such a chance.

"But Imam, we have our wives and farms in the land, most of us." Alfred replied.

"In Islam you are allowed up to 4 wives, now you can see why, who is going to take care of these women?" Bilal made short process of any objection.

He raised his voice as he recited out loud the eternal chant unheard before in this land:

"If ye fear that ye shall not be able to deal justly with the orphans, marry women of your choice, two or three or four; but if ye fear that ye shall not be able to deal justly (with them), then only one, or (a captive) that your right hands possess, that will be more suitable, to prevent you from doing injustice."
Surah 4 (Women), Verse 3

And he chanted in Latin and others translated it into Gaulle.

The women pointed at the soldiers and pointed out to the Imam their preferences already. They understood immediately what they were offered and they were not reluctant or shy about this at all. They knew what they needed, what they had been longing for for a long time.

"The women of the people of the Book are allowed to you, especially Christians and Jews. So marry them, up to 4." He spoke to his newly converted men as well as his fellow soldiers from across the Straight alike.

The men had collected food and had already prepared the barbecue with the animals they had been given by the locals and they were now turning their attention to the women, following the command of the Imam.

"Marriage is a good thing, marriage is easy in Islam and marriage is not to be delayed in Islam. It is not supposed to be a burden or difficult to arrange or be forced upon anyone. So choose freely and without any compulsion. Women are not supposed to be alone, so it's every man's duty to marry one, or two, or three, or four, if he can and wants. Marriage is just the beginning and marriage is compulsory before men and women go alone with each other. We cannot afford any sort of fornication or any type of adultery or we shall loose all blessings in this mission! Intercourse is only for the married, whose company has been blessed through prayer and witnessed and whose offspring have 2 confirmed and committed parents, none of the women is to be left alone to fend for her offspring . . .

"*. . . Kings, when they enter a country, despoil it, and make the noblest of its people its meanest thus do they behave . . . .*"
Surah 27 (the Ant), Verse 24

. . . If I see as much as one rape or one killing I shall take the head of the perpetrator with my own hands, if I hear of one case of fornication I shall lash the couple with my own whip!"

With these strong, concise and piercing words he pulled his mighty sword out of the shaft, a sword that had felt many necks and drunken much blood, yet a sword reluctant to strike without warning, a sword too kind to cut the neck of the innocent. In amazement the locals watched as the stainless steel reached for the stars and as it reflected the bright moonlight, which they had never seen. It seemed to melt together with it in a sparkling dance of the milky-way, the people from the Sahel too were tall, perhaps taller than the Goths, but much slimmer and darker, you could not have seen their faces in the night despite of the bright starlight were it not for the moon and the fire from the grills and flames they had placed alongside the walls of the fortress.

"Therefore marry, if you fear you cannot be abstinent." He added.

All men knew fairly well that pleading for Mercy and Forgiveness was still an option after mutually agreed fornication, of course not in cases of rape, but marriage was also their desire. Immediately as with a push from these vehement words the men lined up, newly converts and their mostly darker freshly arrived brothers from across the sea along the lines of the women who stood against the city walls and after short haggling and wrangling you could see some of the men stepping slowly towards the women and holding hands with smiles in their faces, the newly converts being a bit more hesitant than the old Muslims and after some pushing and pulling they had at that very moment a match of couples along the walls. The light of the barbecue and the torches lighted up their faces. Happiness spread as the hammer hit the nail's head. Not one sad face. Hearts were filled with love and relief as the Imam spoke:

"All couples now line up here in front of me," he laughed and pointed out the way he wanted the queue to be. It grew and grew from where he stood all along the wall spirally. He had a long night's job in front of him. He was full of smiles.

"Tariq and Alfred, you must witness this!" They came along immediately and took position, one to the left, the other to the right of the Imam.

He looked each couple in the eye as each couple was given a cloth for the bride and a coin of gold each, symbolising their share in the booty and the dowry from the soldier to his bride. The first couple stepped towards him as he waved them by and they were the oddest, yet perfect match. A tall Bedouin from the Touareg tribe in Algeria, the mineral traders of the Sahara and a most fair and reddish-blonde princess of the Gaulles. She smiled and looked down in her natural shyness as she was a virgin and orphan, who had lost all she had, family, home, people, this being the happiest moment she could remember. She had seen them fight, she had seen them smile and she had seen them not demanding anything, just defeating the rapists and murderers, who killed all her family. All she wanted was a home and a man. And a man so strange, exotic, so strong, someone who could defend her yet was kind and caring was an adventure and welcome change from these brutal Goths in deed. The Imam spoke:

"I take refuge with Allah's perfect Words which no righteous or unrighteous person can transgress from all the evil He has made, created and originated. I take refuge from the evil that descends from the skies and rises up to them. I take refuge from the evil that is spread on Earth and the evil that springs from her, and I take refuge from the tribulations from night and day, and the evil of one who visits at night except the one who brings good, O Merciful One!"

He took a deep breath and with the twinkling of the stars the Mumins, the most pious Muslims, could see the angels riding the light waves down from Heaven to reach the believers and transmit the blessings directly from their Creator. This is how the Muslims of those times acted, no lengthy and decadent wedding ceremonies that would have lasted for days or even weeks, just the bare necessity of rituals in the Name of Allah, under the immediate guidance of his Words and the example of his Prophet (pbuh).

"Are you ready to join in marriage for this life and the hereafter?" In Islam divorce is allowed but marriage does not end with death. The couple enters paradise together, if they earn it.

The entire crowd nodded the warriors once with a sharp smile, the women repeatedly.

"I seek refuge with Allah from Satan the accursed. In the name of Allah Most Gracious, Most Merciful."

Alfred whispered repeating these words in Gaulle to the first bride as the Imam speedily yet eloquently and beautifully melodiously chanted these verses:

"I seek refuge with Allah from Satan the accursed.
In the Name of Allah, Most Gracious, Most Merciful.
All Praise is Allah's, Guardian of all Beings
Most Forgiving, Full of Mercy
Master of Judgement-Day
Only you we serve and only for Your help we crave
Show us the Straight Way
The way of those to whom you've sent down from your Grace
Those who don't deserve disgrace and who do not go astray"
Surah 1 (The Opening)

He pointed them to the side towards the empty dinner plates on the floor that were lain out on white garment from the sails, saying: "In the Name of Allah". The next couple approached, a woman of age who was to be wed to an Arab warrior a few inches shorter than her. They were happy and the people cheered at the sight of this odd and funny couple, love was stronger than physiology that night. The women had 3 children with her, all of minor age and one older child, a girl of 12 or so. They were all smiling and welcomed their newly won step-father as the pain of the loss of their own father faded away into the night.

With the first Surah of the Quran he pointed them to the side and towards the banquet which had been prepared, they kneeled down in circles around the plates, as couple after couple was wed that very night in this very way and the white garment was spun across the ground under the canopy of tents, where the festive mass wedding was completed within hours. And they ate and drank, groom next to groom, bride next to bride, now covered in white cloth and ready for the first night with a new husband. Children kneeled in between.

Outside the city walls the villagers held their own celebrations dancing around the fire to the tone of the bone-flutes, drums of hide, doodle-sacks and the thirst quenched in wine. The Muslim garrisons placed there watched and clapped in joy, joining in on the drumming, an exotic cross-over jam where East and West, South and North met. And how similar were the sounds, how common the rhythms, Celtic and Bedouin. There too love was born where fathers gave their daughters happily in marriage to the newly arrived warriors, heroes. A few stormed by to the Imam, asking for his permission at last moment. The Imam did not reject a single pair of them, exhausted as he was.

The Gaulles were friendly, peaceful and hospitable people, not as strict about their Catholicism as Romans, although these people were mixed with Romans, Goths and Greeks as well as Byzantines and many other tribes from the North that the Roman and then Vandal Empires had brought in. Some of their roots even reached as far back as Punic or Phoenician times and this essentially gave them an ancient bridge to the tribes of Arabia. Spain had been under Carthage before Roman times, the people of Hannibal, some 900 years before, who themselves were an offshoots of Phoenician colonies that were founded by their Lebanese ancestors. Most of them did not know this, but they felt the ties. And since all of mankind comes from one pair, Adam and Eve, and after that Noah and his family, the bond is natural once the barriers are torn down. And they were certainly torn down that very night. Echoes of the Koran reversing in their minds and the Will of the Prophet (pbuh).

"O mankind! We created you from a single (pair) of a male and a female, and made you into nations and tribes, that ye may know how to love each other. Verily the most honoured of you in the sight of Allah is who is most righteous. And Allah has full knowledge and is well acquainted (with all things)."
Sura 49 (The Private Appartments) Verse 13

". . . All mankind is from Adam and Eve, <u>an Arab has no superiority over a non-Arab nor a non-Arab has any superiority over an Arab; a white man has no superiority over a black man nor a black man has any superiority over a white man</u> . . ."
Prophet Muhammad's Last Sermon, 632 A.D

Words not even 100 years old still fresh in their collective memories. Like a father who gathers his sons to speak to them his will shortly before his death, the most important words he ever says. Words that hit on open ears and minds back in those times lead inevitably to immediate and eternal success as they still would, were they only obeyed.

They ate and drank late into the night and they withdrew into the tents built up around the palace and into the chambers of the palace for the night with fireplaces to keep themselves warm, olive-oil lamps and coal-lit furnaces where condensed green-tea and coffee brew in small steel kettles and small glasses were used to cool and ventilate the drink with air by pouring it from far high into the glass on the plate below repeatedly. The sweet and rosy smell of incense and cinnamon, green-tea and coffee spread far and wide across the valley. Tears of joy and laughter.

The kids were given their own tents for the night and were fast asleep while the sounds of love filled the air around the palace and inside the walls. Thus peace and love had arrived in Iberia and the stars and moon were witness to this fact, just like the angels waiting to carry the new souls into the many wombs after 40 days, once they had witnessed the couples' intercourse. 7 weeks were the period of delay between insemination and insertion of the soul into the embryo by decree as known by the Hadith, the sayings of the Prophet Mohammed (pbuh). During that period mercy is granted to the victims of rape or incest or the perpetrators of adultery if abortion is their decision. These were laws of justice and truth that have now been long forgotten. But those were the rules that were still fresh in the minds of those who were blessed on their journey towards bringing Islam to the tribes of the Land of the Vandals. These rules were the manifestation of the blessings they carried along with them. They did not only bring their women from back home to marry them by arrangement or compulsion. They married there and then as Allah wished it. And that was part of the secret of their success and they knew it. And we know it. But we fear it! We fear the truth! We would rather engage in lengthy courtship, family arrangements or long expensive festivities and along that way loose the eternal collective blessings.

The lack of this same understanding in later generations was the reason for failure, when Muslims began to segregate themselves from anything new and alien, because of fear and compulsion. Fear and compulsion based on false tradition. False tradition based on deviation from the true religion. False tradition masking itself as religion. Hypocrisy. In fact false tradition is the handiwork of none other than the eternal enemy of mankind, who has promised to strive for its failure with his full effort. The Spirit of Evil. If you reject it, you're accepted as fit. Fit for eternal profit. If you accept it, you have deviated. And deviate they did but not until later centuries.

What Tariq and Bilal understood that day was that marriage is the manifestation of the acceptance of one's mission on earth during a conquest, unity of mankind across the boundaries under the banner of truth. How can that happen if one only marries inside one's own family, tribe, race or nation? It can never happen that way. So if they had entered a new country without marrying local women, they would not have been blessed and not conquered and not ruled it. Stayed a minority. If they had taken slaves they would have not fulfilled the will of the

Prophet Mohammed (pbuh), who considered the freeing of slaves as a noble deed and lead by example, not until later generations deviated did they reinstate slavery as an institution. Such as the Sultan had freed them from slavery, they now too refrained from slavery and nurtured an equal relationship in marriage, because in Islam women had rights to witness, divorce and inherit. And if they had not married, much rape and fornication would have taken place.

"It is not righteousness that ye turn your faces Towards East or West; but it is righteousness—to believe in Allah and the Last Day, and the Angels, and the Book, and the Messengers; to spend of your substance, out of love for Him, for your kin, for orphans, for the needy, for the wayfarer, for those who ask, <u>and for the ransom of slaves;</u> to be steadfast in prayer, and practice regular charity; to fulfil the contracts which ye have made; and to be firm and patient, in pain (or suffering) and adversity, and throughout all periods of panic. Such are the people of truth, the Allah fearing."
Surah 2 (the Heifer), Verse 177

And so it goes that during that night new souls were in the making that would have their share in the most prosperous and fruitful of cultures ever in the history of mankind, lineages of gentry and craftsmen, warriors, scholars, doctors, lawyers, judges and scientists were opened that very night. Justice breeds progress and stability. It must do so as it is brought about by truth, a truth based directly on revelation cannot hurt the true believer, the one who has not yet deviated from his way through false culture and conjecture, by following blindly scholars' and parents' words without reading them in the Book of Allah, if he read it in a language he could understand, if he read it without mourning the dead, if only he read it himself!

Around 1000 weddings took place during these festive days, Tariq and Bilal lead by example by taking a wife each. Hence Muslims had planted their seeds in the fertile soil of this new land, those seeds were soon to grow roots in the lush yet barren land, strange yet full of welcoming love. The locals were sweet people, innocent and open. In the second night in this new country the scene was very similar, inside the walls the captives and outside the local villagers eagerly listening to their new friends in amazement to these stories about one God and his last and final Messenger to mankind, who commanded kindness, justice and peace. This was a different breed of men altogether, not the isolated and estranged, celibate monks. These were warriors with intellect, swordsmen with spiritualism, archers with knowledge of the unseen, soldiers with the wisdom of priests, bishops with certain powers of the unseen.

The gate, or rather what was left of it, the gap in the wall became the most frequented place as young girls took their new men back out after the wedding to take them into the family home, to show them off to their families, because even those girls who were local villagers began to grab one of those warriors while they could, taking them into the round Celtic houses with straw roofs around a central fireplace, smoke columns rising from the gaps in the roofs, surrounded by Moorish tents.

One week went by and the men had begun construction work on command of Tariq and Imam Bilal, who had brought along plans from Damascus. The Sultan was a keen architect which he had proven by building the Dome of the Rock and a new mosque in Damascus was in the making. Here in Al-Andalus foundations started to emerge in the muddy ground. A mosque, a hospital, a university, libraries, residences, forts. The ideal location for the hospital was determined by placing pieces of meat on sticks across town systematically and choosing the stake where the meat decayed at the slowest rate over a week as the centre point of the building. In this way micro-climate, spore and bacterial count and clean airflow were all considered carefully. Buildings were in planning, wooden scaffoldings littered the landscape and the surrounding area much to the amazement of the locals. One could see Tariq and Imam Bilal running to and fro instructing the men, soldiers turned engineers and construction workers. They stayed there for a few weeks and completed the fundaments of the many buildings.

On the 7th week, after the Friday prayer in the mosque within the fortified palace Tariq called the men together:

"O men of Allah, you have done well, by the Grace of the Almighty. New souls have been conceived in the wombs of our new sisters. Last night we woke long and sensed the lights descending, by the Grace of the Almighty, the Lord of all Beings. Our first part of the mission has been fulfilled, we have established a kingdom. This is the beginning. You have seen an example of our work, a guideline for the whole country, a blueprint for you to follow and copy. I will now appoint leaders and divide you into armies who are to spread out and found similar cities across the peninsula, if Allah wills. I myself will march along the East-Coast with half the armies. My Brother Bilal will take the other half along the West and we are to meet at the feet of the hills at the North. On the way there we shall await the arrival of another army, fresh from Damascus, which was sent along the coasts of Byzantine and Rome. Along the way we will leave behind garrisons in the places we conquer. We shall leave behind here and now with preference those who married local women to guard the heart of our new Empire, Granada. In this way we will not tear apart the families, this is not our intention. Those who march with us, rest assured, your time to settle down will come. You came with nothing and here you shall find everything.

Once we have surrounded them we will aim for the head of the Beast. At the heart of this land lie two cities called Toledo (Tulaytulah) and Reccopolis where Roderick rules from. We will assemble there and I expect the armies to send delegations for that decisive battle which I anticipate within a year, inshallah, godwilling. We shall stay in touch through pigeons as well as riders and crosslink paths reporting back to Granada. We will not conduct that final strike, we shall not attempt that lethal blow, that necessary evil without establishing our rule firmly over the rest of the country, until we force the lion out of the den, until he has nowhere else to flee within this land. He will be too humiliated to ride North by then, back to his family. They will not welcome him anyway, so we have to make him meet his end there, godwilling.

Toledo (Tulaytulah) and Reccopolis are our final destinations, however, we shall not go there until we free Valencia, Madrid, Alloysious (Isbunah *Arabic*, Lisbon), Braga and Porto, Seville (Isbiliyah, *Arabic*) and Malaga, Cordoba (Qartubah, *Arabic*) and Catalan, Saragossa (Sarakusta, *Arabic*, Aragon, *Latin*), Galicia and Basque. The forts of the Romans and their surrounding monastries. The kingdoms of Pelayo, Wittiza, who is in exile and Roderick until we reach his capital Toledo (Tulaytulah, *Arabic*). 1 year, 3 years, 7 years, no matter how long it takes. We shall stay and conquer. We shall spread justice and truth. Remember this place, remember this day. This is your stronghold, this is your guideline, and this is your home from now on. Follow the lead of Grenada, baptise the places, unite it under the Sultanate of Al-Andalus, the land of the Vandals, Inshallah, Ameen!"

The men cheered and were exhilarated. They were in an ecstasy of success and determination. The morale could not have been higher. And at the same time they knew the task could not have been harder. Tariq knew fairly well that the morale was at its highest now and was going to sink gradually over the years, which is why he was trying to push it as high as possible. He appointed 10 leaders from the noblemen of the tribes and gave them each their garrison of men across different tribes. He appointed an Imam, a doctor, judge and a general among each garrison and gave each garrison its target fort. They would march 5 along the West and 5 along the East and leave behind a garrison at each town. When the last of the 5 garrisons met at the North, they would all send half of their men towards the heart of the land, Toledo and Reccopolis.

During the following weeks like in the first 7 weeks, but now more intensively, troops were sent on expeditions inland and along the cliffs at the coastal areas of the land to explore the routs and draw maps and take astrolabe readings with altitude, longitude, latitude and all results were brought together and integrated in the central admin chamber in the palace of Granada. There the scholars and scientists assembled, pigeons were hatched and reared for posting letters quickly back to Granada, troops were collated from across the Empire that came during the coming weeks from as far as Mail, Syria, India, Azerbaijan, as the story of the conquest spread fast via Mecca. Much laudation was sent and the Sultan planned his visit immediately upon return from Azerbaijan, whilst laying the foundations for a new mosque in Damascus. Word came he was to join the conquest from the North-East after paying a visit to the Emperors of Byzantine and Rome along with the army he had promised already. Tariq and Bilal planned a surprise for him. They would name a city after Alwalid, Vallada, where he first set foot on Spanish land. They also knew that Ibn-Musa, the governor of Africa was to join them from the South with more refreshment as well.

The Grip

"And fight them on until there is no more tumult or oppression, and there prevail justice and faith in Allah altogether and everywhere; but if they cease, verily Allah doth see all that they do. "
Surah 8 (Spoils of War) 39

Every day as dawn broke over the land, what a bright dawn it was, the men came out of the tents and palace, as soon as the call to prayer was heard across this new Islamic Kingdom. They shuffled water form the shallow streams and with white wrappers around their waists washed the private parts and the whole body, then poured the cold fresh water over their hands and mouths and noses and faces and arms and heads and bodies and feet. 2-3 times repeatedly. This was the cleansing from the night, the principle washing, the Ghusl. Ready for prayer, ready for the day.

One day Tariq and Bilal were preparing their march North at the sight of the new moon crescent. Julian-Urban of Ceuta sent his monks to ask them to join him in the Christian camp. They entered the tent where crosses were marking each and every object, including the tent and the entrance itself, one having to bow to the cross while entering. Tariq and Bilal looked at each other and smiled.

"May Peace be upon you and may Allah give you guidance," Tariq and Bilal greeted their Christian Brothers.

"And you, my dear Brothers, and you . . ." replied Julian-Urban in Arabic, being half Arab and having lived with Arabs all his life, his mission in Ceuta as co-Consul of the Vatican, Byzantine and Reccopolis, the religious capitals of 3 Empires, he was an influential and powerful man, a dignity nobody could deny, although he was strange looking to the Romans, he looked very familiar to the Hispanics and Arabs, a typical bridge-person, he could easily have passed as a Jew. One who could have held the peace, had there only not been so much bloodshed already.

Julian had engaged the Arabs for a reason. It was only as a last resort, cool and calculated, not without planning. All the while he kept a firm grip on all actions, monitored each and every move and tactic, kept open lines to the leadership, Ibn Musa, Amir of Al-Afrique and Alwalid, Sultan of Damascus, the pope and Byzantine. He had brought along pigeons of his own and was sending them, reporting regularly to Rome and to Damascus independently from Tariq and Bilal, whilst they had just established a pigeon colony in Granada that was being carefully shipped to Damascus so they could hear back weekly and order fresh pigeons from Damascus as their Damascus-reared pigeons were running out. Throughout the ancient and medieval civilisations pigeons were used for long-distance communication.

Each letter was tied to 3 pigeons independently so it was sure to reach home. These clever little birds navigate by the earth's magnetic field and always find their way home unless intercepted by falcons. And Roderick had sent spies with falcons to every section of the Iberian coastline. But it was a one-way communication with these pigeons anyway, until the eggs in Granada were hatched and the birds were at least a couple of weeks into flight and then shipped to Damascus or Kairouan or Alexandria. That would take a few more months. Julian's pigeons came from Ceuta and were regularly supplied by the Vatican and Byzantine. And Byzantine and Rome had their own connections to Damascus, the local Christian abbots in Damascus being their representants. So they were in touch and Julian had no problem in keeping the lines open since he had boats crossing the Straight every day.

Julian had these dreams though, that were not letting go of his conscience. They were haunting him, even in broad daylight. And bright were the days in Hispania now. He succumbed to fever murmuring his thoughts, laying bare his innermost secrets, while the assistant monks wiped his forehead with wet cloth and did their best to keep him calm. Had he not been such a senior figure they would have surely gotten rid of him easily during these turbulent times.

Charles resided in the corner of the tent next to the barrel of wine. He was somewhat distant to this scene, not approving of what was going on, Julian seemed too amicable with this conquest. Charles was the type who would have openly confronted the Arabs, were it not for the shear number of overwhelming forces they had brought along. He was too late to assemble an army against the Goths himself, which he had tried for many years; this was what was depressing him, almost to a state of permanent frustration. These monks were too subservient to the word. He was of a different creed that would in later generations command to join crusades, inquisition and imperialism, spreading the word by force. So he kept his silence most of the time, only letting off short and sharp comments, like knives into the lines of the Muslims to make known his dismay.

The Muslims knew his type, they had Christians and Jews amongst themselves and they were used to open envy and confrontation, which they mostly replied to with humour and laughs, wiping them off like dust. However, jealousy towards the Muslims was immanent due to their fast dominance across the known world. Umayyads even sent missionaries into the heart of Europe, Switzerland, England, where Anglo-Saxon kings were ordering coins from Damascus with "No God but Allah" stamped on them and Estonia had commissioned a city-wall for protection against the Swedes.

"My Brother Tariq," Julian said ignoring Bilal.

It was no secret that the Catholics still thought of Blacks as Gladiators, slaves essentially, not worthy of equality, depicting Judas and Cain as Black despising the Jews, who were mixed with the Sabaeans (from the marriage of the Queen of Sheba to Solomon, pbuh), declaring racial interbreeding as heresy, calling the children of mixed couples bastards and not approving of the open mixed marriages and conversions to Islam. Bilal knew fairly well how to deal with that. The more someone did that to him, the more he would smile and raise his voice and emphasize his eloquence in Latin, Greek and Hebrew as they swapped languages constantly while debating with Christians and Jews of different origins.

"We hear you", Bilal replied, Tariq and Bilal both smiled along.

"Oh yes, Brothers, heh, I called for you because I want to raise some concerns. This Conquest of yours is a most noble and blessed task and believe me, Rome will be eternally thankful for this service of yours to the pope and the Lord Jesus Christ, our shepherd."

He had to take a break every few sentences because his breath failed him. He was heavily asthmatic and a vapour of herbs and salts was spread around him that the Amir of Afrique, Ibn Musa, had sent as a gift from his herbal-gardens in Rabbat and some came from Ibn Musa's cousins who ruled around Cairo, all close members of the Umayyad clan, who maintained excellent relations to the religious leaders and Kings of all Empires not only politically but also through intermarriage. In fact a noble Arab those days was a more befitting groom for a Roman, Byzantine or Greek princess than a common local peasant or even a rich tradesman from the silk route. The Catholics did not approve marriage to Muslims though. But even the Gaulles and Goths knew very well about the expanding power of Muslims and offered their daughters to the Sultans, Caliphs, Amirs and Wezirs. Ibn Musa was only looking after his potential in-laws when sending these gifts to Julian-Urban and Julian was from Ceuta, he was part of the Maghreb union and had helped them tremendously in crossing the Straight, opened the doors to Al-Andalus for them. Julian approved of intermarriage of Catholics with Arabs and Berbers, relatively light-skinned people, but not any other Muslim tribe.

"We engaged your most generous assistance in order to facilitate re-entrance into Hispanic Rome for our Christian monasteries and clerics. Our utmost longing is to re-establish the Kingdom of Christ and the Cross in these countries. We need your assurance that that will happen and that you will revert this land to the pope and his servants under the banner of the Father, the Son and the Holy Spirit once you are through with your mission."

There was a moment of silence. A silence so dense you could have almost split the air with a knife. Tension rose while Charles and the other abbots of the mission to Damascus stared and focussed their eyes on Tariq, leaving aside Bilal, too dark to stare at for their noble Roman eyes, whilst Tariq was almost fairer than them, him they could tolerate, accept, perhaps. Was he only baptised in the Name of Trinity.

Tariq spoke, Bilal held his silence; it was not the moment to prove them wrong. It was a moment for diplomacy.

"Brothers. We have come here on instructions of the Sultan of Damascus, whom you asked for help, in Command of the forces of Al-Afrique granted by the Amir Ibn Musa. Clearly they did not specify this to us, but asked us to be guided by our Creator, Allah the eternal Almighty under the teachings of our Last and final Messenger Mohammed (pbuh), who was forecasted by Jesus (pbuh) even in the Canonical Gospels as the Comforter,

Al-Hamd, the Trustworthy, John Chapter 14, verse 16, Chapter 15 verse 26 and Chapter 16, Verse 7 to Verse 14. You would say Jesus (pbuh) speaks of the Holy Spirit, but surely the Holy Spirit has been around since before and during Jesus' (pbuh) time, so why does Jesus (pbuh) say, he has to leave for him to come? Since our Prophet Mohammed (pbuh) is also mentioned in the original Hebrew Torah, naturally not the translations, as Ahmad in Haggai, Chapter 2, Verse 7, the Holy one of Pharan in Habakuk Chapter 3, Verse 3, his flight from Mecca to Madina is mentioned in Isiah, as well as the fact that he will not be able to read, Chapter 29 Verse 12. He is also mentioned in Hindu and Zoroastrian scriptures millennia ago, he is mentioned as the Antam-Rashi, the Narashansa, the Bhoji, the final Messenger. Why don't we openly hold a debate in front of the People and let them decide and choose what they want and what is ultimately best for them, which they wish to follow without compulsion and obligation, voluntarily and happily?

Bilal added: "Our Prophet Muhammad (pbuh) is mentioned by name in the Old Testament in the Song of Solomon chapter 5 verse 16, I will recite the original in Hebrew: "Hikko Mamittakim we kullo Muhammadim Zehdoodeh wa Zehraee Bayna Jerusalem." meaning "His mouth is most sweet: yea, he is altogether lovely (Muhammadim). This is my beloved, and this is my friend, O daughters of Jerusalem." So we let you decide . . ."

And Bilal ended with a recitation from the Koran, as in Alexandria they had produced Latin translations of the Bible, so at times he chose Arabic, when especially addressing Julian, who spoke Arabic fairly well, and other times Bilal spoke Latin:

"Let there be no compulsion in religion: Truth stands out clear from Error: whoever rejects evil and believes in Allah hath grasped the most trustworthy hand-hold, that never breaks. And Allah hears and knows all things."
Surah 2 (the Heifer) Verse 256

"Hah, Brothers, you overestimate the common peasant's mind . . . It is true that you follow the path of the righteous and are virtuous in your deeds and have been somewhat blessed by Abrahams' descent via Ishmael, however, the common man cannot come to the truth by himself, for we are like sheep in the sight of our Lord and must be lead to the water. For as our Father and Lord Jesus Christ, the one and only begotten Son of God is our shepherd, the pope, the representant of Christ on Earth is also our shepherd and we abbots and monks and priests are the shepherds of the people. You will understand that one day; I am sure, because you are wise."

Julian gasped for air as he finished the last few words of his.

"We do not interfere with your ways, Brother; do not interfere with ours, unless you wish for an open and honest philosophical debate. And then you will hear the whole Truth manifestly and you will have to accept it." Tariq was firm.

Now Charles took over the word and with his cup of wine in front of him smashing to the floor, he stood up with his whole tall figure and shouted:

"Philosophy? That's the way of the pagans, the ancient Greeks and the old Romans before the time of Christ. Now we are much wiser, wise enough not to reason, reason is worldly delusion, man cannot come to the truth by reason, he needs revelation. What new did your religion bring anyway? What is in it that our Lord Jesus Christ, the Son of God, the flesh and incarnate God would not have taught us already?"

Tariq replied: "See, this is exactly it. We believe revelation and reason go hand in hand and must achieve harmony in order for human and the divine to communicate properly. That is why like Jesus Christ (pbuh) for you is the flesh of God, Mohammed (pbuh) is the word of God to us. Because Christ himself said in the Gospel of John, as I quoted before, he had a lot to say to you but he could not tell it at his time as you were not ready for it. That is why he prayed to the Lord to send his Comforter, who shall not speak out of his own accord but by inspiration, the Holy Spirit put the Lord's words in his mouth and those he shall speak. In John Chapter 16 Verse 7 you can read that the Helper or Comforter can only arrive once Jesus (pbuh) has left, so it cannot be the Holy Spirit, for the Archangel Gabriel, whom you call the Holy Spirit, was already present at the time and during the life of Jesus (pbuh). And the words are not entirely new of course. What the Archangel Gabriel brought to Mohammed (pbuh) is the same message of old, that was revealed to Adam (pbuh) already, the message of One God, Love, Peace, Justice and Truth, from which former generations have deviated, like those who have taken others as partners to God, son of God, even his own messengers are worshiped besides him and even the virgin-Mary, pbuh."

Tariq was careful not to offend anyone but as the Words took the better of him he was sure to at least mellow down his voice in order to sound most calm under the heavy weight his speech would carry.

"How do you know the word of the Lord so well? How dare you quote from the most Holy Gospel, canonical the while? Have you been to Franciscan schools? Are you born and christened in the Name of the Father, the Son and the Holy Spirit?" Charles pushed his mighty eyebrows deep into his eyes as he finished.

And silence again. Julian was breathing hard and Charles staring into the round.

"We have been taught the Torah, the Old Testament, the Gospel, the Psalms, the Vedas, the Upnashaids, the Bhagvadgita, the Puranas and the Book of Zoroaster as well as the Tao Te Ching and the teachings of Buddah. The Koran teaches us that Prophets were sent to all People and were rejected or accepted for a while and then people deviated after subsequent generations. That is why we needed the final and universal reminder, the cleansing, the criterion, the book, the reading, the warning, the word, the sign and the message, the Koran, to come again and be revealed in its entirety and purity and preserved by Allah himself until the Last Day."

Tariq and Bilal stood smiling at each other while Julian tried to mediate:

"Our Lord Jesus Christ teaches us to turn the other cheek and so we did for centuries with these Goths. But what does your Book say about Jesus Christ our Lord?"

"A most righteous Christian King received a delegation from Mecca during the Life of the Prophet Mohammed (pbuh) and asked the same question. King Ajashi of Ethiopia." Tariq stated.

Julian and Charles frowned at the thought of a Black Christian king and the round of monks stared in unrest at each other.

"He got the following answer . . ." Tariq pointed at Bilal to continue. And Tariq was Hafiz as well but Bilal was also a Muezzin and he knew how to chant the Koran in many different ways according to the situation and mood, time of the day and such factors that influence intonation, the converts from India had brought with them their Ragas and Sutras, alongside with arithmetic the mathematical enchantment of souls and the Koran is multi-compatible with all harmony and adaptable to all rhythms and melodies. So he took a deep breath and a mystical-magical flute in company of a whole orchestra released from his mouth, his mesmerising voice converted into an amplified instrument, something so strong the likes not heard in this land before:

"I seek refuge with Allah from Satan the accursed.
In the Name of Allah Most Gracious, Most Merciful.
Relate in the Book (the story of) Mary, when she withdrew from her family to a place in the East.
She placed a screen (to screen herself) from them; then We sent her our angel, and he appeared before her as human.
She said: "I seek refuge from thee to ((Allah)) Most Gracious: (come not near) if thou dost fear Allah."
He said: "Nay, I am only a messenger from thy Lord, (to announce) to thee the gift of a holy son.
She said: "How shall I have a son, seeing that no man has touched me, and I am not unchaste?"
He said: "So (it will be): Thy Lord saith, 'that is easy for Me: and (We wish) to appoint him as a Sign unto men and a Mercy from Us': It is a matter (so) decreed."
So she conceived him, and she retired with him to a remote place.
And the pains of childbirth drove her to the trunk of a dead palm-tree: She cried (in her anguish): "Ah! would that I had died before this! Would that I had been a thing forgotten and out of sight!"

But (a voice) cried to her from beneath the (palm-tree): "Grieve not! for thy Lord hath provided a rivulet beneath thee;

"And shake towards thyself the trunk of the dead palm-tree: It will let fall fresh ripe dates upon thee.

"So eat and drink and cool (thine) eye. And if thou dost see any man, say, 'I have vowed a fast to ((Allah)) Most Gracious, and this day will I enter into not talk with any human being'"

At length she brought the (babe) to her people, carrying him (in her arms). They said: "O Mary! truly an amazing thing hast thou brought!

"O sister of Aaron! Thy father was not a man of evil, nor thy mother a woman unchaste!"

But she pointed to the babe. They said: "How can we talk to one who is a child in the cradle?"

He said: "I am indeed a servant of Allah. He hath given me revelation and made me a prophet;

"And He hath made me blessed wheresoever I be, and hath enjoined on me Prayer and Charity as long as I live;

"(He) hath made me kind to my mother, and not overbearing or miserable;

"So peace is on me the day I was born, the day that I die, and the day that I shall be raised up to life (again)"!

Such (was) Jesus the son of Mary: (it is) a statement of truth, about which they (vainly) dispute.

It is not befitting to (the majesty of) Allah that He should beget a son. Glory be to Him! When He determines a matter, He only says to it, "Be", and it is.

Verily Allah is my Lord and your Lord: Him therefore serve ye: this is a Way that is straight.

But the sects differ among themselves: and woe to the unbelievers because of the (coming) Judgment of a Momentous Day!

How plainly will they see and hear, the Day that they will appear before Us! But the unjust today are in error manifest!

But warn them of the Day of Distress, when the matter will be determined: for (behold,) they are negligent and they do not believe!

It is We Who will inherit the earth, and all beings thereon: to Us will they all be returned!"

Surah 19 (Mary) Verses 19-40.

Julian of course understood fairly well, as he spoke Arabic and was reflecting on these ideas as Bilal repeated his words in the most eloquent and posh Latin like that spoken in the Vatican and by all the monks in the round. They were amazed and suspended in a state of shock.

"Do you not teach your slaves to control their tongues? Blasphemy! How can you say Jesus is not the only begotten Son of our Father? By the Holy mother of God!" Charles reached for his sword, while Julian rolled down from his bed and placed his hand over that of Charles, gasping for air, but forcing himself to smile at Tariq.

"Please excuse him, he has fought hard and seen many losses at the hands of the Goths!"

"So have we," replied Bilal.

"Please forgive his youthful ignorance!" Julian ended the discourse.

As Tariq and Bilal turned around and left the tent, Bilal said loud and clear:

"At least now we know what we are at!"

Julian followed them with heavy steps and his monks tried to hold him back, but he insisted and tore himself off:

"Brothers, please forgive us, we have suffered much hardship. I actually need to inform you about some things. Please listen to me. We were told by a few local monks here in Granada that the Byzantines have established colonies on islands off the coast of Hispania towards the East, the Balearics, and they are planning to storm in from the South-East to capture as much land as they can. We are not loyal to them anymore as the late Julain dynasty abandoned the pope in his hours of distress and established a truce with the Goths, the Ostrigoths, but we maintain ties of communication with the Heraclian dynasty. Here in Hispania we are dealing with Visigoths though, who are only distantly related to the Ostrigoths.

By now Tariq and Bilal had stopped and were listening very carefully as this could be crucial to their mission and could not only influence but even jeopardise their whole plan. Julian continued:

"So, like I was saying, the Byzantines have been hostile to the pope ever since they have been in a pact with the Goths who occupied the land and always plotted against him. Now that they see that you are in confrontation with the Goths they sent garrisons of their Viking guards to the Balearics in order to prepare for an offensive. The Vikings of the Normandy and elsewhere in Europe have converted to Christianity and are the only match for the Goths in Europe apart from the Franks. I want you to be aware of that."

"All right, it is very noble of you in deed to tell us about these developments and it is much appreciated. We shall appoint an expedition towards those islands with local guides in order to monitor the situation and developments carefully; perhaps offence is the best defence in this case," Tariq spoke

"It might be worth appointing a separate unit, perhaps order reinforcements directly from Damascus for this purpose," Bilal added.

"You are very wise for a Moor," added Julian, despite of his nature, having seen Blacks all his life as lower-rank slaves for petty-services such as cleaning and washing, if not just sweeping the yard and heavy-duty lifting of water as well as tilling the soil.

"Was not the Queen of Sheba Black and the Pharaoh at the times of Abraham (pbuh)? Whites were his slaves. You might be surprised how dark Jesus (pbuh) was himself and perhaps even Adam (pbuh)." Bilal spoke. "Islam teaches us equality and many of the first Muslims and companions of the Prophet Mohammed (pbuh) were Black as was the first King to embrace Islam, Ajashi of Ethiopia. He converted from Christianity. Hager is very likely to have been Black and Ishmael (pbuh) subsequently mixed, therefore the Arabs, including Mohammed (pbuh) of racially mixed descent, although they may have forgotten that by now." Bilal added. "We have evidence that Adam (pbuh) must have been Black and Eve, they gave birth to the people of the Southern mountains in Africa, Kilimanjaro, a tribe called the Maasai, who call themselves fathers of all people, tall and handsome they have very diverse features and colours between the darkest of dark and the lightest of brown. And then after the Great flood of Noah perhaps some 100,000 years ago around the Black Sea region came a long Age of Ice during which North and South were divided and the Northern people developed white colour to cope with the lack of sunshine, since the blood needs sunlight to survive and white skin is more transparent. Black skin on the other hand protects the blood from harmful light from the sun. We have discovered a disease of the skin and blood that light coloured people develop, if they don't cover themselves in Southern regions and another disease that our dark people develop in the North, if they don't eat enough fish and don't get any sunshine it leads to a deformation of their bones. They also gain weight and become obese."

Bilal was of course talking about skin-cancer caused by excessive UV-light from the sun, rickets caused by a lack vitamin D and obesity caused by high cholesterol. Sunlight turns cholesterol into vitamin D.

Julian was staring at him with eyes wide open. He was never spoken to directly by a Black man. He was smiling gently as if relieved from a burden; a burden of ignorance was lifted from his shoulders. Delegations from Abyssinia, Ghana and Nubia had reached Rome and Ceuta but they were all rejected and the Copts and Ethiopians like the Byzantines, Greeks and Eastern regions, which had to fend for themselves and found their own churches. They were to become the Orthodox churches later on and Rome had lost their support in its war against the Goths.

"Julian, we have been on our way together for quite some time. We need you to see one of our medics regarding your condition. I suspect it can be treated. You have kindly assisted us across the waters and shown us the way. We honour your congregation and we recite these words from our Creator to you because we love you like our Brother:

"From those, too, who call themselves Christians, We did take a covenant, but they forgot (hid) a good part of the message that was sent them: so we estranged them, with enmity and hatred between the one and the other,

to the Day of Judgment. And soon will Allah show them what it is they have done.

O people of the Book! There hath come to you our Messenger, revealing to you much that ye used to hide in the Book, and passing over much (that is now unnecessary). There hath come to you from Allah a (new) light and a perspicuous Book,-

Wherewith Allah guides all who seek His good pleasure to ways of peace and safety, and leads them out of darkness, by His will, into the light,—guides them to a path that is straight.

In blasphemy indeed are those that say that Allah is Christ the son of Mary. Say: "Who then has the least power against Allah, if His will were to destroy Christ the son of Mary, his mother, and all every-one that is on the earth? For to Allah belongs the dominion of the heavens and the earth, and all that is between. He creates what He pleases. For Allah hath power over all things."

Surah 5. (The Table) Verses 14-17

Julian's eyes became watery, tears dropped from them uncontrollably; he stared silently towards the ground and turned away breathing heavily, back to his camp.

The March

"By the (Steeds) that run, with panting (breath),
And strike sparks of fire,
And push home the charge in the morning,
And raise the dust in clouds the while,
And penetrate forthwith into the midst (of the foe) en masse;-
Truly man is, to his Lord, ungrateful;
And to that (fact) he bears witness (by his deeds);
And violent is he in his love of wealth.
Does he not know,—when that which is in the graves is scattered abroad
And that which is (locked up) in (human) breasts is made manifest-
That their Lord had been Well-acquainted with them, (even to) that Day?"
Surah 100 (The Chargers)

On the following morning after the prayer Tariq and Bilal marched off and left behind a garrison of over 1000 locally married men with the houses and farms that had been developed around the local settlement and the seeds were planted and one could see the crops sprouting out of the ground. Old Roman olive-stems were carefully attended to and showed signs of recovery, this resilient but reluctant tree, even Roderick's fires could not kill it entirely as they were to find out on their way. He had burnt everything apart from Grenada because he was planning this to be his seat in the South. Irrigation channels had been dug now for dry seasons and the locals were somewhat amused at the idea of the wells and rivers running dry in the valley although they felt the change. An old Roman aqueduct was being repaired. It had suffered much neglect and all that had remained were the columns, so Tariq had ordered for the gaps to be filled with newly cut stones from a nearby quarry, limestone pits were being uncovered for cement production.

These sunny days changed the climate entirely. Water was getting scarcer. It was up to 30 degrees hot and the locals had a hard time fighting dehydration, much of the sicknesses that developed were cured simply by a diet of fruit or berries, yoghurt and water as well as tying a wet cloth around the head, something the Muslims had no issues with as their turbans always soaked up the sweat and kept the heads nice and cool in the heat and warm in the cold at night and one could additionally wash them at least once a day and soak them full of water to keep cool during the hard construction work. Even the non-Muslims started wearing them.

Now that many foundations were laid, the 1000 men who had married locally were left to complete the construction work in Granada and it was to be the cradle of this new civilisation. The other 7000 men, the 5000 who had crossed originally were now joined by many locals, both converts and Christians, now took seat on the horses in their light armour, while the heavy armour was left behind or pulled in wagons.

And thus they took off North, the Sierra Neveda in their faces, they split at its feet, half West, half East, it was a difficult Good Bye for 2 men who had grown up together, never been separated, Bilal and Tariq, with tears in their eyes and a quick embrace from horseback to horseback to push each other away, in order not to extend this painful moment. Tariq went along the East, through what was the Roman-Gothic province of Carthagensis named after the Phoenician Carthagians, ironically also originally from Arabia, only around 1000 years before, conquering the same route as the Umayyads via Ceuta. The Carthagians had ruled it before the Romans and even tried to attack Rome when Hannibal famously took his elephant army across the Alps. It lay in ruins now burnt down by Roderick all the way to Valencia. Barcelona, the Northern target of the conquest was in fact named after Hannibal Barca, the father of Hannibal the conqueror of Rome. Bilal went West, the unknown hills and plains of what was to become Portugal and Galicia, which was mainly a reminiscent of Greek colonies.

As one would expect, Roderick had left behind his spies among the civilian population, who were ducking and covering while the long line of men marched their way along the coast up North. Running by with curiosity in their eyes were the children, from the settlements and villages, the soldiers reading out the same message again and again to them in local dialects, Latin, Greek and Gaulle, through a brass-funnel to amplify the noise up along the slopes of the hillsides where the locals had fled up to, "You are safe, your land is safe, your cattle is safe, your crops are safe, your children are safe, your women are safe, we come in peace, we mean no harm."

And the people believed it as companies of villagers stormed by in relief, jumping, singing and dancing all along the way, cheering up the growing lines of soldiers, half of whom were locals by now, such was the vehemence with which the news of the conquest had spread far and wide, that local young men stormed by to join the new forces against Roderick to avenge their wives, sisters, fathers, children, who had been killed or raped, taken slaves or tortured to death by bloody-eagle. You could still follow the trail of destruction Roderick had left behind, the charred corpses standing like dead raven on the stakes by the wayside along this old Roman road that they took, by now a slim highway, more for means of orientation than a speedy ride, such was the state of this once flawless tarred highway that took chariots of stallions with consuls and wagons pulled by oxen for heavy loads of farmers up and down the land. Even Hannibal's elephants once upon a time, for centuries in a prosperous age of trade and commerce as long as Romans ruled it after taking it from Phoenicia since Hannibal had fallen around 200 B.C., Carthage burnt to the ground by Rome.

So they made their way from village to village, leaving behind a dozen or so guards for each settlement, to monitor, administer, pass on messages, commence construction and planning to repair the road-section and nurture, organise and spiritually tend to the people. Partly these guards were complemented by the scouts and spies that Tariq had sent to explore the land before crossing it. These spies saw no reason to mistrust the locals, as they saw the houses along the way being charred and burnt, plundered and destroyed. So they had openly declared their presence and intentions. The locals had to flee from Roderick up the hills into the land and where it was flat, just as far into the land as possible, since Roderick rode along the coast and then at Valencia he took a sharp turn West, away from the coast, inland to the seat of Gothic power, Reccopolis and Toledo. Tariq sent a small delegation to Cordoba, an old Roman fort with a huge olive orchard brunt down to its roots before Roderick had advanced to Grenada. Tariq's delegation had witnessed Roderick's march back to Toledo, because Roderick had refrained from conquering Cordoba, while passing it in a hurry on the path back from Valencia to Toledo. Basically Tariq followed his trail.

So the spies had already taken over most of the empty villages and mended the locals of Iberia, these most sweet and kind people, naive but strong, weak but resilient through centuries of invasion, mixing their way through changes in power and trade-centres, taxation and liberation. The land along the way was lush but barren, it was ideal to be turned into fertile orchards and farmland for crops, so they left behind seeds and seedlings and the port piers along the coast were quickly repaired for reinforcements that would be expected from across the Empire, who could hit the coast any day from now.

Everywhere they went the scene was repeated, sunlight broke through the clouds and the weather and climate literally changed as gradually as their march progressed. The locals were staring at the skies and were amazed as if a miracle had happened, which it definitely was. The sun and the blue skies by day and the stars and the moon by night, all a sight new to the generations that inhabited this land and had only heard of such miracles from their elders.

All in all it was an easy march so far, no resistance was to be expected, the locals had no reason to resist, and things could only get better after this storm of Vandals had vanished. And so they swiftly reached the Roman town of Valencia, shattered in ruins, the mosaics and Roman bath, cellars and temples all stood empty and desolate. As the army spread across the market squares and roads, they were astonished and looked on in wonder at this first large Roman city they had seen outside Africa, Alexandria, Tripoli, Hamamet and Rabbat were the only ones they knew and Carthage. And those had been transformed into sizzling Arab metropoles by now. The mosaics on the walls, the columns of the temples and baths, all ideal to form a new civilisation, built upon these ruins, after centuries of neglect and downfall, now finally, culture and civilisation had returned to this place of arts and architecture.

It was the first week of their march and they had arrived in time for the Friday prayer, so the temple of Jupiter was cleared of the old statues, who stood lost, headless, the floor was swiped off the dust, the place rid of the weed and grass to make it a clean surface inside and around which the congregation formed, thousands of men, new converts and conquerors shoulder to shoulder, sat, listening to Tariq and what he had to say about this amazing progress in his sermon before the congregational prayer:

"Men of Allah! I am extremely pleased, and the more pleased and secure I feel, the more I fear overconfidence and failure. You know fairly well that this life is not for enjoyment and pleasure only. It is a test. Therefore do not think for one second that this is a walk in the park. Be weary. Be very cautious. For over-confidence is the concept for disaster. Many an accident and downfall is rooted in comfort and ease. The true Believer dwells between Fear and Hope. Fear of Hellfire and Hope for Paradise. Otherwise one gets arrogant, if one is too certain of paradise. Know that Satan is after your souls, he possesses that of the Unbelievers already so he leaves them alone to be deluded by their worldly achievements and good deeds. It is us whom he wants to seduce by making us lie, unfocussed, cheat, fearful, feel arrogant and proud.

Please be not too worried either, but know that around the corner lies the next battle. We have heard of killings by Roderick's spies who have intermixed with the local population and some of your Brothers whom we left behind along the way have died senselessly at their hands already, cowardly the snakes crept up out of the woodwork and disappeared, leaving them to bleed in the sand. We cannot afford such losses. We either die in battle or of age and sickness, but not through carelessness. So from now on, I want you to be cautious, attentive, weary, alert. At all times. I have already appointed some men among you who are going to ride back to the settlements along the coast we have passed for reinforcement. And more forces will come from across the Empire, but we do not know when. So assume you are alone for now.

Moving on to what you are probably waiting for most. News has reached us from Grenada that the first pigeons have arrived from Bilal. Bilal has reached an old Phoenician city called Ollisius (Isbunah, *Arabic*, Lisbon, *English*) in a land West of the hills where the Greeks dwelt and the Romans made it their own, a land he says is ideal for orange plantage, we will name it Bordughal (Portugal), land of the orange. He sends his greetings and is looking forward to the day we meet in the North, reunite to storm against Roderick in union.

And we ourselves have of course reported back to Granada and heard from riders who have arrived from there just yesterday the news that Alwalid is going to arrive in the North coming along the coast from Rome, attempting to make peace between the pope and the Ostrigoths, the cousins of Roderick who have surrounded the Vatican and occupied Rome and the whole land, putting the pope under house arrest. Sultan Alwalid should be in Rome by now; he had left Damascus after returning from Azerbaijan a few weeks ago.

And this is all I can tell you about the situation, we will set camp and establish a settlement here until we hear of his arrival. He wishes for us to wait until he arrives before confronting Roderick again as he perhaps thinks that peace would be the better solution and diplomacy. I would agree, if Roderick did."

That very evening much to Tariq's surprise sails started to appear on the horizon across the sea, the watchmen who had been pulled by ropes on top of the empty columns shouted down as they spun their brass-rods with pieces of glass like grapes inside to stare far into the distance, further than the eyes could reach. The sun was about to go down in their back to the West and so the light was bright hitting the clean white sails at a particular angle which allowed them to see the ships' sails from far away, before the deck became visible. All night they feared the worst, an invasion from Byzantine forces from the Balearics. They stood waiting, anticipating a battle. The ships did not arrive until the next morning.

When dawn broke the Call to prayer sounded and after the prayer the first boats came rowing in. They saw it clearly and Tariq breathed a sigh of relief as he had commanded the men of Allah to take position along the coast, bows up and arrows pulled, when he gazed upon the crystal-white banners. These were Umayyad delegations, what a brilliant timing. What a speedy arrival. They had made their way along the Northern coast all the way from Rome, a hundred ships, sails were pulled down and empty masts reached into the sky along the coast at around a mile's distance, these vessels were too precious to risk a landing in these shallows full of corals and under water rocks. They sent the men to land gradually in groups of a dozen or so by rowing-boats and the rocky coastline was filled with cheers and celebratory calls as native Berber, Arabs and Africans do. A loud joudling filled the air and quick embraces followed to welcome the fresh men from Damascus.

Immediately they started handing across sacks of goods, hard and soft, all types hidden in the bags as gifts, surprises, essentials for the time ahead, made to order, the letters had gone through, their plea for medicines, herbs, seeds and seedlings, oils, spices but also strings, thread, powder, steel, clothes and colours was heard. It was like an Eid-celebration, the smell of fresh incense, saffron, olive-oil and rosemary, ginger, mint and cinnamon, menthol, peppermint and lemon. What else could they wish for? Well, there it was ...

Women from the palaces, dancers in their most beautiful garments, fully covered in silk and brocade, transparent face and head scarves, no overloaded designs but unicolour uniforms, red, white, green and blue, yellow and orange, a delight to the eyes. The local men were more amazed than ever before. Colours of purple and cream they had never seen, boats full of ladies came in from all sides, were delicately guarded to the shore and big tents built up there on lush cloth that was spread out on the old mosaics that were cleared of the dust and rubbish. Where emptiness had reigned before for decades now a scene of pleasure, playful young dancers and potential brides, with eyes as pretty as those of children, dark and shining, long lashes, glistening in the morning sun, a bizarre mirage in the sparkling jewels of the water. As the boats came in one by one the sun was blinding the men who were frozen at the shore and apart from one step to the right or left they were not able to do much for the girls, reluctant to touch these valuable, pure and fragile doll-like creatures.

It was a massage for the senses when they started singing their welcome songs after their shrill joudling had seized, with the bells attached to their waists, ankles and knuckles, the drums they played, the smells that filled the air and the colours that tickled the eyes. An early celebration of victory. The men of Allah stood there smiling, all they could do since they were exhausted from the many days of marching and standing awake all night, not knowing who was to be expected, how many of them or how quick they would arrive, stared in delight at this overwhelming arrival of hope and support.

By midday the beach was filled with goods and the empty ruins of the town were full of activity, trading, haggling, bargaining, greeting, people meeting after years of separation, the dancers in their midst from place to place being wooed to by the men, in courtship with the warriors, smiling at them and looking down in shyness. It was not the kind of prostitutional belly-dance that was known in the pre-Islamic and later Arab world but much rather an innocent jumping around by these young teenaged girls, whose slight clumsiness in their moves made them the more attractive and pure in their intentions, because their bodies were not under their full control erotically, not the type of dominas that were widespread in the ancient world and at medieval orgies in Rome. These were noble creatures, clean and divine. The brightest of alabaster and the darkest of night were the colours of their skins to choose from, across the known world they had been collected, even Rome and Byzantine sent some of their maidens, as well as Greece, China, Arabia, Africa and

India. They came fresh from the Hajj in Mecca, souls purified, taught the rites of Islam, intended for marriage.

So they had already established a new colony by shear numbers and thousands of people lined the streets in queues for the latest essence, the new arrivals and the brides to be. And then he came, in a much guarded congregation of boats, surrounded by white banners and announced by the loudest but sweetest of trumpets, high pitched and low tone, played by servants from all sides, when his boat hit the coast, carried on a board on the shoulders of his closest guards, who held up shields to protect him. There he was clothed in simple dark clothes, silent and strong, restful and content, Al-Hajj Sultan Alwalid ibn Abdulhakim al Umayya, ruler of the Muslims, Caliph of Arabia, King of the Umayyad Empire reaching from Spain to India, architect of peace and prosperity, guardian of the Holy Mosque of Medina, custodian of the Holy Kaaba in Mecca. He still held these titles although the Abbasids were fast taking over the holy sites.

He was neither tall nor short, had dark brown hair, brown skin and a long nose with no moustache but a beard carefully trimmed at the top of the whiskers and lengthy towards the bottom, plated with pearls. But most of all his eyebrows, long and thick, strong and distinctive, a piercing look complemented by a thorough smile that reached from one ear to the other. His face was athletically symmetrical. His turban was dark blue and his glistening black gown was covered in golden calligraphy with verses from the Koran, the colours archaic, simple patterns but strong like the stars, shimmering in the midday sun. With his pitch-black eyes he stared gently at everyone in the crowd, a gift he had inherited from his lineage, to mesmerise the people, to unite them in love and peace, one look convincing them that this was the man for the job, doubtless. His aura spread far and wide. The people were coming from all directions, so fast had the news spread into the hills of the arrival of the new King of the conquerors, that they wanted to test him and confirm what they had heard, and strangely enough, one look was enough to comfort them that yes, things were to get better. One look and nothing more was needed, they almost turned away, not in disappointment, but in relief that this was the man they could trust to be different, to be better, to be good. The contrast to Roderick could not have been bigger.

"In the Name of Allah, Most Gracious, Most Merciful." With these words he stepped with his right foot first on to the rocky shore of this new pearl of his Empire, surrounded by the guards, as the crowd cheered and greeted him.

Tariq worked his way out of the crowd from next to the tanks of water where the horses lay for rest and hay had been collected, to mend the newborn stallions and gazed at his step-brother since childhood while tears of joy and happiness rolled down his face. Alwalid was working his eyes in search along the lines of people at the coast who were cheering; even the new converts knew immediately who this man was, while he was carried across the waves towards the coastline and stepped on to the mosaic. He looked up again and saw him, his childhood friend and companion, Tariq ibn Ziyad.

He opened his arms wide apart and after waving to the crowd, his guards pushing the people to the side gently, while fixing their eyes at each of them and checking the lines thoroughly with hands holding the swords that rested firmly in the shafts, let him step to the front towards the victorious general, whose name was written in ink and hammered on walls across the Empire within weeks, newly promoted Amir of Al-Andalus, Al-Hajj Tariq ibn Ziyad Al-Barbar Al-Andalus, Wezir to be of the Sultan of Damascus. They walked towards each other smiling and weeping tears of joy, ended in an embrace.

"My dear friend and Brother! May the Peace and Blessings of Allah be upon you this day and for all eternity" Alwalid had broken his silence.

"And on you be the Peace and Blessings and Mercy of Allah the Almighty this day, during your life and in the hereafter, my dear Sultan!"

"Oh Allah, Lord of the seven layers of the atmosphere and all that they envelop, Lord of the seven inside layers of the Earth and all that they carry, Lord of the devils and all whom they misguide, Lord of the Winds and all whom they whisk away. I ask you for the goodness of this land, the goodness of its people and for all the goodness found within it. And I take refuge with you from the evil in this land, the evil of its inhabitants and from the evil found within it."

The Sultan completed these prayers upon the entrance into the gates and in this way ensured the divine blessings, The Prophetic sayings were intense, full of wisdom and knowledge of the unseen, even the unknown inside structure of the earth, much stronger than the ink of the poet clotted in the well, the blood of the poet casting its spell. This was divine magic. This was decree. This was a sign. This was the formula of success.

"None has the right to be worshiped except Allah, alone, without associates, to him belongs all sovereignty and Praise. He gives life and causes death, and He is living and does not die. In His Hand is all good and He is over all things, omnipotent!"

"I witness there is no God but Allah and I witness Mohammed is his servant and Messenger."

With these last words Tariq joined in and they said a quick prayer standing in a circle with the guards holding shields to protect from arrows from potential assassins, all raising their hands to Heaven and vehemently asking Allah for forgiveness, guidance and blessings as well as quick progress, rectification and completion of the mission. They could feel the embrace of the angels appointed and sensed the spots of light when closing their eyes, stepping towards eternity; time became irrelevant, the morning flawless, the mind pure and clean, free!

"The angels and the spirit ascend unto him in a Day the measure whereof is (as) fifty thousand years"
Surah 70 (The Ascending Stairways) Verse 4

They walked hand in hand as Brothers do along the coast and through the town talking, followed closely by the guards, who reached one by one for Tariq's shoulders to tap them and wave to him while he recognised them from the years back in Damascus, where he was know in the streets and neighbourhoods, not able to walk even 10 steps without having to exchange excessive greetings all along during market days and festivals alike. Here they did not want to disturb his reunion with the Sultan. Where they would have punched his shoulders and waited for the hardest of punches back to test their friendship, they now held their hands back, these young boys by nature, playful and cheerful. Tariq was their idol and so was he the one they all aspired to, the Whites to him and the Blacks to Bilal. That was the significance of having all races covered in your closest circle of guards and Tariq and Bilal had been in charge of the palace guards, the elite-forces of Damascus, before they were sent to the West.

"Where is my Night-like-Brother?" Alwalid asked looking around towards the back over his shoulders. It was clear whom he meant, the night was a very precious time for Muslims as they woke long for prayer, so there was no discrimination whatsoever in these words, much rather respect and honour.

"We decided to send him West with half the armies at Granada we split, so we can surround Toledo and Reccopolis before striking the final blow, godwilling, if we survive."

"Wise move, I knew we could rely entirely on you two, Rome and Byzantine are set ablaze by fury and jealousy, Arabia sends its daughters to the men of Allah, our own men are somewhat decimated after the many battles amongst ourselves and my missions towards the North and the East, even the Abbasids and their patriarchs selected their sisters, daughters and widows, setting their differences with us aside, some divorced their 3rd and 4th wives for you and dressed them in the nicest garments with plentiful gifts. I wish I had come here instead of the East, but then Allah knows best."

"Yes, we can see, the maidens are in deed lovely, the gifts very pleasing. We did not expect anything and now we are delighted, overwhelmed."

With these brief words he swung up on top of an old column which was standing half broken at the height of his waist so the crowd could see him and reached for the Sultan's hands to pull him up, but the guards shook their heads and pulled him back, too dangerous was the risk of hidden archers from Roderick in the crowd, so Tariq nodded agreeably and glanced at the flood of heads all the way to the edge of the city. They had come by from the surrounding hills, peasants, traders, farmers, recruits, converts, local men and women and children and elders, the men of Allah and the colourful maidens and men newly arrived via the sea. He spoke Arabic for this occasion and throughout the crowd men were translating into Latin and local converts from Latin into Gaulle:

"Men and women of Allah." He held silence for a few moments and let them collect and clam down.

"This is a joyful day for all of us, a celebration we all deserve, an achievement we have been waiting for, a huge step ahead. My dear beloved Brother, Al-Hajj Sultan Alwalid ibn Abdulhakim al Umayya, ruler of the Muslims, Caliph of Arabia, King of the Ummayads, guardian of the Holy Mosque of Medina, custodian of the Holy Kaaba in Mecca, has finally arrived and is here with us as you might have gathered and has brought along prayers and support, blessings and help, success and happiness. This is him and I wish he would address you this day, but we do not want to risk hidden men of Roderick striking an early blow. So you are welcome to visit him, his tent will be standing next to the main mosque to be, the former temple of Jupiter, where you can admit yourselves to the guards and make an appointment with your requests and leave behind letters.

People of Iberia, Al-Andalus, Hispania, West-Rome, Byzantine, Goths, Vandals, Berbers, Africans, Normans, Europeans, Arabs, Muslims, Christians, Jews, Pagans and Atheists, this is your ruler, I declare this city this day henceforth to be his city, we call it AL-VALLADA, City of Alwalid. I declare a week of festivals and market trading!"

A united and bursting sound emerged slowly and then peaking from the crowd, a sigh of relief from the locals mixed with a dominating and proud shout from the men of Allah intertwined with a high-pitched joudling from the maidens and an end to all of that with a clear-cut:

"Allah, the Greatest, No God apart from Allah, Mohammed Messenger of Allah!"

The crowd reluctantly dispersed as Tariq stepped down and both Alwalid and Tariq walked slowly surrounded by guards who were carrying sacks of garments and sticks for the tents of the Sultan towards the central square, the former temple of Jupiter.

"We are extremely grateful for your assistance and the honour you have given us by naming this city after us. It has been long since we have met such a welcoming congregation. Rome was cold and grey. Constantinople unwelcoming, so I was told by my fleet that travelled there before me and warded me off. Damascus was still, engulfed in silent envy from the Abbasids and the Shiite, who are kindling their fury, I fear a riot every day. And the East is harsh, my friend, the people are stubborn polytheists, an ancient culture so rich that we cannot match it, Persia and India and China, they have their very own religions, very different from our Monotheistic stem of Jews, Christians and Muslims. They still have idols that are not even human and some of them even worship nothing. Even their kings are atheist and still Satan has been able to achieve great works of technology with them. Big dams and canals, irrigation, water mills, astronomy, astrology, arithmetics, medicine, and so on. Some of them heal people by just looking at them, some others can make the heart disappear right out of the chest and they meditate in front of fire for decades and eat and drink nothing for years. If I had not the fear of Allah in my heart I would have surrendered, some of our generals did. My general Mohammed Ibn Qasim has told me they tame elephants, which they have there locally and tigers for warfare, have you ever seen an army of armoured elephants? Like once the mighty Abyssinians and Carthaginians. Unbreakable, unless Allah sends his own warriors, which he did repeatedly for us, as for you as I heard! Praise be to Him only in all past, present and eternity, Praises full of Glory and Majesty!"

"Seest thou not how thy Lord dealt with the Companions of the Elephant?
Did He not make their treacherous plan go astray?
And He sent against them Flights of Birds,
Striking them with stones of baked clay.
Then did He make them like an empty field of stalks and straw,
(of which the corn) has been eaten up."
Surah 105 (The Elephant)

"By Allah, what happened to you in India sounds impossible, but I believe it because you say it. Satan is powerful, even foretells the future, many false Prophets are among us and many are to come." Tariq could only imagine.

"Well, we took many women who were widowed during the fighting with local tribes back with us, many of them are here. The most precious pearls from India. They have this cruel custom to burn those poor souls alive with their husband's dead bodies. We saved them from this fate. Believe me; we did not even scratch the surface. They have so many different tribes and languages, they work like ants and achieve great things, very well organised, these Indians and Chinese, within weeks they build castles and dig miles of tunnels and walls. The Chinese built a wall across their whole country. Some can fly with cloth they fill with hot air and others come back to life after death on the battlefield, as if they were Jinns, I have seen it with my own eyes. Satan has been granted much success there. We need more of your likes, but you will stay here for now and end your mission. It is your honour and nobody can take it away, not even my cousin Ibn Musa. The East and North are eternally big, we would get lost at this stage and it requires careful planning. And neither do we want to conquer for no reason, only if people call us for help. Regarding our mission, we have sent errands, scholars and translators into Hindi and Farsi, translated the Koran, all with some limited success. But people there speak many tongues and are extremely loyal to their rulers although their rulers leave them hungry for weeks and collect all the harvest for tax during many years. Enough of that, now you, tell me, what is new, the last message I read came by pigeon shortly before I left. It said you had established Granada and were on your way North, so I figured out I should progress via Rome towards the South along the Gothic coastline. Rome by the way is lost, nothing I can do there, basically peaceful but the pope is not happy until the Ostrigoths become Catholic and you know them, they stick to Arianism. Many are converting to the Byzantine way of ruling called Orthodox . . ."

"Were they only Arianic here, Brother Alwalid, they have resulted to full-scale barbarism, cannibalism and blood-culture. Satanism pure."

"What?" Alwalid burst out into tears, covering his eyes with a piece of cloth and both his hands for a few minutes, sobbing. He was sensitive in his nature because he and his father had sworn off his grandfather's ways in a lengthy 40 day fast. His grandfather Marwan great-grandfather Muwaiyah 1st, who was the scribe of Prophet Mohammed (pbuh), had been accused of being very cruel to Muslims as well as Yazid, one of his great-uncles. This had further split the Muslims into Sunni and Shia. And the Shiah backed the Abassids. But Allah guided Abdulmalik and Alwalid to a better way than their ancestors They couldn't stand violence outside the battlefield.

"Yes, in deed, they have devastated the locals, especially after the delegation from Julian reached Damascus. Julian is ill. We are worried. He is essential for our ties to Rome. You remember Charles, the tall fellow; he has been fighting them for years, now he will tell you all."

"Oh yes, my Christian brothers, how are they getting on? My abbot from Damascus has come along, he will be keen to meet them, let us visit their camp".

Tariq took him by the hand and guided him towards the old church that Roderick had burnt down where the monks were still building the camp, Tariq immediately appointed a few men to assist them as the abbot of Damascus, Benedict-Augustine was guided along the way, he went right past Tariq leaving him aside like a child and fell into the arms of Julian-Urban, kissing his hands. Charles came out of a tent, with a smile for the first time since the Muslim army set foot in his land.

They had exchanged the vows and greetings surrounded by monks when Alwalid and Tariq reached the delegation. Immediately the round fell to their knees and greeted him by nodding the heads down towards the ground, not meeting him eye to eye. They spoke Arabic.

"Welcome to Hispania, O Great King!" Julian spoke for the whole round except of Charles who turned around and went back into his tent.

Benedict joined Alwalid since he was his in law and his sister had been wed to the Sultan as one of 4 wives. No harm could be done to him and he had not to welcome him, he had accompanied him.

"My dear Julian, Peace be upon you, stand up, how did my Brother treat you?" He glanced at Tariq and smiled while his eyes twinkled.

"No complaints at all, my King, none at all!" Julian joined the tips of his fingers from the right and left hand together and looked down towards the ground at the feet of Alwalid hesitating to stand up.

"The pope sends his greetings; I enjoyed his hospitality for a night. Will you join us for dinner?" Alwalid asked.

"Certainly, if he insists."

"Bring the tall fellow along; I need his views as well." Alwalid pointed at the tent along the ruined walls of the old Church where they had provisionally mounted a golden Cross as if to make a statement.

"Certainly, Sire, we will."

Alwalid turned around and stepped back out of the churchyard, a reminder of the present Roman decline, people here were more loyal to Rome than Rome itself, and all he had seen there were orgies and feasts. He was amazed.

Tariq was sad: "I am sorry about this fellow, Charles, we were not able to appease him and we tried but saw no reason to bend over backwards".

"You did the right thing, do not worry, I know these people well." With these words he put his hand over the shoulders of Benedict, his brother in law and laughed. "They have managed to infiltrate my family."

"My sister has joined your religion, what are you complaining about?" Benedict murmered.

"Nothing, I love her very much!" The Sultan laughed, a happy and bright man, wise and content, while he looked from side to side, Benedict to his left, Tariq to his right.

Tariq was smiling carefully towards Benedict.

91

"Now take me to my other Brothers." Said Alwalid and Tariq looked somewhat dazzled.

"Who?" He asked.

"The Rabbis. Never underestimate and never forget those who carry the collective memory of the Stories of our Prophets from the offspring of our cousin Isaac, (pbuh) because they confirm our message that was revealed to my Great-Uncle, Mohammed (pbuh), even though they have deviated, still they worship one God, the same God!"

"Oh yes, they have been very silent, almost hidden, reluctant, stealthy. I could not even tell them from the masses and I would not be able to find them for you."

"You should have asked for them and given them equal treatment with the Christians. They rioted against Roderick and they were decimated here in Al-Andalus. We have to keep them in honour. The Rabbi lost his family to the sword of Roderick. What is past is past, when a tribe of theirs sided with the infidels at Medina and fell into our backs. The other Jewish tribes pleaded for their death. My uncle Usman (may Allah be pleased with him), when he was Caliph, gave them justice equal to our own and our beloved Prophet Mohammed (pbuh) asked us to pay them respite and married among them. I will not deviate from that."

"Sorry, Brother, please rectify me." Tariq was ashamed.

"Hassan," he called his chief-guard, "please search for Rabbi Samuel Benitoch of Rabbat, I long to see my big Brother! He too could have a share in the Garden beneath which rivers flow. What was revealed against them was for the stubborn Jews at the times of Moses and those tribes who failed in Medina, not for those who side with us, the likes will be around until Judgement Day." With these words he took a deep breath and sounded like Bilal when the angels accompany him after midnight for the festive reading:

"I seek refuge with Allah from Satan the accursed.
In the Name of Allah, Most Gracious, Most Merciful.

Those who believe (in the Qur'an), and those who follow the Jewish (scriptures), and the Christians and the Sabians,—any who believe in Allah and the Last Day, and work righteousness, shall have their reward with their Lord; on them shall be no fear, nor shall they grieve."
Surah 2 (the Heifer) Verse 62

Tariq and everyone around was entirely humbled not only by the recitation but also by the justice and the almost vehement longing for the implementation of it that the Sultan brought along which even Tariq could not match. That was what set the true Muslim ruler apart. That was what was worth inheriting. That was what lineage was good for. Nothing else! The secret to success. Aspiring to the same level as your righteous ancestors. Competing for justice.

As they found the Rabbis and Jewish mercenaries covered in cloaks humbly like the other soldiers, they were somewhat ashamed that the Rabbi had to fight alongside average soldiers and Alwalid showed signs of despair, while hiding his anger at Tariq and Bilal as deep down as he could, he smiled:

"Peace be on you, o Rabbi, what were you hiding from, why did you not make yourself known? We missed you. We need to know you are well!"

"We are well, o King, we are well, we are at your service and Ibn Musa has been very generous and so has your Brother Tariq ibn Ziyad, we owe him a lot. He has avenged our defeat at Toledo already and is on the best way to strike the head of the Beast off."

The Rabbi nodded with his head sunken into his chest and shaking from front to back, a movement that had become second nature from studying the Torah for decades while standing upright in front of the wall in Jerusalem when he was young.

"Yes, but . . . where is your camp, why are you not within your own congregation?"

"We are fine; we are well with your people. We enjoy their company and their food."

"No, you will not do this to us, Rabbi. Hassan! Unload a boat of garments and tents, your best guards and your strongest incense. I want them here right now!"

Hassan rushed out with a drawn sword and commanded a group of sailors to the vessels. They brought in haste the goods to the temple of Jupiter which was by now more resembling a mosque and the mosaic was torn out carefully and they began to piece it together in a geometrical pattern rather than a luscious scene of feast on grapes and wine as Jupiter was depicted like a bearded old man with a long mane ruling over the clouds. Later this concept was to be reborn during the Renaissance by Michelangelo and his likes. Alwalid was looking at the ground until they returned.

"Here take this, I insist!" Spoke the Sultan.

"You are too generous." The Rabbi gave in.

"Choose the best place for your synagogue. Choose freely." Alwalid raised his voice.

"That will not be necessary; we will fight till Toledo." Replied the Rabbi.

"I command you." Alwalid said somewhat strictly.

"Ok, you choose, please." The Rabbi carefully agreed.

Alwalid took hold of his hand and lead the Rabbi whom he had known for many years as a delegate to his father's palace. He was like an uncle to him and Alwalid had of course married into his noble clan, the tribe of Solomon (pbuh) taken a wife from the Jews, a princess from Marrakech, who converted to Islam later. So essentially this man was his in law and he had been playing with his children since he could think and later on competing healthily against them in the sports and the arts. This is how they did it in those times, this is how conflicts were quenched in their ashes before they broke out. And the Jews were also important because they had wide reaching connections across the Empire deep into the Northern and Western territories, not so much towards the East, since they were scarce in number. So they had to build communities that stretched across the regions and trade and communicate. Much knowledge and talent came from them and the Sultan knew the importance of that. In fact it was essential to his rule, the way Allah wanted it, the way Allah tested the sense of justice, by placing minority groups into societies. The same attitude would many generations later forbid the Muslims of Palestine to repel the Jewish immigrants from Europe much to their disadvantage, since those were no longer the practicing Jews but in fact secularised Bolsheviks and later on right-wing nationalists, who would not appreciate that hospitality as they did not fear God the way the Rabbi Benitoch did and his congregation.

So Alwalid lead him walking around and eventually, followed hastily by the guards all along, to the temple of Venus and saw the shining marbles and pillars rising high, a place at the edge of town that people had avoided because it was not central enough for trade right then and far too noble for the common peasant, its stones and fallen pillars far too heavy to move aside without wooden hinges and mechanical cranes. The men had started hacking them apart for building material. There he pointed to and commanded:

"This is to be your synagogue and your resting place, your camp, your place of festivals and your quarter in Vallada." Tariq watched carefully but amicably from the distance and the Rabbi thanked with one nod.

"Help him unpack and collect the Jews. Assist them in clearing the ground and lifting the stones and putting together the tents." Thus was the command of the Sultan and none could resist the command of the Sultan.

"That is that dealt with", the Sultan breathed a sigh of relief raising his eyebrows towards Tariq, who agreed silently. "Allah will ask us on the last day!" Added the Sultan.

Whenever he got angry he occupied himself and ran around doing things to the extent of digging trenches and building fortifications by working alongside common peasants and mercenaries and this was his nature, until he was calm again and during the process he rectified what was wrong with his own two hands. Same in warfare and inter-governmental affairs. He had not slept one night in Damascus since he returned from the East. In fact he never slept much, 4 hours maximum. He always stayed on the move. The older he got, the less sleep he needed and the younger he looked, on a diet of fresh grilled fish or birds, lemons, ginger and herbs with a careful selection of vegetables and fruit, rarely meat, once a week, since it was custom at the clans of the Umayyads. They sacrificed once a month for each wife, he had 4.

He had left Damascus two weeks ago and rested in Rome for a day. His fleet had left much earlier from Alexandria and he joined them at Rome as he had strong trade-winds driving him West and rowers but most importantly he took a shortcut along Cyprus, Crete, Malta and Sicily and up the Italian West-Coast. The stars guided him over days at sea where one lost sight of any coast between Cyprus and Crete and between Crete and Sicily at high sea.

"It is He Who maketh the stars (as beacons) for you, that ye may guide yourselves, with their help, through the dark spaces of land and sea: We detail Our signs for people who know."
Surah 6 (Cattle) Verse 97

The Sultan was telling stories of the high seas how they passed lofty vessels from Byzantine with tall fearsome ghost-type warriors who had long gold-white hair although they were young and helmets like devil's horns. They thought them to be Jinn and they ducked and hid in the waves, extinguishing their lights. He was a keen and entertaining story-teller. But the Byzantine threat was real, not to be taken lightly.

"I saw on the high seas between the main islands Cyprus and Crete and later again between Crete and Sicily as if it was a ghost ship with a dragon spitting fire from the front, they call it Greek fire and it comes from a big brass kettle and sets ablaze anything in its way. The fearsome Viking guards of Constantinople roam the seas for any enemy and let none pass as a friend. They are violent and rumour speaks they eat people after roasting them alive with their ships. We cannot afford a sea-to-sea battle with these people and they are all over the islands in the sea. Thank God they are distracted with interior matters and with their dealings with the Goths. Otherwise, I am sure, they would have attacked us already."

In the meantime darkness had fallen and the Sultan lead the prayers in the newly founded mosque, the floor was hastily covered with garments and the canopies built up in the shallow evening breeze from the sea, a refreshing breath from the East, while the locals lit their fires and the markets became more crowded, singers, dancers, Beasts from the South, being traded, cattle and oxen, sheep and cows. Wagons of beer and wine were held back at the edge of town and so were swine and bears. They were not to be traded in the newly sanctified enclave. Meanwhile appointed Imams started their wedding ceremonies, the first of many, the newly arrived girls were too sweet to resist even for a day, local converts keen to grab one of the born Muslim girls delicious as they looked and dressed, melodious as they sounded.

The locals traded keenly their harvest, or what Roderick had left of it, and the cattle. They were entirely dazzled at the lights, colours, rich garments, smells and spices and the stars and they learned there and then while the arrived. Damascene and Alexandrian traders had built up their grills and stands and were busy trading and giving cooking lessons to get the locals acquainted with culinary pleasures and addicted to the pristine Arab cuisine. The ruins were converted into a Kasbah and a Medina, through out the night the feast lasted, celebrations of weddings and dances of courtship under the close guard of the soldiers who watched carefully that the limits were not exceeded in terms of chastity and behaviour. But the people knew their limits. They had never been lewd, even during Gothic rule, even during Roman periods of decadence, Rome's misbehaviour had not spilled over to these distant outposts; these were humble people, content with the little they had.

By now the festival was in full bloom. Special tents had been pulled up, lofty, tall, like halls inside, high canopies with congregations, merchants from across the Empire establishing local links and opening new markets by introducing the need for their goods and services, debating with local tribal chiefs and village elders, while hefty gesticulation was exchanged, bonds of brotherhood formed and pigeons left behind for placing orders that would be fulfilled within a month. The fleet would establish regular routes coming along the North African coast and more pigeons would be brought along, while some local pigeons that Tariq had brought along from Granada were to be taken back to Alexandria and Damascus.

The big central tent was that of Alwalid. He called for dinner with Julian, Charles and the Rabbi. The guards were sent to all directions while a handful stayed back to make sure he was safe in the midst of the crowds passing, the acrobats and fire shows. The food was brought in, large silver plates with several courses in one, lined next to each other, seared salted camel meat in the middle, surrounded by cous-cous, lean breast of pheasant, vegetables and fish stuffed with herbs and spices. Mild yoghurt and bread accompanied the dishes. Bowls of hot water were served and slices of lemon to wash the hands before touching the food.

"In the Name of Allah," the Sultan commanded, his way of asking the round to begin, once the congregation had arrived, even Romans and Jews used to eat sitting on the floor at that time using their right hands, the fork in the left hand and table-manners did not come about until the Inquisition ordered everything to be done in the opposite manner to the Muslims. The eyes of the monks sparkled at the food and they thanked God and crossed themselves, not having seen much luxury for many months.

"How do you always look so young, Sultan?" Julian-Urban broke the silence.

"My Dear Julian, by the Grace of Allah, we watch our diet, fast twice a week on Mondays and Thursdays and do regular sports, hunting the scavengers and predators. We always travel, we never rest. As you know we raise our own sheep and cattle with our own hands, milking them, stroking their skins every day saying our prayers for them. Then when they are due, we sacrifice them to Allah, only then are they a true sacrifice and blessed, as you put the love for Allah above the love for the animal. The prerogative for that is that you love the animals. They too are Muslims. Then it is blessed as it was raised with love and a tear is shed for them and we are reluctant to kill them, hence we value the meat and sacrifice as little as possible. We keep a variety in diet, fish, birds and vegetables, herbs, lemon, ginger, fruit and so on. On top of that we use our skills in riding, archery, swordsmanship and running mixed with heavy and light exercise, breathing, swimming, lifting weights, jumping and stretching the way we have learnt it in India and China. We also like to give charity and pray."

"Very impressive. We could do with such discipline among our own rulers. Surely you know of John the Baptist, he was ascetic like you and so was our Lord Jesus Christ, a strong carpenter and impressive man. I wish you would join our quest in the Name of the Father, the Son and the Holy Spirit. None shall enter the Kingdom of Heaven unless . . ."

The Sultan interrupted Julian with a deep breath to recite vehemently:

"And they say: "None shall enter Paradise unless he is a Jew or a Christian." Those are their desires. Say: "Produce your proof if ye are truthful."
Nay,-whoever submits His whole self to Allah and is a doer of good,—He will get his reward with his Lord; on such shall be no fear, nor shall they grieve.
The Jews say: "The Christians have naught (to stand) upon; and the Christians say: "The Jews have naught (To stand) upon." Yet they (Profess to) study the (same) Book. Like unto their word is what those say who know not; but Allah will judge between them in their quarrel on the Day of Judgment.
Surah 2 (The Heifer) Verses 111-113

"It is true that we do not agree with those who do not accept our Lord and Saviour Jesus Christ as the Messiah." Julian replied pointing his hand towards the Rabbi.

The Rabbi did not respond to him directly but looked at Alwalid and said:

"Even you my King know that we are the chosen people of God and that we will enter Paradise".

The King knew fairly well, why they were the chosen people:

"Children of Israel! Call to mind the (special) favour which I bestowed upon you, and that I preferred you to all other (for My Message).
Then guard yourselves against a day when one soul shall not avail another nor shall intercession be accepted for her, nor shall compensation be taken from her, nor shall anyone be helped (from outside).
And remember, We delivered you from the people of Pharaoh: They set you hard tasks and punishments, slaughtered your sons and let your women-folk live; therein was a tremendous trial from your Lord.
And remember We divided the sea for you and saved you and drowned Pharaoh's people within your very sight.
And remember We appointed forty nights for Moses, and in his absence ye took the calf (for worship), and ye did grievous wrong.
Even then We did forgive you; there was a chance for you to be grateful.
And remember We gave Moses the Scripture and the Criterion (Between right and wrong): There was a chance for you to be guided aright.
And remember Moses said to his people: "O my people! Ye have indeed wronged yourselves by your worship of the calf: So turn (in repentance) to your Maker, and slay yourselves (the wrong-doers); that will be better for you in the sight of your Maker." Then He turned towards you (in forgiveness): For He is Oft-Returning, Most Merciful."
Surah 2 (the Heifer), Verses 47-54

"You will enter it, if you deserve it and you will be judged. You were chosen yes, aforetime for the Message, a burden which was lain upon you, to spread the Message, which has now been lifted and put upon us, your Brothers, as the last Message was promised to Ishmael's clan" The Sultan continued with a deep breath again:

"Say: "If the last Home, with Allah, be for you specially, and not for anyone else, then seek ye for death, if ye are sincere."
But they will never seek for death, on account of the (sins) which their hands have sent on before them. And Allah is well-acquainted with the wrong-doers.
Thou wilt indeed find them, of all people, most greedy of life,-even more than the idolaters: Each one of them wishes He could be given a life of a thousand years: But the grant of such life will not save him from (due) punishment. For Allah sees well all that they do."
Surah 2 (The Heifer) Verses 94-96

"We have no quarrel with you. You go your way and we go ours. You have agreed to protect us and grant us freedom and so have you granted freedom to the Romans." The Rabbi said.

"We also gave you freedom, much more than you gave us. You killed our Lord Jesus Christ, Son of God!" Julian spoke with anger in his voice.

"We did no such thing said the Rabbi. It was your people, the Romans, who did that. We stayed out of their matter and merely recommended he stop preaching and the Romans agreed."

By now the tension rose high, so the Sultan took a deep breath in again:

They said (in boast), "We killed Christ Jesus the son of Mary, the Messenger of Allah.;—but they killed him not, nor crucified him, but so it was made to appear to them, and those who differ therein are full of doubts, with no (certain) knowledge, but only conjecture to follow, for of a surety they killed him not:-
Nay, Allah raised him up unto Himself; and Allah is Exalted in Power, Wise;-
And there is none of the People of the Book but must believe in him before his death; and on the Day of Judgment he will be a witness against them;-
Surah 4 (Women) Verses 157-159

"Yes, we believe in His return!" Said Julian."But he is divine, he is Spirit and Flesh, his soul is pure light and his blood is red-wine."

By now the Sultan was in a state of trance and only spoke with recitative hymns from the Koran:

"The similitude of Jesus before Allah is as that of Adam; He created him from dust, then said to him: "Be". And he was.
The Truth (comes) from Allah alone; so be not of those who doubt.
If any one disputes in this matter with thee, now after (full) knowledge hath come to thee, say: "Come! let us gather together,—our sons and your

sons, our women and your women, ourselves and yourselves: Then let us earnestly pray, and invoke the curse of Allah on those who lie!"
Surah 3 (The Family Of 'Imran) Verses 59-61

"We will pray" Said Julian reluctantly. "But we only pray in the Name of the Father, the Son and the Holy Spirit". He coughed loudly and excessively at the end of this sentence and his handkerchief was covered in blood. The monks helped him up.

"Please see one of our medics, Sire! We worry for you!" Said Sultan Alwalid.

Charles had been watching the round with much fury in his eyes as he picked up bits and pieces of the little Arabic he knew, Julian and the Rabbi were of course fluent in Arabic. Now he stood up and wanted to turn around, when the Sultan stopped him and spoke to him in Latin:

"Charles of Montril, please don't leave us so soon, we need your assistance. We heard that you have been fighting these Vandals for many years, We admire your bravery. What can you tell us about them? Their strengths, their weaknesses, their ways, their routes, how to best overcome them. Where were you successful? Where did you fail? How could we do it better?"

Charles looked back over his shoulder:

"If I knew all these intricate details I would not have called for your army to enter my land. The Goths are a mystery to us all, they change their ways all the time and do not follow one clear-cut strategy. They stick to their laws when it suits them and next time they don't. They fight each other more than us and they kill one day and are silent the next. You never know what to expect. They are savages and I cannot expect anything better from people who do not follow the pope and our Lord Jesus Christ as the Canonical Gospels state and the congregation of bishops dictates. My loyalty is to Rome and it always will be as I told you, so please do not expect me to act any differently."

With these clear but yet for his person surprisingly diplomatic words he swiped aside the cloth that was covering the tent's entrance and pushed aside the spears of the guards that were crossed in front of it. He then pushed and pulled his way through the crowds swiftly back to the church with his head lifted high above the crowds followed by the monks and Julian. Once at the church he reached for the holy water and sprayed it over his hands and face, kneeled at the altar and put his hands together in prayer, praying in silence.

"Sultan, I am again impressed by your knowledge of the Koran and how you choose the most suitable verses according to the situation." Tariq smiled.

Tariq was in a state of bliss, happiness to the level of fascination. The Sultan was an inspiring man as he always had been, Tariq was confirmed in each and every step he had taken as soon as he had left Damascus a year ago with a thousand men who had grown to 5000 along the way to Ceuta where Julian had congregated the boats from as far as the Lebanese forests and the soldiers who joined them in Cairo, Alexandria and Rabat came from across the Empire. But this was his source of motivation; he was following the right leader, fighting for the right cause, Allah's men at his command!

All night the Sultan sat with Tariq and the appointed leaders of the 5 armies and 3 commanders from the newly arrived 3000 men from Damascus, planning and debating, philosophising about the next best move, about supplies and reinforcements, about Bilal's progress and plans. They also planned an assault on the Balearics:

"As I was saying earlier, it is imperative that we appoint a significant chunk of our fleet to deal with the Byzantines on land rather than on sea, their vessels are far too dangerous for us, they nearly got us on high seas. Technically we are in a truce with them but it is no secret that that does not count for much on sea. But they are themselves engulfed in a civil war since the Heraclian Dynasty has been ousted and an Armenian general called Phillipikos is fighting to come to power. When our fleet passed their capital they made it pretty clear to us that we were not welcome at the docks and also that were they to find us on sea they would make a quick job of us. We rushed off before we got into the Bosporus. Their mentality is more that of Romans than Greeks, worse, they have totally declared any type of reasoning for heresy. I suggest we attack them as soon as possible before they start invading. They have assembled at the Balearics, I am sure."

The Sultan was confirmed by Tariq as soon as he finished, since he had heard it from Julian. The Sultan's main concern was to secure the back of this conquest and last but not least, the trading on the Mediterranean. His goods arrived via the silk route, the Red Sea, Yemen and Sinai, incense, silk, brocade, spices, carpets, coffee, tea, gold, silver, diamonds. He could not afford for them to be jammed at revolt stricken Damascus and Alexandria, where the goods were loaded on ships and spread across the Empires and via land to the Baltic and Africa. Rome relied on supplies from him and so did Iberia now. The Byzantines had their own connections with China and Persia, so they were not too interested in his trade, perhaps even competing against him. But his clear dominance in the Southern Mediterranean was a thorn in their eyes and now they knew that he could cross the high seas even right under their noses and this they did not like.

The Astronomers they appointed were not as skilled as his. Before they had a silent arrangement with him, that any place South of Cyprus, Crete, Sicily and the Balearics was Alwalid's and any place north of these islands was Constantine's. What was happening now, especially after Spain was about to fall to the Moors, did not suit them at all. They were competing with him for the favour of Rome and she was not happy about the rise of Constantine. A power shift was immanent and they could feel it. Hence they had sent their fleet West towards Spain.

"We must appoint a fleet of 50 vessels and 3000 men with horses especially for Majorca, Menorca and Fuerteventura! There are Roman, Phoenician and Greek forts they have occupied and they want to cut us right off our new trading routes to Spain and Rome so we would be restricted to the land route via the Southern Rocks. I will take care of that on my way back. By the way, I too have a surprise for you, my dear friend Tariq. The people of Ceuta and Tangier have assembled under command of Ibn Musa and baptised the Rocks that face their country. Guess how they have named them."

Tariq was clueless as to this event.

"Gibel Tariq. The Mount of Tariq. The honour is yours. And Ibn Musa set foot there and would have set camp at Granada by now. He is assembling an army to reinforce yours. Not many, just symbolical, some 1000 men to march North through the mountains, the Atlas elite force, and join you at Toledo."

"Really?" Tariq smiled somewhat shy, but yet he felt the pride and the satisfaction inside, as well as comfort due to the reinforcements. He answered with a clear cut: "All Praise be to Allah."

"Ibn Musa and I have fond childhood memories of Toledo from the time before you and Bilal came to Damascus. Always cloudy in cool shade, a welcome change from the harsh desert climate back home. Ergica and my father, Sultan Abdulmalik, were very close. We used to stay there for weeks under the rule of Roderick's father, Ergica. Wittiza was always friendly and his sister, now Roderick's wife. Yes, the Arianic Christians were in deed closer to us than the Romans. But Roderick . . . He always used to chase us out and push and bully us around. An unpleasant fellow. Funny how people can be predictable. Wittiza's sister fell in love with Ibn Musa and Roderick was so jealous that he did not even shy away from marrying his own half-sister just to prove his point. Rome was furious, incest was also in breech of their own Gothic code, the Gothorum Legum Hispaniae, but then so was polygamy, and Ergica practiced it and Roderick too. Just imagine, that poor soul, what was her name again, Egilon, she has managed to somehow stay in touch with Ibn Musa over the years. It is the main reason why he is coming. Not to take your honour away, but to make sure she is safe. Roderick has locked her up in the dungeon."

Alwalid spoke in a nostalgic manner about those years but his mood changed whenever he touched on the subject of Roderick.

"I wish you could have been with us, those years in Toledo were lovely, I miss that place. It is one of the reasons why Ibn Musa and I decided not to invade ourselves. We would be too reluctant to strike at Roderick's forces, many of his commanders are our childhood friends, many of the gardens our cradle, many of the roads our routes from back then."

"O, I see and understand. What you tell me about him though sounds much like him. I saw his portrait at the palace in Granada and his cowardice. I offered him a one-to-one combat, but he refused. Come with us, you will see Toledo again and lead the march. Perhaps you can talk some sense into Roderick."

"No, Tariq, I will not. I will leave by dawn and will not do any such thing."

"But why?" Tariq was so shocked he stood up from around the fireplace and a few glasses of grape-juice fell over, red staining the white garment on the floor. The Sultan ignored that completely although his guards were a bit concerned and got ready to draw the swords. The Sultan waved them back:

"This honour is yours. I have had my chances in India and Azerbaijan. You take this land and I expect you back in Damascus once you have satisfactorily established reign here for yourself, you are now Amir of Al-Andalus. After your service here, and you decide when that will end, you are welcome at Damascus anytime as my personal Wezir until you meet your maker, godwilling, and I will not forgive you, if you die here or if I die before you return! I want your children to take this land as theirs! Yours and Bilal's and whomever you appoint!"

"How can we know when we are to die? How can I be sure to see you again?" Tariq was sad and worried.

"We don't, but it is my wish and prayer. So fight hard and Ibn Musa I have briefed, he is here to merely face Roderick and save his love Egilon, but will not interfere with your command and leave immediately upon the battle, whatever the result." Alwalid was determined.

106

"Alwalid, I beg you to stay with us, we need you here. We need Ibn Musa too." Tariq pleaded.

"No way. No chance. Stop. I command you. This battle is as good as won, it is just a question of time. So why should I cowardly steal your honour? I will do my job at Majorca and cover your back from the Ostrigoths and Byzantine." The Sultan finished the debate.

Tariq held his silence but turned away in anger and disappointment, walked out of the Sultan's camp, more because he would miss him rather than being in despair that he would not fight alongside him. He did not return until dawn broke and did not say goodbye when their eyes met while Alwalid was carried back on the boat after the Morning Prayer the next morning. One day was all he had stayed after years of absence. A year was to pass before they would meet again. He just saw the back of him while the guards and the troops silently rowed away towards the vessels, half of which were destined for the Balearics and the other half back along the African North-coast towards Damascus, expected there in 2-3 weeks.

The men lined up along the coastline and shouted and screamed:

"Allah the Greatest, No God apart from Allah, Mohammed Messenger of Allah!"

The best goodbye they could have given such a wise and pious leader. It was a painful goodbye for Tariq and he saw the Sultan's tears glistening in the morning sun that just appeared at the horizon across the sea when Alwalid turned his head half back and took a last glance over his shoulder at this new land of his Empire. He was never to return after conquering the Balearics with 3000 men, 1000 of whom were to stay in Majorca and the rest back to the mainland of Al-Andalus and to be stationed in Vallada in permanent contact with Damascus and the rest of the new Andalusian force. Alwalid did a good job in the Baleraics they heard later on, the Viking guards were destroyed and the islands occupied, the 2000 men who returned caught up with them at Toledo to join them in the siege with the men from Ibn Musa 3 weeks later. A surprise was waiting for them at Cordoba though that would put them into a very awkward situation.

And so it happened that after the week of festivities in Al-Vallada, during which Tariq was somewhat withdrawn, they hastily marched across the fields, past the hills and villages sharp westward towards Toledo, unstoppable, steadily and determined. They sent two thousand men North towards Barcus (Barcelona) and the hills towards Gaulle who were then to march West past Sarakusta (Saragossa) and join him at Tulaytulah (Toledo).

The Struggle

"They have made their oaths a screen (for their misdeeds): thus they obstruct (men) from the Path of Allah. Truly evil are their deeds.
That is because they believed, then they rejected Faith: So a seal was set on their hearts: therefore they understand not.
When thou look at them, their exteriors please you; and when they speak, thou listen to their words. They are as (worthless as hollow) pieces of timber propped up, (unable to stand on their own). They think that every cry is against them. They are the enemies; so beware of them. The curse of Allah be on them! How are they deluded (away from the Truth)!"
Surah 63 (The Hypocrites) Verses 2-4

Bilal's march North was progressing from day to day. Bilal followed a very different strategy as he was not bound to a particular meeting point with the Sultan. His approach was that of swiftly conquer and leave behind a garrison at each major fortification. And so he stuck to the coast and as soon as he had passed Isbunah, the scarcely populated once Greek fortress of future Lisbon, where he had left a garrison of 1000 men to fend for themselves, equipped with all the necessary goods and skills, he made his way hastily to Porto an Braga, the Northern Hispanic forts of the Romans, leaving behind another 1000 men for that region, after which there were only impenetrable mountains. At Porto and Braga he made a quick turn East and approached Sarakusta, later known as Saragossa, where he was to meet with the Northern flank of Tariq, the 2000 men Tariq had sent along Barcelona and Saragossa. He wanted to regroup with them there in order to jointly approach Toledo but later on decided to progress to Toledo without meeting them beforehand. During his conquest he sent only a small delegation to the Northern coast of Galicia and Asturias as well as Basque as these areas were scarcely populated. How was he to know that that was going to be the last enclave of resistance by the Goths later?

Following this strategy he had, just like Tariq, passed many settlements that were amicable to the Moorish conquest as they were not too pleased with Roderick's rule, who had not held his promises, overtaxed, broken his own law where it suited him and plundered all the monasteries after stripping them of their land. This was the part of Hispania that belonged to Roderick even before he had violently taken the rest of the land from Wittiza, but he had neglected his own kingdom and famously he was not a friend of the soft-soft approach anyway. He made an example of letting people suffer and threatened others with the same fortune. He had practiced the violence in his own land before carrying it to Wittiza's kingdom in the South-East.

Therefore basically one town surrendered after the other to Bilal, Allah made the path easy for him, smooth to follow, although the abbots and knights, commanders and gentry of Roderick as well as the Roman consuls were quite baffled to see a most formidable army lead by the darkest of dark Moors they had come across, a Black man on a horse, an African dressed in brocade with the sword of a knight, the armour of a legionnaire, better, a general of the Romans did not even own such intricately chained armour and weaponry. But they bowed and paved the way for him and listened carefully to the delegates he left behind and the sermons he held. He was an object of fascination, a much awaited contrast to these supremacist Goths, the Moor was compassionate and humble, taller and nobler than they had ever seen any Goth to be.

So Bilal let the sword rest firmly in the shaft and his tongue do the job with the most eloquent of Latin speeches, the likes not heard in the land of the Vandals since Cesar's times, "De Bello Gallico", Gaius Julius Caesar's account of the war against the Gaulles and Tacitus' report on the Germans, partly the ancestors of the Goth, were standard literature preserved in Alexandria where Bilal had studied for many years under Greek and Roman scholars, science, arts and literature of Homer, the Aeneis, the battle of Troy and the Odyssey, philosophy of Aristotle and Socrates, politics of Pericles and medicine of Galen and Hippocrates. And of course the scholars of the Christian era, the Gospels and the Torah. This paid out now, Alwalid had sent the right man for the job because this area was densely populated by Hispano-Roman Catholics and Gaulles who were very welcoming to begin with and even more so once they heard Bilal speak of their own history and theology while building bridges to Islamic teachings. Many converted to Islam, especially the lower ranking soldiers of the Goths and the Gaulles, less so the Catholic clergy, who nevertheless maintained ties of friendship in their own interest, especially because so far West they had received merchant delegations from West-Africa, who had navigated along the Atlantic coast and into the land through the rivers and among them were Blacks.

Meanwhile across the valleys and hills to the South in the distant the clouds of dust were rising up in a smoky column when across the horizon they came. These sunny days had significantly dried out the soil and there was clearly a difference now whenever armies approached, one could see them from afar and everyone was warned, took shelter, just in case the Goths returned. But they did not. It was an abandoned old olive orchard of the Roman type with many country-estates lining the shallow valleys and hills across which were olive trees lined up one after the other as far as the eye could reach with paths riddling the landscape all across.

All farmyards had their own well and farmhouse. It was a once wealthy region which was now lying desolate in the late summer sun, not a sign of life but the birds singing in the Cypress trees that once had marked the boundaries between the properties, long before the darkness came and the harvest failed. Bones of cattles were scattered where even flies had given up hope of finding the least bit of flesh for their eggs to lay, their maggots to feed on, olives lay on the ground, unharvested and dried out like small grind stones, as olives do, decades after they had ripened. The trees held new sprouts for the coming year, so resilient was this blessed tree, it just continued its life-cycle once the sun had returned.

The riders approached in a company of thousands of footsoldiers marching slowly but steadily into the region, settling across the barns and fields, laying camp and surrounding the castle in the midst of the area. Cordoba. The pearl of the West. The glory it was to rise back to one day could already be marked out by the meticulously planned canals and waterways, the orderly agricultural basis and the natural richness of this chain of valleys. The Romans had left behind what the Goths could not value, the Moors now invaded, what the Goths did not dare to keep.

But somehow these men were different. These were not the highly skilled archers, the masterly swordsmen and the new converts from the Gothic and Gaulle gentry that marched under Tariq or Bilal. They were clearly Moorish, but much older at the average. The riders were somewhat less determined, their posture lacked the natural confidence and the horses the stamina and obedience. The weapons were not as fine and carefully crafted. They had no mastersmiths with them and no clear order in the lines. They did not obey the regularity in congregational prayer and timekeeping. Neither did they have astrolabes or telescopes. But what they lacked in skill and fitness they seemed to be making up by shear numbers. They poured into the valley and poured and poured until night fell and they did not seem to stop. From all sides and slopes they descended, no clear command or organisation, the landscape was filled with them like flies laying their eggs on a dead body. These men were elderly and had a leader above them who was old as well.

It was Musa ibn Nusayr. The father of Abdul-Aziz Ibn Musa, the governor of Africa. He had left his post 10 years ago but refused to retire, stubbornly clinging to his veterinary forces, whom he had now taken to Iberia, following the shadow of his son's 1000 men strong elite-troop of the Maghreb. Of course Ibn Musa knew about his father's plans. Musa was there to cover his son's back, but also, they did not set any limits as to where this back-covering was to stop or end or whether there was any limit to the activities of Musa at all. The men Musa now brought in were long retired soldiers of the Maghreb, they were alongside with their fathers and grandfathers the conquerors of the Maghreb, the peasants from the Berbers and Bedouins, the Arabs from the deserts who had no hope in Arabia, collected from across the Empire and now settled in the Atlas region all the way from Marrkesh, Rabbat, Fez and Tangier, what was to later on become Morocco, even as far south as the West-Sahara, Mauritania and Senegal. In later centuries the Almoravids would invade Al-Andalus and they too came from there. Al-Mooravids, Mooritania, Moorocco, hence the name Moors.

Ibn Musa in the meantime surrounded the valley, setting camp on the hills and overviewing the scenario. He was relieved that they had arrived early. Earlier than Tariq. Long before Bilal. And so they made their way into the desolate fort and began repair works reluctantly, Pelayo and Roderick had taken what they could on their retreat from the South and Ibn Musa and Musa were not sure, if it was worth the effort to rebuild this place. So they hesitated and just rested in the empty palace, which was easily taken, a few local guides offering their services to them immediately made way for the horsemen. But such a big army posed a challenge in itself, a huge vacuum in the supply-lines, a destructive factor for the local resources. These were farmers who had all hands full tilling the soil at home and had to leave their younger sons to tend the farms alone and they were forced to bring along their elder untrained sons.

In any case, far more men arrived than requested by Alwalid, some 20,000! This was surely going to cause confusion and conflict, put pressure on Tariq and Bilal, raise the tension between Tariq and Ibn Musa. Anyway, Ibn Musa stuck to 1000 men. Ibn Musa's father was grabbed by greed in his old years:

"Son, you must take over command, you are from the tribe of Solomon, he is just a Berber".

Ibn Musa's father was a convert from Judaism and he had converted back to Judaism, which was the reason why Alwalid had sent him into early retirement. In Damascus he would have been sure to be executed for heresy, but he was spared as he had served well in his years and was now taken by some type of dementia, that caused his face to drop down on one side, which is why his reconversion was seen as a sign of fading mental power, therefore he was granted amnesty. But now apparently he wanted to take Spain for himself as a Jewish kingdom, he was the one who had funded the revolt at Toledo. It was pretty clear what father and son were up to.

"When do we show them our forces?" Musa started as soon as they had settled down after the sunset prayer that was combined with the night-prayer, Musa, abstaining from it, sitting and resting, turning a few pages of the Torah, moving to and fro.

""I am not so sure this is a good idea, father!"

"Son, never be afraid to show your strength, flex your muscles. One day you will understand, keep in mind your noble lineage and that you are superior to them. You always will be. You are a Jew."

"Father, we have had this discussion so many times now, I believe, No God apart from Allah, Mohammed Messenger of Allah."

"I know you are saying that to please the Sultan, to show your loyalty to him. Son, we can have our very own kingdom here in Hispania. Have you not seen the land? If you were not so stubbornly in love with that Gothic-girl, you would open your eyes and see. Your friend Roderick has impregnated her twice already, she will be barren and old by now. I for myself have tasted the pleasure of these young redheads and blond-locks. They are sweet as honey."

"Father, please, can we stick to the subject. I need to plan and manage this my way. I let you come along . . ."

"You let me do nothing. I am here because I wanted to; I need no permission from anybody! If I say a word my men will take the head of each of your men."

"I doubt it", Ibn Musa laughed. He knew his father's humour.

During the crossing where they had commissioned just 50 vessels hastily that were operating like a ferry service for days, they had many conflicts between the two armies and Ibn Musa had sought some distance immediately marching into Granada to admit himself and report to Tariq by rider-post when Tariq had just left Vallada, congratulating him to the victory. In the meantime Musa had cowardly crawled through the valleys in darkness and made his way North by appointing local guides and taking their families captive, even if they had no clue about local paths and orientation. Most people at that time never left their vicinity throughout their entire lives. So after many heads of locals were taken, many widows and orphans left behind, most of whom were carelessly raped and plundered, finally Musa and Ibn Musa had regrouped some 15 km South of Cordoba to approach it jointly, while Ibn Musa had behaved like an absolute gentleman and was determined and noble.

"Father, I heard rumours of killings outside battle and harsh justice. What is wrong with you?"

"Don't question me. We are God's chosen people. You are my son, like Solomon to David. We are from his clan. Be obedient and loyal to me! Why do you care about these gentiles anyway? They are gentiles to you as well or not?"

"Father, they are potential Muslims, not if you kill them, but if you treat them kindly." All the while the generals were listening into the conversation from the background.

"Kindness will not heal them, they worship 3 gods, don't you know?"

"I know, I know, but they are mislead."

"There you go, so what harm is done, if I take a few for my pleasure? I joined this new cult of Mohammed many years ago because I thought it was more offensive, manly. But they are a bunch of softies; they are going to fall hard!"

Ibn Musa was tired of this lifelong argumentation. He would have cut ties long ago, but the Koran forbade him to do so and he had to follow it in front of his men. He decided to send scouts out to find Tariq and Bilal's army before they approached so he could accompany the first one and prepare him for the news about his father and the 20,000 men, as this would come as a shock to them, if they were to just stumble upon it without any preparation and diplomacy and clearly his father was not going to move.

And news came on the second day upon their arrival and they were out of reserves and it was about time for them to leave Cordoba to search for farms that were in tact and livestock to feed the men and keep up the morale. Not that these older men were in any way to be lured into thinking that they had some sort of bright future so far away from home, some were grandfathers and would have been content with new land, but most were too wise to be lead into believing that they were going to be rewarded generously against the will of the Sultan, as rumour had spread that this second invasion was not what Alwalid wanted. Many of the men were in their 50s and still fit and wise enough not to act it out and show off their strength. They had used their skills to hunt and gather whatever they could, in extreme situations pork, predatory animals and even carrion was allowed as food, and the fields were scattered with flocks of raven and seagulls along the riverside just like swarms of pigeons and bees nests for honey after years of neglect in the fields, these eager little creatures had managed to gather nectar from flowers on the hills that were growing wild above the cloud level and make homes in the trees.

News came of Tariq's approach from the East and Ibn Musa rode out with his advisors to welcome Tariq but his father was adamant to follow much to Ibn Musa's despair. They rode along the hilltops and the rocky tracks of the mountain passes, a group of 5 men when they saw the valley chain underneath filling up steadily with the troops from the East, the riders and footsoldiers, colourful and strong, intimidating and confident, at ease in foreign land, partially consisting of locals, a strength Musa and Ibn Musa could not claim, and skills they did not possess. So they rode back along the hilltops, reluctant to descent and meet the mighty general, now officially Amir of Al-Andalus, Al Hadj Tariq ibn Ziyad.

In the meantime down in the valley Tariq rode next to Alfred, the former Gaulle general Fredric, his appointed local Wezir, who was alarmed as he noticed the riders on top of the hills, but Tariq spread his hands to wave him into pretending he had seen nothing:

"Sire, why do you not send troops against them, they must be Roderick's spies?"

"No such reason, I know who they are, I sense they are Moors, Ibn Musa has arrived in Cordoba, we will wait for him to make the first move."

"Very well, but if you wish I will go up myself and take them out, we should not let them think we are inferior in any way. But if you know them of course ..."

"I know them well, I have served alongside Ibn Musa for years, I trained with him, I was in charge of some of his troops around Ceuta, we are friends from long ago. He has always been loyal and even took his own father out of his position when the Sultan ordered him."

"Well, you know best, but I thought we are doing a very good job on our own."

"We are, we are, he is here only for his childhood sweetheart, Egilon, Roderick's wife, who has been locked up in the dungeon at Toledo since Roderick found out about their love letters."

"Are you telling me that he loves the Queen?"

"Yes, in deed, they have been very close since they were children and Roderick's father Ergica and Musa were close, Ibn Musa has been travelling here for many years."

"So why did they not come themselves to do this job?"

"Well, it was thought to be restrictive since Musa financed the Jewish revolt in Toledo and has his own interests, which is why he was taken out and his son succeeded him prematurely. Also, they have history in this land and would be prejudiced, perhaps reluctant to strike, hesitant, or the other way around, overly revengeful. In my case, it was to me an entirely new approach, unprejudiced, neutral."

"But you did a great job, nobody could have done it better."

"By the Grace of Allah, the Almighty Creator of the Universe and the Earth, we are where we are, all Praise is to Him."

"Ameen". Alfred had learned to say.

"There they are . . ."

Dust was raised and the low evening sun blinded them as the riders descended the slopes along the rocky Celtic paths that had been laid centuries ago, where wild olive trees were eating their way into the rocks at the hillsides, themselves standing like bizarre statues of stone, their seed stones brought here in the stomachs of birds from the valleys full of orchards around Cordoba.

"May the Peace and Blessings of Allah be on you!" Greeted Ibn Musa, his father sticking behind him like a shadow.

"And likewise may the Peace and Blessings of Allah be on you in this Life and the Hereafter, be on you under any circumstance and his Mercy and Forgiveness and Guidance." Replied Tariq in a manner as the Sunnah of the Prophet Mohammed (pbuh) dictated, one should reply to a greeting in a way that exceeds the wording of the greeter.

"Finally you have come, we have been waiting for you for a few days already, my father and I."

"We were in no rush. We had a week of festivities in Vallada, we named the old Roman port of Valencia after our Sultan, may Allah's Mercy be on him."

"O, festivities, yes I heard, what a delightful occasion, you are claiming victory, but the King still sits on his Throne in Toledo." Musa commented sarcastically from behind Ibn Musa.

"We will get him as we got his half-brother's kingdom he had stolen from him, if Allah wills, sooner or later, winter or summer, as long as it takes, we are here to stay."

"Yes, in deed, we are, we are very thankful for your services, Tariq ibn Ziyad!" Ibn Musa was quick to add since he did not want to offend Tariq in any way and make up for diplomatic damage caused by his father

"We are surprised to see you, Musa, as you will be surprised to hear about my outstanding promotion."

"What promotion?" Asked Ibn Musa as if out of the same mouth with Musa.

"Tariq is Amir of Al-Andalus!" Said Alfred in broken Arabic.

"And who is that?" Musa looked at Tariq when asking that question, he was not used to speaking to gentiles and non-Arabs.

"My Wezir Alfred, the former Gaullic general of Wittiza who had been captured and forced to fight for Roderick after he seized his own brother's land."

"Half-brother, I know, I have been in touch with, my dear brother-in-law to be for very long, Roderick has blinded the poor fellow and put him in the dungeon with his sister. I am here to avenge them" Stated Ibn Musa. But Musa was not so diplomatic:

"O, we are here for a lot more."

"Father, I beg you, let me do the talking . . ." Tariq and Alfred looked at each other and smiled with a frown . . .

"I have assembled my most formidable men of the Maghreb and lead them here to take over the task of conquering the land since you have not managed to hunt down Roderick and his hoards and let them escape back to Toledo from Granada, where you nearly had him!" Musa explained.

"Who told you we are not going to get him. We strike the lion in his den, we wanted to cut his supplies and take his kingdom first and mobilise his own people against him. You can hardly face the full might of the Gothic army at Toledo with a few thousand people, we have collected local mercenaries and peasants and put them through our training. Most are friendly and support us, many of them have embraced Islam and the few who stayed loyal to Roderick are being looked after."

"Embraced Islam . . . from one heresy to the other." Musa made things clear.

"Father, I beg you." Ibn Musa ended the debate.

"So how many have you brought?" Tariq asked.

"I brought my 1000 elite guard." Ibn Musa was quick to make clear. "Father thought it was necessary to . . ."

"I brought 20,000 men" Musa's eyes were glistening with pride and he stretched his chest while Ibn Musa held his head and bit his lips.

"How are you going to feed them?" Tariq asked.

"We know this land better than you. Your father was still tilling the land in the hills of the Atlas when we came here for State visits and built diplomatic ties."

"What diplomatic ties? Not very effective ones, obviously!" Tariq could not but smile at the old fool, although Tariq usually was not like that.

"Well, this bastard Roderick messed it all up. You let him escape, we will seek revenge for his deeds, his people took many of my vessels."

"Yes in deed, he is a troublesome fellow and we should do our best to make him pay."

"So, we are on the same side, hand over command and we shall put you and your Black and White slaves in charge of a garrison each."

"I will do no such thing!" Tariq smiled at this thought and Alfred and his frontal ranks drew the swords, but Tariq pointed them back.

"I will ride to Toledo and lay siege and nobody will hold me back, if Allah wills, neither will anyone accompany us, we will act as independent armies until the Sultan instructs us otherwise." Tariq concluded. "We will set camp outside Cordoba on the hills."

"But . . ." It was too late for Ibn Musa to use his diplomatic skills.

"Let me come with you." Ibn Musa felt that Alwalid would not be happy and it could be heard in his voice.

Meanwhile a group of riders progressed from the back ranks and the leader approached Musa. Rabbi Benitoch.

"Peace on you!" He embraced Musa from horse to horse.

"And on you my Brother, how did these people treat you?" Asked Musa.

"They were generous."

"Are you sure?"

"We are sure, what are you doing here, Sire? You should be resting at Rabbat."

"How can I rest while my son and you are out here continuing my work, am I that old?"

"Not at all, but I thought . . ."

"Do not think so much, Rabbi, you are to do what Jahve wishes, not think." Musa was happy to see his old friend and cousin. "You will come with me. I have assembled 20,000 men and wish to march along with you to Toledo."

"We will all march." Replied the Rabbi.

"I will march with my men, you are coming with me. Now I am here!"

There was silence in the air and the air was thick, one could have split it with the sharp blade of the stainless African steel of Tariq's sword as the dust was rising and the sun was hitting the slim valley pass from the West while sinking surely and indifferently to this argumentation still heating up the air intolerably in this late-summer evening.

"I cannot" The Rabbi ended the argument. "I have clear orders from the King." And with King he meant Alwalid, his brother in-law. Musa was disappointed and angry. An anger he would have liked to show but his son made an end to it.

"Let us leave, we have much catching up to do and Tariq needs to set camp before sunset."

They rode in rows of three while the army stretched all through the narrow valley-pass that started widening each cubit towards the end and ended in this beautiful green valley of Cordoba, the palace stood out in the middle of the wide basin while the orchards and farmyards were sizzling with men, men not very well fed and looked after, demoralised, reluctant to move, indifferent to the arrival of the new army.

The men of Allah set camp at that very hillside where the narrow valley-pass ended and kept their distance from the men of Musa and Ibn Musa, while Musa rode back to the palace and Ibn Musa nervously kept riding to and fro after conducting the sunset prayer in Tariq's congregation where he was offered to lead it, Tariq clearly respecting him as Amir of Afrique and the Maghreb while Ibn Musa fearing his each and every breath in the neck and Musa despising his very existence.

The night passed quickly as the men were tired and they woke to the break of dawn surprisingly not by the call of the locals to prayer, prayer was not being observed in much of Musa's camp, it was Ibn Musa who hastily gathered the men together as the guards of the men of Allah urged him to arrange for the call as dawn broke, shocked at the sight of old farmers using their slingshots at the trees hoping to catch the odd raven or two or a handful of pigeons. The same men who had ignored them at arrival were now begging the men of Allah from Vallada for food, but how could they have cared for so many men, their own supplies dwindling by the day as the fish and seafood caught at Vallada was dried for the journey and the local game scarce, the men having to resort to wild boar and bear, even wolves at times. Although they did not like that it was a completely reasonable way of eating on a conquest so far from home, even the Koran allowed it under such extreme circumstances and over half the army consisted of recent local converts anyway, so to them this diet was nothing new.

But Tariq was so shocked at the state of this "army" that Musa had brought along and felt such pity for the men that he ordered all the food they had brought to be distributed. They thankfully accepted, while Musa's guards were fighting their own men back and lashing them with a whip each time they reached out for the dry bread and the sundried fish that Tariq ordered his men to throw across the lines of the guards, by which he risked a rebellion from his own ranks. Who would have given up food so easily in these meagre times? Tariq ordered the tents to be torn off and an immediate departure, rejecting any of Ibn Musa's hospitality.

The army marched North on an empty stomach and game got scarcer as local farmers were reluctant to give up crops in these now arid regions, rivers running low since the sun had broken through. All the while Tariq felt in his back the pursuance of Musa and Ibn Musa, who had hastily ordered their forces to follow Tariq's command, wishing for reconciliation with Alwalid as soon as he would find out about his father.

And he did. Tariq had sent off a few carrier-pigeons reporting about this event at Cordoba and how worried he was about the veterans of the Maghreb, who were partly from his own tribe and deserved to rest in their late days and by no means to take part in a lengthy siege through winter with constant battle with Gothic forces, who were sure not to surrender at their capital without a fierce resistance. By the time they passed Reccopolis, Tariq decided to make a big circle around it and deal with this religious capital of the Goths later. They heard news from scouts that Bilal was known to approach from the North and was merely one day's ride from Toledo. So they sped up.

The deeper they penetrated into the land the more the climate changed. It was not only the transition to autumn that gave their bones a chill, it was also the rugged landscape, the more continental and mountainous climate and the darkness that still reigned this part of Iberia, almost as if the rule of the Goths still caused nature to be reluctant to reveal its full splendour. The cloud of darkness still engulfed the cliffs and the elements and plants here still abhorred the rule of the Goths, so they prayed against them to their Creator and He held back the sun from breaking through the clouds here in the core of the Vandal Empire.

Meanwhile Musa had left behind a few thousand men at Cordoba to fend for themselves and a few thousand in the vicinity around Reccopolis, following Tariq a day later and Ibn Musa caught up with Tariq at Toledo, where Bilal was already awaiting them having passed Toledo by circumventing it, now he stood there with a big smile facing the South, he had been waiting for days. This smile faded when he saw Ibn Musa, but came back immediately when his friend Tariq took hold of his hands:

"The Peace and Blessings of Allah be upon you, my dear Brother and friend." Tariq approached him happily.

"May the Peace, Blessings, Mercy and Forgiveness of Allah be upon you in all eternity, Amir of Al-Andalus!" Replied the overwhelmed Imam Bilal Al-Din, defender of the faith in Al-Andalus, who had heard rumours, but not seen facts about the other side, so he was very excited and anticipating to be enlightened by the now present Amir, whoever that was ...

Now Ibn Musa and Bilal exchanged greetings hastily, Ibn Musa was good in overcoming his inhibitions and hide his background as a monarch of his own rights, his father had brainwashed him constantly with the inferiority of other races and the infidel gentiles, but his book and his belief told him otherwise.

"What brings you here, Amir of the Maghreb?" Bilal was still surprised to see him.

"We are here for moral support and to free our wife to be." Ibn Musa replied hastily.

"And you bring along many men?"

"1000."

"And his father is here too, with 20,000 more." Tariq added.

"But ..."

Tariq put his finger over his mouth and indicated to Bilal that this was no time to talk this out, Bilal bit his tongue. They had met some 15 km South of Toledo, in a plain that consisted of fertile soil and lush fields next to a lake, where the locals had gathered to celebrate and Bilal's men were hidden in the forest to keep their numbers ambiguous as they were still fearing Gothic scouts but at the arrival of Tariq they started pouring out of the woods and embraced their brothers whom they recognised through ties of old friendship reaching far back to Damascus and the Atlas mountains, the Sahara and the oasis of Egypt and of course the local converts.

The thousand men of ibn-Musa had blended in with the men of Allah and Musa's men were lagging behind. They decided to set camp at the lakeside surrounded by forests and the climate in this region was misty and cool, a welcome change from the now arid late-summer heat. In the distance rose the hills of Toledo and the rivers flowing down the slopes gradually towards this inland lake. There was welcome local fish and fishermen gathered their nets to trade in their catch of salmon for knives and garments, spices and perfumes, luxuries they had not seen for a long time, a small market opened at this occasion and locals came by from all sides out of the woods with game stuck on their spears and rabbits and boar.

The climate was somewhat different here so far inland and Bilal brought knowledge of the North and so did the 2000 men Tariq had sent North from Vallada. Cold winds blew in and it was misty and cool, cloudy and rainy, a welcome change but also the first signs of autumn. The men began collecting the hides from the animals they ate and established leather tanning and impregnation basins filled with faeces, excrements as well as urine. This was the common way of treating hide for strengthening and softening at the same time. The stench filled the air but it was a necessary evil to equip the troops for the coming autumn storms, since they had seen the locals do it and they knew harsh winters from the Atlas mountains. Of course the weight they were allowed to bring along on the vessels did not allow for year round provisions and they were asked to arrange locally for seasonal preparations.

And autumn came soon enough; the next day a heavy rain drew in, soaking the men knee deep into the mud and leaving the tents to cover from water as they had been carefully waxed as there was no need for protection from sunlight anymore. The horses too were sheltered under waxed canopies and so were the men. Now was the time to rest and plan the manoeuvre, not the time to march. Tariq and Bilal took seat in one central tent and closed themselves in with Ibn-Musa and Alfred. Tariq began:

"My dear Brothers, we are here to plan the best possible approach in order to not only swiftly, but also thoroughly subdue Roderick's forces and wipe out his power once and for all. He has shown his inability to compromise, debate or even fight properly for that matter and now he is back in his capital surrounded by our armies, like a lion in a den, dangerous and cowardly, his commanders by his side. Amir of Afrique, you know him best and his commanders. Alfred, you have served in his army and that of his half-Brother Wittiza who is now blind and locked up. Please make your suggestions."

After a moment of silence and meditational prayer Ibn Musa broke the suspense:

"We have heard of their fight during the Jewish revolt at Toledo. As soon as the Jews formed alliances with the locals and threatened to take out Roderick, the inner walls were locked and the revolting masses taken into the enclave between inner and outer walls. Then the outer walls were locked and the masses cut off from their supply line. There they were kept for hours being fired on with burning arrows and boiled with hot water and oil. He showed no mercy until they were all dead, no negotiations, no talks, no asylum. The paths on top of the outer walls are connected with the inside of the castle somehow, either underground or by a bridge. The place between the two walls is filled with mud and only a stony path allows crossing. The mud must be now riddled with rotting corpses after last year's revolt."

Alfred was the next one:

"The same happened to Charles' army a few years back. He had no chance and withdrew after fighting his way out of the enclave and apparently they opened the gate for him for some reason, but he will not tell us why. He might have had someone on his side in Roderick's lines or even arranged a truce or a pact. I myself stood on the walls that day and was hindered from looking down at the gate. As you know some of the commanders converted to Catholicism like Ergica had and Roderick was baptised as a child but he always rejected it. The vast majority though as well as Wittiza remained Arianic and rejected the monks. If Wittiza had sided with Charles, they would have perhaps stood a chance against Roderick. Charles never wanted to fight alongside Arianic Christians who do not pray in the Name of Trinity. As far as I know Pelayo is entirely loyal to Roderick we think, mainly for the booty, we don't know yet, how far this loyalty goes . . ."

"I am sure there is a limit to that," Ibn Musa interrupted him. "We can offer him some sort of truce or compensation, but we have to get through to him. That won't be easy. Perhaps we can use some of the locals or spies at night to invade the castle."

"We can always dig a tunnel, but that will take years as it is as all rocky ground." Tariq pondered on the best way ahead. "How thick are the walls?"

"They are enormous." Alfred looked worried.

"Yes, I remember from childhood years when they were building the second wall that it was thicker than the first one, perhaps a horse's length or two." Ibn Musa rejected the idea of a siege completely. Bilal spoke now:

"There was a heavily fortified city called Isbaliyah (Seville) on my way West, where a similar fort was standing. We had to leave it with some delegates, perhaps a few dozen of our men stayed behind as messengers to communicate between the local chiefs and Granada as we would never have made it here in time otherwise. Roderick never took it either. It was the first city I remember after Granada when we progressed westward. These are old Roman forts, partly reaching back to Carthaginian times and the Greeks also built some of them and the Romans cherished them. Now the Goths have maintained them well, perhaps the only thing they maintained as it was essential to their rule. Toledo was their own foundation around this old fort as it is the only one on top of a hill with a view over the whole surrounding vicinity, 150 degrees. The steep cliffs don't allow any tower to be pulled beside the walls. Behind it are steep mountains. A strong river flows around the hill and forms a natural barrier. It also keeps the space between the two walls moist and soggy, impenetrable. I heard they can flood it and release the water on demand to wash out the dirt and the corpses. They use it as a rubbish dump and perhaps for human excrement and remains as well as dead horses, food-waste, sewage and so on. So the filthy smell and repelling disgusting nature of this fort alone is a reason to stay away from it. They seem to enjoy being surrounded by death, sort of a necrophilistic cult."

Bilal spoke with much hate and disrespect, the like that was new to his person, he had learned a lot about the way the Goths had dwelt in the

North and West of the land and the local elders, the monks and gentry had warned him and alarmed him of their ways and how ruthless they were when it came to maintaining power. Tariq summed up:

"My dear friends and brothers, so I take it that the only way out of this is a lengthy and painful siege that is going to last . . . however long it takes. We have to hunger them out and ensure they are cut off from any supplies, secret exits through tunnels and any armies attacking us. But as far as I know there are no more troops loyal to Roderick anymore outside this fort. They have all lain down their arms and work with us in all major cities of this land, apart from the ones over there in Tulaytulah (Toldeo), who have agreed to a truce with us. So basically we are in no particular rush and we have the benefit of time, while he is dependent on his reserves inside the walls. How long do you think are they going to last?"

Alfred spoke: "They could last for a very long time. Don't forget, they have a natural stream entering the walls, so they can fish, they have wildlife and birds, pig-stables, they have a silo of flour and they eat anything that moves anyway. My best guess is a year."

"One whole year. Are you sure?" Tariq was astonished.

"Maybe more, they will, as I am sure, start eating their own. Each other. From bottom to top!" Alfred knew that all too well. He had seen their cannibalism first hand at Montril.

Ibn Musa was frozen and the others shivered at this idea, but it was nothing new, some African tribes were said to eat human flesh ritually, the Vikings did it for sure and in emergency cases it was even a law at sea. One could argue that in extreme situations it was forgiven and even allowed by God. The desert dwellers knew very well, first the reserves, then the camels, then game and pork, then carrion and then . . . it was the law of nature in the wilderness. And this rock in the heart of Iberia, this fort on top of a hill, this huge complex was the last bit of wilderness left in this new part of the Empire where limits and inhibitions did not count for much anymore. Survival was imperative to them, therefore the law at sea was their law perhaps.

"How many are they anyway?" Bilal asked.

Alfred knew best: "Perhaps 15,000 or even 20,000 now, even after over half the army has deserted and come over to our side!"

"O Allah be merciful!" Tariq shivered, not for fear of his life but for those men.

"What would be the best way to attack them?" Tariq added this question reluctantly as he really did not want any confrontation, the walls and the numbers inside forbade it. Also this shear number inside an enclave meant a lot of suffering among them, which was not what either Tariq or Bilal wanted.

"Our black powder is useless against these walls and we have not found any local sulphur-mines yet so we are limited to the reserves we have managed to keep dry and bring along. We would have to decimate the local forests for siege-towers, which are useless against these walls and along these slopes anyway and burnt down easily. Ladders would be useless as the walls are far too high. Basically catapults would be good, but they are too random and at these slopes, how do you position them? Arrows, arrows and again arrows. That would be my recipe." Bilal had already studied all types of scenarios and had the best experience in this respect because he had tried this at a few smaller forts and it had worked. Of course that was after intense negotiations and only as a last resort.

"We do not want to loose too many men just for the sake of attacking. They work with fire and tar, oil and boiling water. The black powder we used at Granada is only for destruction of building work and we are running out of it. We are not allowed to kill with fire anyway! But merely for penetrating the wall perhaps we can order some more from Damascus, Tangier or Ceuta. But the supply that the Sultan brought at Vallada is not sufficient to take out the heavy gate and certainly not a second gate." Tariq finished the debate with a prayer and Bilal and Alfred and Ibn Musa all had their say in it. They ended with a few verses from the Koran:

"By Time! Verily Man is in Loss
Except such as have Faith And do Righteous Deeds
And join in the mutual Teaching of Truth
And of Patience and Constancy."
Surah 103 (Time)

The Betrayal

"Let not the unbelievers think that they can get the better (of the godly): they will never frustrate (them).

Against them make ready your strength to the utmost of your power, including steeds of war, to strike terror into (the hearts of) the enemies of Allah and your enemies, and others besides, whom ye may not know, but whom Allah doth know. Whatever ye shall spend in the cause of Allah, shall be repaid unto you, and ye shall not be treated unjustly.

But if the enemy inclines towards peace, do thou (also) incline towards peace, and trust in Allah. For He is One that hears and knows (all things)."

Surah 8 (The Spoils of War), Verses 59-6

All these weeks the Goths had been surprisingly passive and quiet. The men of Allah knew fairly well that they were scouting the land and underground with guerrilla tactics here and there, camouflaged as civilians. Apart from reports of killings in the surrounding villages and among the delegates they left behind on their marches there had been only one major confrontation with them after Granada, the one at Seville, where after a few days of siege they had basically come to a peaceful arrangement and abandoned their loyalty to Roderick, taking delegations into their city and keeping ties with Granada. That had gone unexpectedly well. Nothing of that type was to be expected here at Toledo.

All this changed vehemently and with one hard blow when that same night a troop of scouts from the Goths fell in from the surrounding hills and forests in the hundreds and overtook the guards and spies that had been placed by Tariq and Bilal on the hilltops. The whistle post failed as their throats were slashed before they could report down the slopes and when they heard the first few interrupted whistles it was too late to form for battle. Also, there was no particular pattern as to the attacks and no frontline, no enemy to confront; they were falling in sporadically, a burning arrow here a spear there, hidden in the forests and running past only on suicide-missions. Hundreds of men died unnecessarily that night, burnt inside the tents. Some of the Goths were caught alive but did not talk and Ibn Musa took some of them to the side and used his very own interrogation techniques not approved by Tariq and Bilal, dipping the hands into boiling water and pulling out nails and teeth ... they talked.

Basically they had been sent in a wide flank to surround the troops and had a few confrontations with Musa's army that was camping further South when they decided they could not close the circle and retreated, some of them breaking away to conduct these un-tactical attacks against Roderick's approval. Roderick was not a guerrilla-person. He was an army-to-army type leader, while he avoided the frontlines himself. This looked more like the handiwork of Pelayo, but both stayed behind in palaces, reclining on thrones, apart from small villages, where they could taste the blood of innocent young girls and where they were sure not to be confronted. There were not many girls here, they had left them all in settlements far away and the rest of the land was too scarcely populated for him to conduct raids from Toledo.

This devastating blow to the morale of the men of Allah urged Tariq, Bilal, Ibn Musa and Alfred to act, especially when they found that the men were deprived of sleep and nervous. Also, they could not afford for Roderick to escape, because the landscape and the underground of the city were known to be riddled with caves and secret underground passages and waterways. Furthermore there had been reports of troop movements inside and outside the city walls, exercises.

It was the month of Shaban and some of the men were fasting, starting preparations for Ramadan. Eventually the New Moon was sighted on a clear night and all the men stood in Taraweeh-Prayer late into the night, while fasting commenced the next day. On travel fasting is forbidden but not once you have settled for a few weeks it is all right to do so. And judging by the lack of food it was recommended to fast and fasting also heightened the alertness of the senses.

On the 3rd week upon setting camp 15km South of Toledo they formed garrisons of 500 men each and marched in several waves North towards the city to face the might of the Gothic army in a full-scale confrontation:

"O men of Allah. The time has come. This is what you all have been waiting for. This is the moment of Truth. We have come to the lion's den to strike the final blow, the last battle of Hispania, the war of Al-Andalus, the conquest of Iberia! It is near and we long to seize it. Roderick sits over there, cowardly on his Throne inside the walls and has sent his men out alone without any leadership from his side. You know fairly well our leader Sultan Alwalid ibn Abdulmalik Al-Hadj Al-Umayyah, ruler of the Muslim World, King of Damascus, guardian of the Holy Mosque at Madina and custodian of the Holy Kaaba in Mekka is a different character. Our leader is a hands on man and has fought hard to cover our backs from the Byzantines and for that we are thankful. He has battled himself hard for many more years in Sindh and Azerbaijan to protect the locals form cruel tyrants such as Roderick and worse. He has only left this for us as an honour, not as a cowardly retreat like that fellow over there, whom I have offered a one-on-one combat repeatedly before to spare your and his men's lives, but he rejected it. Arrogance is his motto, cowardice is his style, honour is his fear! O men of Allah, you have come so far, now I ask you for a last time:

ARE YOU READY FOR THIS BATTLE?"

An all deafening shout filled the valley and funnelled and echoed all across the place deep into Toledo:

"Allah the Greatest, No God apart from Allah, Mohammed Messenger of Allah!"

By this time they had already approached Toledo and the city grew in their eyes, the background was filled with the misty slopes and the fort rising from the fog, the forests had turned from green to display a spectacular mix of colours, yellow, red and brown, the sun was rising slowly from their right and autumn had moved in over night, leaving a chill in the air that was no longer ignorable, they had to put on a layer of leather-coated hide to keep the wind out.

And so they marched slowly but determined and confidently with their eyes fixed on this fort of all forts, this mighty castle of the Goths, the subject of myths, surrounded by Roderick's backyard and hunting ground that was no longer his, step by step they approached in blocks of 500, subdivided in rows of 5, then 7, then 10 as the road grew in width before it spread out to finally become the fields that surrounded the hill-fort of Toledo, where history was in the making. But how long would victory await them? How far was the final battle? How close was the end to the conquest? Little did they know that there would be no real battle . . .

By midday the well-oiled war-machine had set camp in the fields and woods all around the area, beige waxed tents now additionally covered in hide in well-ordered ranks facing the slopes, with horses around them to be watered from the rivers, white banner-waving spears next to them, guards surrounding each block of 100 tents or so with strong armour the likes not seen here since Roman times, in fact perhaps never seen, mastersmiths at their work praying, blowing, striking, repairing,

moulding and blessing the swords, sharpening and cleaning the steel here in this place that was soon to be known to produce the best steel in Europe, based on the principles introduced by these very pioneers, who created there a centre of learning and teaching, a multi-faith university, the first of its like in Europe, to which groups of nobility would travel from afar to learn and Brahe, Kepler, Kopernikus, Newton, Bruno, da Vinci and Galilei would take their theories from. Even Thomas Aquinas would bow to the wisdom from the East in this very place, although he would deliberately translate "No God apart from Allah, Mohammed Messenger of Allah", as "No God but Mohammed", leaving the Christian world to think that Muslims worship Mohammed (pbuh) like many of them worship Jesus (pbuh) and hence justifying the crusades.

But the establishment of this guild of the mastersmiths at Toledo was the real significance of this day that changed history forever, leaving behind a light of progress that would not fade until the times we know now. A light without which the darkness of Roderick's reign would still cast its cruel shadow that was later on manifested in the return of his spirit in shape of the Inquisition, echoing throughout the centuries in form of the Crusades, Imperialism and last but not least the mighty World Wars that Europeans were to fight unfortunately.

None of that was the immediate concern of the men who had now settled in the valley to stay there, not to be moved for many centuries and brought with them everything they needed to await the surrender or confrontation, whatever it may be, a peaceful union or an epic battle of biblical proportions. 11,000 men filled the valley that day and more were to come during the following weeks as the news spread across Iberia that the Siege was laid, Roderick surrounded, the troops collected around Toledo. Time for the kill, the final blow.

Tariq tried in vain to solve this issue diplomatically, again and again sending in his messengers with letters knitted around arrows, who shot the arrows across the mighty walls, having to climb up the slopes for hours before being able to shoot far enough and many of them being taken prisoners or just violently shot at by the Gothic guards and scouts that were spread across the hills, none of them dared to descend into the valley though. And so it came on the 2nd week of the siege that Tariq gave up all diplomatic activity after loosing nearly 15 men in this way and the men of Allah looking at him with challenging eyes and somewhat disappointed. That disappointment grew when they heard news in the 3rd week that Roderick had escaped. Ibn Musa heard from his father's riders who arrived frequently at the camp that they had seen Roderick march South towards Toledo.

Tariq and Bilal both were in a State of shock that day. They had done all they could to avoid that from happening, searched the hills for entrances and gaps in the rocks, asked the Goths and Gaulles and Hispano-Romans among their own for secret passages, but none of them knew anything about it. This was a well-kept secret among Gothic gentry and they were known to kill those who dug the tunnels in years of hard labour, so that the exact passages were unknown to anyone but the closest comrades of Roderick. Still the fort-city lay far up on the hills, impenetrable, distant, mighty and mystical. All that came down were the wild springs and rivers, all that ascended up was the vapour, mist and fog, surrounded by clouds, engulfed in mystery. Spies and messengers who climbed up only ended up tumbling down like rockslides.

Adding insult to injury Musa came riding in on the Friday of the 3rd week and barked out at Tariq's tent, while the guards held their spears into his face:

"You idiot, I always knew we could not count on a simple Berber from the hills, you will always be what you were born to be, a peasant farmer tilling the hillside, not able to grasp the likeness of the gentry residing on top of it. You let him escape again, you let Roderick ride off to Reccopolis, you had victory and you chose defeat!"

The guards asked Tariq to give them permission, but he held them back and just looked away, turning his face to the sky, the by now cloudy, rainy and cold heaven above them. Allah would be merciful again some time and He demands patience. That is Allah's habit. He is time and he takes time. His own time. In fact he is endless, eternal and everlasting, so what was the rush, the worldly haste, the useless stress. Rest is peace. Rest is eternity. Before Allah split the heavens and the Earth asunder there was no movement, no time, no question about eternity or creation.

"Do not the Unbelievers see that the heavens and the earth were joined,
before we clove them asunder? We made from water every living thing.
Will they not then believe?"
Surah 21 (The Prophets) Verse 30

The next day, as Tariq was getting ready to march off to Reccopolis with
a troop of 1000 men, news came from Vallada. A rider brought in a letter
from Sultan Alwalid that had been flown in by a pigeon:

"In the Name of Allah, most Gracious, most Merciful. The Peace and
Blessings of Allah be on you, my dear friend and Brother Tariq. We have
heard of the recent developments and Musa's move that went against my
instructions. Do not fear, the land is yours, we will send him instructions
independently and send an army to take him out, if we have to, but we
command you and his son to strip him off his powers, take over the
command over his troops, send as many as possible back to their farms
in the Maghreb and collate all efforts against Roderick. For striking
Roderick is your first and foremost goal. Do it by any means necessary,
you have my blessings, within the limits set by Allah. I expect Musa back
and Roderick's head, soonest!"

This impatience was unlike Alwalid and the tide had turned, Musa's
moves were the cause of it all and they might be a factor that would
divide the Empire, people like him were dangerous. Musa also got a
letter from the Sultan but ignored it. Ibn Musa on the other hand, in
whose camp Musa had stayed, naturally took his father aside:

"Father, it is time to act reasonably, before we divide the Empire, cause
civil-war to break out. We need to compromise or we endanger our
mission!"

"Son, I will do anything for you, even lay down my sword, but let me do
it my way, I will ride to Damascus myself! Promise me only so much, you
will take this land as yours and continue our lineage and establish our
name here as regents!"

"Father, you can count on me in your absence. Our eyes will meet
again."

With this they parted and Musa left the tent, but unexpectedly Tariq had sent his guards already to stripe him of his Power, take his sword and his armour, arrest his guards and tie him to a horse.

"I curse you, Berber-boy!" Musa was furious, the fury of a lion in chain and he jumped, strong for an old man like him, from side to side pushing and pulling the guards who had a hard time holding him still. Even Tariq took a few steps back.

"Tariq, untie my father. He will make his way to Damascus with his own congregation."

Demoralised as Tariq was he had no will to resist this plea and without words he just waved his guards back and Musa kissed his son's forehead, climbed on his horse, called his guards and slaves and marched off South, leaving Ibn Musa in charge of 17,000 men that day, who were scattered between Cordoba, around Reccopolis and all the way to Toledo in the field, woods and valleys, along rivers, lakes and streams. The remaining 3000 from his army rested at Cordoba.

Tariq and Ibn Musa were now in possession of an approximate equal amount of men in the area, while Tariq's troops were 15,000 in number, young and strong but somewhat demoralised in the valley and another 10,000-20,000 across the land, Ibn Musa's troops were his 1000 strong elite force, the 20,000 veterinary forces and another 10-15,000 back in the Atlas. Tariq tactically did not want to ask him to send his men back to the Maghreb yet, as this would have made Ibn Musa angry and challenged him, instead Tariq left Bilal in charge of the men in the valley and took 5000 men in clear cut formations South towards Reccopolis, the place they had left out, ignored, circumvented on their march North from Cordoba. Somehow he had known that this would come back to haunt him, but not so soon. Now Roderick had made it his retreat and it was not very convenient to be facing 2 armies instead of one. If Toledo had fallen, Reccopolis would have automatically surrendered. But now that Roderick was at Reccoplois and Pelayo perhaps still in Toledo, this chance was minute. There was still a chance that this was only a bluff and that Musa had fabricated the information to distract Tariq away from Toledo. How could he be sure? In any case he put his full trust in Bilal to guard the position at Toledo.

Tariq could have been mean and sent in Musa's troops in advance to feed them to the Goths, but this was not his style. He cared too much about the lives of old veterans and if it was up to him they would be tilling the soil back home and not marching or fighting here in Al-Andalus. He just didn't feel he could make any good use of them other than as settlers in the land to fill the vacuum the Gothic massacres had left behind, especially in the former regions of Wittiza.

As soon as Tariq had departed, Ibn Musa sent a delegate to the city of Toledo via the moutainpassess around the other side of the valley where outposts had been placed. He knew that region fairly well, it was the hunting ground of Ergica and Musa when they used to visit many years ago, and so he knew the secret passageways and alleys through the woods and something very intriguing was happening back there. One night Ibn Musa set out into the fog when heavy rain was moving in and the thunderstorms of autumn and the winds had started to settle in, leaves blowing across the fields and swiping the landscape, painting it yellow and red.

He made his way past the guards unnoticed and rode through the mist and the fog and darkness of the wood in a big circle around the valley and to the other side where a less steep but still impossible high road lead up the hill towards the back of the fort. There he tied his horse to the trees and continued to walk through the pine forest that was far too dense for his horse to get through. He had to cut his way through the dry pine-needles and towards the rocky cliffs that hugged the forest closely. Pushing aside a few branched he uncovered a cave entrance with a few guards who knew him and lead him past. He went underground past the watery floor and streams; he seemed to know very well where he was going. There he ascended into a passageway that was lit with torch-flames and lead slightly uphill. He walked a few hundred metres and at the end the light was getting brighter, he continued. At the end of the tunnel was a chamber, heavily dressed with garments and hide, paintings and mosaic. The richness of the whole Gothic Empire seemed to be collected here, gold and silver, a festive-banquet and a fireplace with a huge portrait of Roderick overviewing the chamber. It was in deed the royal palace at Toledo .

What was he up to? Why had he not used the knowledge of this passage in order to facilitate the conquest? Why was he there now?

While he made himself comfortable at the fireplace and warmed his fingers and dried his coat, pulled off his wet turban, suddenly the big portrait moved and with a squeaking sound immediately a few people started stepping into the room, dressed in black hide accompanied by sparely-dressed women that were giggling and pouring the wine down their throats, these men tumbled towards the banquet slowly, drunken to the bone. When they saw Ibn Musa they were more amused than shocked. Pelayo was in their midst:

"There you are, finally!"

"Pelayo", Ibn Musa stepped towards him and they shook both hands while Pelayo pushed away the girls. "Shall I get you one of them?"

"No thanks, I have come in haste, Tariq left behind his Black-slave when he ran after your cousin."

"You are not seriously scared of him, are you?"

"Not at all, but we cannot be too careful. Father has been ordered back to Damascus and had to follow, he is planning a revolt with the Abbasids and this underground-cult who call themselves Shiite. I have called my cousin Al-Lakhmi from Rabbat with 10,000 men. When did Roderick leave? Why was I not informed? And father?"

"We do not have to tell you about our every move. We thought it wiser not to disclose the date."

Meanwhile they had taken place around the table and started to chew away on meats. Ibn Musa abstained.

"Where do we go from here?" Ibn Musa was lost. "Can I see Egilon?"

"I am in no mood to break my loyalty to Roderick or to surrender. I cannot let you see the Queen. Neither would I stay here in this place, if I were you. It is doomed. We are celebrating its downfall. I feel like returning to Asturias, the maritime climate suits me better, I can establish and regroup. We have to do without our friend Roderick I am afraid. He chose Reccopolis, he feels some sort of connection there. He even left Egilon to rot in the dungeon down here with Wittiza and their sons."

"What are you suggesting?"

"We are not going to get past your forces. Our forces are in no mood of fighting here. Your Arabs are not going to move. Let me take them North. I would ride alone but I do not want to risk my best men to side with Tariq and fight against me in the North. I want to take Roderick's men and my men. He only took 3000 last week, as many as he could fit through the tunnel during one night. The rest are vegetating away in the yards and caserns. Roderick chose to abandon this place, why should I stay? I offer it to you, if you let me go. Talk to that Black slave, he will let me go. If not, cover my back and I will take 10,000 men with me, leave the rest here."

"I don't think he will barge. We will have to cover your back while you take them through the tunnel."

"How can I fit 10,000 men through the tunnel? It will take days! How will we escape North? We do not have enough horses."

"If you give me all the rest of your men in this city and brief them as to their loyalty, I promise, I will fight Tariq's men until you have escaped with as many as you can."

"Surely they will send troops after me."

"They will be too busy fighting Roderick and us." Ibn Musa was determined to get Toledo at any cost.

"Ok it is done. I would not stand another week in this place anyway. Neither could Roderick, that coward. Why should I cover for him in his absence anyway. I'm off."

Ibn Musa had not eaten from this banquet and stood up in haste, turned around towards the exit and left with the words:

"Get ready to leave. Tomorrow we strike at sunset."

"Filius." Said Pelayo, he meant Ibn Musa. "Go to your love."

He appointed guards to lead him to the dungeon and Ibn Musa met his love after many years, they held hands and kissed, spent some valuable and tender moments together while he promised her liberation was soon to come. And then he left the same way he had come, in the dark, unnoticed.

All the following day it rained terribly and the fields became muddy, the rivers burst through their banks turned into gigantic currents, the rocky slopes became even more slippery and the men of Allah had to break of at least half of the tents and camp them more densely together with other camps on dry patches or seek for higher ground. Basically the garrisons became cut off from each other and were stranded on small islands surrounded by the endless flow of water from the slopes around the fortified city on the hills that seemed even more impenetrable and distant, engulfed in a cloud of mist and rain, permanently cut off from the valleys below. The hills behind it were far too steep for any army to get across. This being the situation, all day was dark and misty, the men of Allah did not even know how to follow the course of the sun and prayers were cut short and the camps were rebuilt where a constant line of men was bucketing out the water from the fields. Night set in.

When it was pitch-dark a bunch of riders approached out of the mist from the woods towards the East and broke news of an escape taking place on the other side of the forest. Immediately Bilal ordered 5 garrisons to make their way and follow those men, no matter what it takes, whether they would have to sink into the knee-deep mud, swim across the streams with their horses, who were intimidated and extremely stressed resting in the rain and morale was naturally low.

The fires outside the tents had been extinguished by the rain for long and the men had been fasting for many weeks in a row, only breaking it at sunset with pieces of dried fish and chick-peas. Reluctantly they packed their gear and horses and set across the fields and marshes, through the waters and woods after the spies who had brought the bad news. Bilal rode with them. In fact he rode ahead and when they broke through the dense forest on the other side of the valley he could not believe his eyes. A steady stream of men was breaking out of the stretch of wood along the slope and rushing towards the North into a forest path right past the positions of ibn-Musa, in fact right under the eyes of his commanders without them acting against it. Bilal kept silent as he had hidden in the undergrowth and left his horse behind.

He immediately rushed back to his men and ordered them back as this would have surely been their death, a trap set by ibn-Musa, it must be, he was furious but hid his anger and he knew at that moment exactly what was going on. Like father like son. Bilal had been betrayed. On the way back he ordered a retreat and the men were very confused but they saw with their own eyes what happened then: ibn-Musa cut them off from the retreat and collected at least 5 garrisons of his father's men to block their way back so they could not recruit any reinforcements.

Bilal reacted promptly and under a hail-shower of arrows that he blocked off with his mighty shield:

"Men of Allah, a snake is in your midst, fight for your lives, fight for justice, attack, now!"

There were many minutes of arrow-showers, whooshing and swishing through the dense forest past the faces and ears exchanged and men fell on both sides, their shields marking the place they had stood and the rain shattering on them like drumsticks on a can. Hundred's of men fell in this useless battle on both sides and by Allah, even on ibn-Musa's side many fell and were possibly martyred as well since they had no idea, who was right and who was wrong. They had mere orders from their commander in charge, the "Amir of Afrique", Ibn Musa. And so they fought bravely, just as bravely as the others, Ibn Musa had brought his elite troops to the battle.

Meanwhile back at base camp nobody even could imagine what was going on in the forest right across the edge of the valley. They were doing their best to keep still and endure the rain and the cold while many were engaged in prayer and meditation, in a state of hibernation, almost in a realm between life and death.

This battle was fierce and short, in vain for Bilal as he could not see anything, arrows flying around him, screams here and there from front and behind, he was lost and confused and so he fought to control his horse and covered himself with armour and prayed:

"I seek refuge with Allah from Satan the accursed.
In the Name of Allah, the most Gracious, the most Merciful.
Allah, there is not God but He, the Living, self-subsiting, Eternal.
No slumber can seize him nor sleep.
His are all things in the Heavens and the Earth, who is there that can intercede
In His presence except as he permits?
He knows what appears to his creatures as before or after or behind them.
Nor shall they compass ought of His knowledge, except as He wills.
His Throne extends over the Heavens and the Earth and he feels no fatigue
In guarding and preserving them
For He is the Most High, supreme in Glory."
Surah 2 (the Heifer), Verse (The Throne Prayer)

At that very moment a cloud parted and let the moon shine through and the white milky rays hit the helmets of the party opposite him and he could see Ibn Musa and his men and immediately he ordered a group of men to ride with him and they stormed, unnoticed by Ibn Musa until the last moment through dense trees towards him and at the last moment broke out of the woodwork into his lines, swords drawn and swinging fast as in a state of ecstasy, battle stance they had practiced for years unleashed that very moment breaking the lines of ibn-Musa, killing many of his guards and storming right at him, only to at last second before reaching him to learn that it was a double and not ibn-Musa himself. He had resorted to these types of methods now and was quite blatantly using cowardly tactics. They immediately dispersed but it was too late to find him.

The group of other men, diminished though they were in numbers by now, a few hundred or so, regrouped and pushed hard through Bilal's lines and past his archers, who grabbed their swords, but as archers are not particularly good at swordfighting, they were overwhelmed and the men of ibn-Musa poured in from all sides in one flank pressing and pressing through the woods towards the other side of the valley, unstoppable. Behind them they set alight the forest with flames on arrows, that burnt well despite of the heavy rains, blocking any sort of passage in the narrow valley and used the time they won in that way to escape to the other side and having the advantage of time entered the cave passage to the city while Ibn Musa and his guards were holding the entrance open uncovering it from the leafs and branches.

Bilal was devastated. He had never been stabbed in the back like that. Hundred's of men killed within minutes, hundreds more burning inside the forest, the pine-needles burnt like lighters even in the rain that had stopped by now. Had it not been for the moonlight breaking through, he was sure to have been martyred at that very moment. Allah had sent his angels and heard his prayer. Still, it was a devastating defeat, the meaning of which he was not able to grasp at that time, but the implication of which he would soon learn to understand. It was for the better that Ibn Musa was no longer among them. And as to mock Bilal and his men, a loud overwhelming explosion was heard from the hillside, the entrance had been bombed by ibn-Musa deliberately to cover the entrance behind him so nobody could follow him.

All through the night and into the next morning the men of Allah were busy carrying the corpses of their comrades and by now the men from the camp had joined them, who had been alarmed as to this development, that ibn-Musa had betrayed them, let Pelayo escape and many Goths with him and taken possession of Toledo while abandoning his own men, well the eldest among them, in the valley. This news was just beginning to sink into their minds, as much as their knees were sunken deep into the mud and the swamps.

The funeral prayers lasted long into the night and the funerals were short and sharp. Not really useful for the already low morale they were suffering from. But man endures more than he can imagine, and in defeat there is victory, very often the turning point comes at the very point that you are about to loose all hope, many of them knew this, but that knowledge being put to the test is another matter altogether. Bilal knew it best of all of them. But even he was sunken deep in mourning and recovering from the fighting, chewing on cad-leafs from Yemen to kill the pain and the sorrow and pondering.

Alfred approached him:

"Sir, we have to storm the fort, we have to smoke them out, we have to pursue Pelayo and his troops. I heard rumours that there are still guards of ibn-Musa on the other side of the valley guarding the secret entrance, we have to send for them."

"We have to do many things, but we are not able to at the moment. I will surely send for a troop to pursue Pelayo, but as for the local guards and secret entrances, we need to comb ibn-Musa's men, whom he has left behind, for information. But chances are they have no idea. And we cannot use torture against innocent old men. We need to search the area, you are right."

Bilal sent troops and put Alfred in charge to comb the valley on the other side of the wood that was devastated by the fire that had burnt all night. There they set camp and searched for many days, while the main troops were recovering from the days of rain and bucketing the water from the fields into the streams that were slowly retreating into their banks. Had there been no flood, this would certainly not have happened; ibn-Musa and Pelayo had taken advantage of the moment.

The following week Alfred returned with news:

"Sire we have found the entrance, but it is no more. They have used black-powder and heavy stones are covering it, digging through it would be like digging a new tunnel altogether. We are now back to zero. The only entrance known is again the main one up the hill along the winding path up the slope through the heavy main gate and the second one after that. But I have good news as well. The men we sent North from Vallada are finally here and bring reinforcement with local troops and we have news that Granada also sent reinforcements, in fact the whole land has mobilised against Roderick upon hearing the news that he and Pelayo were inside Toldeo. They are grouping up and coming from all across."

A smile was immediately recognisable on Bilal's face. And the troops came. And they came. And they came. For days and days they poured in from all sides and valleys, across the hills, down the slopes through the valley-chains, form the North, South East and West. The valley was packed and morale rose to an all-time high, especially as the last 10 days of Ramadan began and one of these nights was the "Night of Destiny", which is better than 1000 months! And finally they returned from Reccopolis, Tariq came back as well:

"Welcome back my Brother, may the Peace and Blessings of Allah be upon you." Bilal walked towards him to welcome him a second time in the field.

"And the Peace, Blessings, Mercy and Prosperity of Allah be upon you in all eternity."

"What news have you?" They both asked almost simultaneously.

"Excellent, Roderick fell at the blade of my sword; it was an all exhilarating experience. After a week of siege and many smaller battles, we smoked him out, we burnt the walls to the ground and poured into the city, rode across the paths and people just surrendered, many of the women and children were there. I can see why Roderick chose that for a final resting place rather than this cold-hell-hole up there. But I saw him in his last moments and he was dug in blankets in his palace in the darkest dungeon, unable to move, ill with fever, not able to even take his own life anymore, feverish and half-dead, not even Satan himself could look worse, when he drew his sword and I decided to free him from his misery, having given him the chance to confess the truth which he rejected and tried reluctantly to raise the sword against me. All his commanders abandoned him. It was not even an honour or anything the like. A broken soul, waiting to be broken from the string of life, dragged down into the deepest dungeons of hell. Had he surrendered and not tried to put up a fight I would have asked him to take the Shahada, confess that there is no God but Allah and that Mohammed is Messenger of Allah. It might have saved him from hellfire. The Mercy of Allah is so strong, that even an evildoer like him confessing at the moment of death could go to paradise, even if he was misguided all his life".

"Well, great, not so good here, my friend, I am afraid. Ibn-Musa used the shadow of the rain to break through the forest while Pelayo was fleeing. He covered his back and took the city! We tried our best but we got caught up in the woods. Hundreds died for nothing." The tears stood in Bilal's eyes, but his spirit was already lifted as he saw the many armies and Tariq back.

"Oh by Allah", Tariq jumped from his horse, "when I get that man, that hypocrite, I will take his head. Do not fear. You know what, the Sultan wrote to him to hand over command to us and await his cousin's arrival. The Sultan lost all trust in his family. He is waiting for Musa's arrival as we speak. The pigeon just arrived in Granada yesterday."

"By Allah, had I know one day earlier, I would have stripped him of his command and tied him up." Bilal replied.

"It was meant to be this way, he cannot win now, we have all the forces in the land, he is stuck with some, what, 18,000 men up there. What can he do?"

"He did a lot yesterday. He killed half of my best men!"

"He will pay for this cowardly betrayal. Believe me. By the Grace of the Almighty!"

Meanwhile some 3000 miles towards the East across the Mediterranean Sea Sultan Alwalid was sitting with his round of Wezirs and generals awaiting a banquet for breaking the fast later that evening that was prepared as a surprise by his family for his success in the East and the conquest of Iberia. It was the late afternoon. Therewhile outside the city came the news of the arrival of a hoard of riders from Cairo, who were claiming to be the Iberian delegation. Alwalid knew fairly well who it was. He stood up and gazed out of the windows facing his newly completed magnificent mosque while the dust rose in the alleys and narrow passageways of the Kasbah over the market. The fading late-autumn sun was blinding him and he held his shade just over his eyes, while his expression changed from worse to worst as he saw the sunrays breaking the dust clouds over the sparkling white roofs and heard the crowds shouting and screaming along with this congregation surrounded by the people hailing them when they poured out from the narrow paths into the palace front yard and collated in rows of 5 with the old decadent figure at their front looking at the new mosque first and then across to Alwalid at the window where he stood far up above the scenery.

"Here we are back at your service, o Sultan, we have completed our mission." Musa spoke with great pride in his eyes and smiled at the crowd.

"What have you completed?" Alwalid was short and sharp.

"We have conquered Iberia for you, my army has surrounded Toledo and Roderick was about to fall when you called me back."

"Roderick has fallen and we have heard of your betrayal."

"How?"

"My Brother Tariq smoked him out at Reccopolis. Fetch him, men, we will deal with him now."

Upon this command Musa was surrounded from all sides by guards who stormed out of the palace and pulled him from his horse, put him in chains with his men together and pushed him into the courtyard at the other end of the palace, a long and painful march for this old man, across the broad alleyway surrounding the palace. The guards were furious at him and kept spiking him with the spears, they had heard the rumours, but Alwalid, who had joined them held them back. He sent for Qazi, the Judge. Musa's troops surrendered and put down the weapons.

At the courtyard, they sat and placed Musa and his men in the middle while along the edges of the huge, two-layered chamber the crowd gathered en-masse, the palace-guards had to make an end to the masses pouring in from all sides. They had not seen anything like it for a long time, since the first Abbasid revolt at the time of Abdulmalik some 15 years ago. Nobody liked to be called to duty during Ramadan, still the Judge arrived and all stood up:

"May the Peace and Blessings of Allah be upon you," began the Judge. "I seek refuge with Allah from Satan the accursed. In the Name of Allah Most Gracious Most Merciful. So what are we here for, Sultan?"

The Judge was an old man with a long beard, a stereo-typical old wise judge with a long gown and a high turban, simple black-and-white dress, who was on stand-by duty for every occasion of the palace or the generals. He was also the specially appointed judge for war-trials and his responsibility was not to the Sultan but to Allah only and for this the Sultan made sure he came from a distant tribe and was neutral in lineage. These men were sought after. They were learned and known for their sense of justice, even their distance to the palace and the Umayyad clan.

All Alwalid could do was to make sure that they were not in line with the Abbasid policies for that would have meant his downfall. It might come as a surprise, but the Sultans of that time were, especially since the Abbasid revolts, no longer immune or exhalted. They were responsible to many worldly entities. In fact the respect for the Abbassids was great among the crowd. Mohammed II stepped into the courtyard, the son of the Prophet's (pbuh) nephew Ali (may Allah be pleased with Him), whose mother was the Prophet's (pbuh) daughter Fatima (may Allah be pleased with Her). Everyone stepped aside, made space and Mohammed II watched the trial in silence. He was somewhat uncomfortable with his position as the head of the Abbasid clan and rebellion was not in his nature. He was pressurised by others. Still Alwalid had to put up a fight to make sure the Judge was not working against him, needless to say that it was tough enough to ensure the Judge was neutral. In many cases he deliberately judged against him. And so he reluctantly began to speak:

"This man is Musa, our former delegate governor to Africa and the Maghreb whom we sent into retirement some 10 years ago and put his son in his place. He has now, against my instructions fallen into Iberia with a veterinary force of 20,000 men who have made the conquest more difficult than anything. Yesterday a pigeon arrived telling me of his son betraying my general and siding with the Goths by offering them free exit to the land further North and taking over the capital fort-city, effectively inciting a civil-war among the troops." The Sultan passed the tiny piece of cloth across to the judge that had come by carrier-pigeon.

"Lies." Musa smiled down on the Sultan.

"It is not your turn yet." The Judge said taking a glance at the letter. "His son's deeds are irrelevant to my judgement. What is your accusation? Anyway, if you are finished, Sultan, Musa may continue."

"Treason. I am finished." The Sultan concluded concisely.

"We have not done anything but to protect our son's life from the irresponsibility of the slaves whom the Sultan put in charge, incompetent, incapable and unable to capture Roderick since they landed some 5 months ago and they let him escape again and again. My son and I came in to rectify the situation."

"If I may add, we commanded Ibn Musa only to march in with a 1000 men strong elite troop to merely assist the siege of Toledo and as a favour for him, as he is longing for the hand of Egilon, the Queen, after Roderick's death." Added Alwalid.

"My son would never marry a second-hand infidel!" Musa shouted out.

"Why did you return?" Asked the Judge.

"On command of the Sultan and because we had done our job, leaving my son to complete the siege."

"How was the conquest?"

"It was easy enough, the locals have bowed to our rule and we had surrounded Roderick and his palace where he was rotting away."

"What is your view, how should I judge?"

"I am innocent as I did nothing to endanger the mission or the Empire."

"What is your view, Sultan?"

"Death for treason!"

After a deep breath the judge decided:

"We will keep you and your top-men locked up until we have news from Iberia of the final development. If they are successful, you are free but shall not enjoy the riches of your retirement and be stripped of all your possessions. You shall remain in Arabia and not return to the Maghreb. If however the conquest is unsuccessful and Toledo does not fall, you will be put to death by the sword for treason. This is my judgement and it is final but there will be a retrial upon the return of the generals which I order for an early date upon completion of their mission or its failure."

The Sultan was not pleased and neither was Musa, but that was a sign for a wise judgement and the crowd cheered "Allah the Greatest, No God but Allah!" They slowly dispersed, gazing upon Musa and the Sultan who were both looking to the ground and not moving, unhappy. Mohammed II looked at Musa and then at the Sultan from above on the balcony where he had watched, turned around with one swing and made his way out. If it was not for the unity of the Empire, he would have been influential enough to establish his own Abbasid kingdom around Mecca. And he had the full support from the Byzantines, whose interests were heavily infringed by the activities of Alwalid on the Mediterranean and their defeat from the Balearics at his hand, which they were too ashamed to be let known as their presence there in the first place was a secret. But their presence in Damascus was no secret, they had ambassadors and lobbies omnipresent among Arab Christians and Jews.

"Take him away," said the Judge to the guards and they pushed and pulled again, Musa and his men towards the other side of the city through the narrow alleys of the market to the dungeons they had built for all folk, common or noble alike, where bread and water were the diet and sunlight blocked out as it was mostly underground. All they way they were accompanied by crowds of people, children jumping, teasing, grown ups partly paying their respect, partly hitting Musa with stones, the guards doing their best to hold them back from doing either.

Back at base-camp around the valleys of Toledo the snowflakes danced in the wind and in rare number reluctantly settled on the frozen ground, while blown across the field around the tents from which columns of smoke rose immediately blown from side to side, broken up by the wind from all directions, dazzling with a welcoming dance to winter. It had arrived early. The breath could be seen and the men of Allah were now all mixed in one big congregation with the new arrivals from the North, Musa's former men, the reinforcements from Granada and all the local supporters across the land and the Balearics had arrived, leaving behind only a minimum number to defend in case of attack from the outside which was unlikely. All had settled in and were ready for battle, morale rising by the day as they saw signs of weakness from the top of the hill. Bodies of the dead were pushed down the slopes, the enclave between the two walls was overfilled and the frozen streams not enough to wash out the corpses stacked there for months. Death was immanent and decay and the smell of rotting remains was omnipresent in Toledo. It is a smell you never get used to, leave alone the sight of people around you dying day by day slowly, painfully, weakening, those nearest to you, those closest to you. And your forces. Only the winter-chill and the steady wind up on the hill made it tolerable, in summer they would have had to surrender immediately.

Ibn Musa stood on top of the palace roof and had an overview over the entire valley and the hills behind him. He was looking happy. Strangely happy. Behind him was the slope. In his hands were the hands of a woman as beautiful as the land. She had hair as golden as the sun and eyes as deep as the sky. Her dress was white and glistening in the winter-sun, subtly sparkling jewels all around her neck and head, the hair tied up in a long piece, tall, handsome and stunningly beautiful. Extraordinary, many men would have dropped at this sight, if she had ever left the palace. The years in the dungeon had not faded her beauty. She was used to being captured and to suffering, but the worry had not marked her face, however, neither was she overly cheerful. She was cold like a queen in an icy land, far away, where her ancestry came from, Germany, Norway, perhaps Iceland or even Svalbard North of Norway.

"Abdul-Aziz. I am delighted that you are back with me after all these years, every letter from you I have kept as a treasure. I am glad about the death of my husband who was a tyrant and I despise the years I suffered under him. But what hope have you brought me, o Abdul? We are surrounded from all sides from people you have made your enemy. What power have we got?" A tear escaped her eyes and her harmonious voice crackled towards the end of her speech and ended in a hissing breath in and out to disclose her fear and sadness in a cry.

"Please marry me, it has been my wish eversince." Ibn Musa insisted. They had retrieved into this chamber with a breathtaking view of the surroundings, a large fireplace, a terrace, an early form of penthouse over a most magnificent mountain spectacle at sunset where Musa proposed for the 3rd time.

"Of course I will marry you, what choice have I left, but what will happen to my sons, how are we going to get out of here before the rations are finished?"

"Do not worry, my dear, my cousin is approaching with 10,000 men to aide us."

"What massacre will there be between them and these forces from all over the land? How do they even stand a chance?"

"Leave that to us, we have made arrangements with father to overthrow Alwalid at Damascus and with Pelayo to assemble forces from the

North, even the Ostrigoths from Byzantine and the Vikings from the Sea are ready to assist us."

"How long will it take them?" Egilon looked more hopeful now and the tears that had flown like a stream were now resting around her eyes making them glisten in the red light of the sunset and the sparkling fireplace shun on them from the other side, while Ibn Musa held her hands and pulled her closer for an embrace.

"How long have we waited for this moment?" He ordered his men to call for the priests and crossed himself together with Egilon they kneeled in front of the large cross over the fireplace and put their hands together to pray. The priests came with incense and holy water and sprayed the room while the knights of the Gothic palace guards assembled, the closest to Roderick, who had during the last few weeks encouraged Roderick and Pelayo to leave as they hoped for a better chance with Ibn Musa. Ibn Musa had been christened secretly in his youth while visiting.

And so it happened that on that very evening they were wed in the Name of the Father, the Son and the Holy Spirit till death would part them. And death was to most certainly part them soon enough. Perhaps sooner than they had hoped for. The following morning Ibn Musa woke as a new man. His lifelong dream had been fulfilled and it was not only an elixir of love and passion that drove him but also a big burden that was lifted from his shoulders that gave him strength and made him bold in the face of defeat so that he, having heard news of his cousin approaching across the fields near Reccopolis, assembled hastily a force of 10,000 men to line them up at the gate and equipped them ready for battle. They waited in the noon day sun that was now shallow and pale without any heat, while the morning mist had settled and a bright winter day manifested itself. The snow had melted as fast over night as it had come.

The men in the valley were under instruction of Bilal Al-Din keeping a strict diet of sundried sea-fish and smoked sweet-water fish for breaking the fast in the evenings at sunset that was brought in from the lakes and even as far as Vallada and Gibraltar, which they boiled in a soup every evening while some local beans and vegetable served as a supplement with dark bread as it was custom in those days. This broth gave them all they needed and they had been preparing it for breakfast before sunrise, before the fast as they had woken late, the sun was rising later and later and gave them much time to sleep during these long nights, leaving the guards on duty. Busy with the broth as usual they heard a crackling of many hoofs up on the slopes. The men fell out of the tents and grabbed their spears and swords, armour and helmets, ran to their horses and fetched their bows and arrows that were mounted on the saddles waiting for such an occasion. They had kept warm with early morning exercise and archery training.

"To the swords, men, to the swords, form for battle, form for battle, no God but Allah, Allah, the Greatest!" Bilal and Tariq were riding to and fro and the generals pushing and pulling and riding to the front lines to face the full force of the Gothic elite troops from the palace. They were ready for this but it can never be the right moment, the valuable broth for the evening pouring into the frozen ground and the bread trampled under the hoofs of the steeds.

Much panic broke out as they realised that there was an army approaching from the South that the spies announced who were riding in now and joining the ranks, while the Goths and Ibn Musa's troops had built a most respectable force that was storming down the slopes exchanging hail-showers of arrows with the men of Allah and when they reached the lower end of the slopes, hitting the centre of the camp, their front engaged in a fierce battle as the swords crashed and rattled against each other, thousands of them, spread out into the valley. They seemed to never end, the mighty gate up on the hill-fort stood open for an hour and the forces were coming and coming, while intermixing with the white banners in the valley, theirs being the dragon and the cross, the men of Allah carrying the declaration of faith "no God but Allah" written on a golden banner with black calligraphy, the new banner of Al-Andalus.

Bilal and Tariq rode to the front where the dense formations were engaged in battle already and if they had not been careful while swinging the sword, they would have been sure to hit their own men, all the while dodging arrows that hissed past their ears and armour, closely, hitting the men randomly, screams from all sides, many martyrs were made.

Many tents were set alight and were burning, some men were fetching water but too late to save the majority of those that burnt.

The troops from the South arrived and it was a two-front battle all of a sudden, Bilal turned around to face the flank at the back and Tariq commanded him to keep the situation under control, as far as possible on that front. But it was all far too chaotic. It was all in the Hands of Allah. To his surprise Bilal realised very soon that the army from the South was not engaging in battle, no arrows, a white blanc banner flying and their leader holding his shield high and asking for safe passage to Tariq.

"I am Ayyub ibn Habib al-Lakhmi, vice-Amir of Al-Afrique and the Maghreb, I wish to see General and Amir Tariq ibn Ziyad!" Bilal rode by him and guided him towards the front by grabbing hold of his horse's rope.

"Sire, I come in peace, I have ordered my men not to strike against yours and I shall not support the endeavours of my cousin Abdul-Aziz Ibn Musa, although he sent for me. My loyalty is to Sultan Alwalid."

"Praise be to Allah. We are extremely pleased to hear such pleasant news, especially during the last days of Ramadan, especially during this battle." Bilal was delighted. Both men were holding their shields high and catching off many arrows as they approach the front of the lines while the men had realised very quickly that the army at the back posed no danger so they focussed again on the front and the Goths and Ibn Musa's men were under immense pressure to retreat.

When they approached the front of the lines Alfred rode by pushing them back and pointing them towards the central medical-camp, Tariq had been shot. Bilal was shocked and in tears as he pulled al-Lakhmi towards the tent and jumped from the horse falling into the tent, while the staff tried to hold him back to keep maximum hygienic conditions. But he freed himself and fought across the beds where many fine men were lying blood-covered and more were being carried in by the minute, both Ibn Musa's men and the men of Allah.

There he saw him, the arrow stretching out from his face, as he moved closer, he saw it sticking into his eye. This eye was no more, but the medics were working on removing it as Tariq lay half-unconscious, bleeding, every move hurting like a spear in his face. He waved Bilal to the other side so he could see him and Bilal took al-Lakhmi's hands and pulled him by.

When Tariq saw al-Lakhmi, he was astonished and relieved at the same time. They were old friends and he was closer to him than ibn-Musa had been. In fact Tariq had suggested to Alwalid to put al-Lakhmi in charge 10 years ago instead of Ibn Musa but that would have cost Alwalid the Throne for sure, as Musa and Ibn Musa were under the umbrella of the Abbasid lobby, whose strength and influence grew day by day. All decisions were formed by mutual consent, albeit subtly.

"The Peace of Allah on you. You have come to support us, for sure!" Tariq was in pain but such immense pain can be debilitating, almost like endorphin, as many nerves had been cut, along them some of those sensory ones that are responsible for causing pain.

"And on you. My orders from ibn-Musa were different, but as I am Amir in his absence, I made my own decision. We see your tragic loss, you fight most bravely."

"Thank you, Ayyub, we will forever be grateful for your loyalty, friendship and support, may Allah bless you in this life and the hereafter!" Tariq fell into a coma at that moment and the medics pushed Bilal and al-Lakhmi out of the tent, it was too painful a sight for them and too hard a task for the medics. Bilal pointed his right hand towards Tariq'a wound while leaving his side and said three times:

"In the name of Allah", then seven times: "I seek refuge with Allah and His omnipotence from the evil that I fear and that I am weary of." This was the appropriate Sunnah-prayer for pain and injury and whispering these prayers he left the tent praying for minimum damage and a swift recovery.

Bilal was devastated. He should not have left Tariq's side in the battle earlier. But it was the will of Allah and what is the sacrifice of an eye in the face of victory, he thought, Tariq had fulfilled many tasks, killed Roderick, conquered the whole land with him together and now Bilal had just followed his command. But Bilal was also happy knowing that Tariq would die a happy death as a martyr, was he to leave them now. And he was also happy because during the following hour the retreat of the Toledo army was unstoppable, while ibn-Musa was burning with anger at the sight of the battle from far above looking through his long pipe with grape-shaped glass and saw the betrayal, as he saw it, from his cousin. He ordered a full-scale retreat. Another day, he thought and he would have to send for reinforcements from the North, Pelayo perhaps even Byzantine or Damascus, if Alwalid fell, if his father managed to incite a revolt with the Abbasids. For that he prayed.

In the early afternoon the last troops had retreated back up the slopes and some were even locked out by their own and taken captive by the Muslims, while others were killed in anger and interrogated by torture against Bilal's and al-Lakhmi's permission. They sat and spoke and planned together until late night after a welcoming bath in a nearby warm spring and dinner had been served, the prayers conducted. Fast was broken earlier on, before sunset, as bloodshed causes a fast to be broken, the use of the blade against a body.

As it had happened before Roderick plundered the South, his half-brother Wittiza, the vice-King of the South-East Iberian provinces, whom Roderick had stripped of power and seized his kingdom, was caught during his flight to Germany and also locked in a dungeon at Toledo, while Roderick had blinded him with hot water. He had been promised justice for his people by him, if he lay down his sword, but apparently that was a wrong promise. Wittiza was Egilon's full-brother and both were from the same father as Roderick, which made him their half-brother. So Roderick had married his own half-sister, against the law of God and the law of his own land and much to the disgust of all the gentry and Rome.

Now one week after her second marriage Egilon asked Ibn Musa as a wedding favour to free her brother Wittiza from that dungeon where she had spent many years with him and his and her sons under Roderick's cruel rule. That very day Wittiza left the palace through another secret entrance through an underground stream in the company of his sons. They were captured by the men of Allah at the other side of the woods that were burnt down by Pelayo and Ibn Musa and taken to Bilal's tent.

"Who are you?" Bilal was very interested.

"My name is Wittiza, king of Southern-Hispania, these are my sons. Roderick took my land and my sight and locked me up since last year while plundering all my people."

"You were a just king, we heard", Bilal had stood up by now in excitement and offered the group a seat and some food and drink, commanding his guards to untie him and his sons.

"Justice did not prevent me from my own half-brother." Wittiza had grown bitter, he was of the wise old type though and nothing could shake him, apart from suffering of others.

"So how did you escape?" Bilal was eager to know.

"My sister Egilon freed us after marrying your deserter, Ibn Musa." He looked into the air as blind people do and Bilal feared that Tariq would suffer the same fate, if not worse. "There is an underground stream that leads from underneath the palace and breaks out on the other side of the valley, one would think it to be a fountain or a source as it comes out from the ground at the end, but if one holds the breath at the right time and ducks into the canoe, one breaks out swimming. Unfortunately it is a one way, because it flows steeply down the hill underground. Much work would be needed to dig through it and it is almost mystical how it flows."

"We have to find a way soon before winter settles in, a siege through winter will cause too much suffering, especially inside the fort, I am not so worried about us, we will survive, we can rotate now as we have the whole land and send people on leave."

Bilal thought aloud while he was breaking the fast, the sun had set. He had already sent for troops to permanently dig through the rocks on the other side of the valley and try to uncover hidden passages and waterways, but it had been in vain. Any attempt to climb up the steep cliffs and burn down the gate was met with fierce resistance through burning arrows and boiling water that caused hundreds of men to be martyred and thousands were already wounded that way, not to mention the many good men who had fallen in the wood that traumatic day that was still giving Bilal nightmares and then the direct attack by Ibn Musa's troops from the front-gate. All in all some 5000 martyrs. While it was good for those men's eternal dwelling, it was not much good for the cause, because their ultimate mission was to take Toledo. Such steep cliffs could not be reached by archers effectively and catapults were in vain too, leave alone siege towers or ladders.

"Well, you will be delighted to learn then that we have made an appointment with my nephews. They are prepared to risk their lives and Egilon is happy to participate in our plan. She only married as a last resort, in reality she does not approve of Ibn Musa's treachery and we are all enemies of Pelayo. She also tried her best to avoid the assault on your troops yesterday." Wittiza spoke with confidence.

Bilal moved around hastily and was eager to understand.

"Please tell me."

All of a sudden the door opened and a man with an eye-pouch made his way into the tent, unbroken, full of life, steady. It was Tariq. Immediately Bilal stood up:

"My Brother, the Peace of Allah on you, I am delighted to see you back on your feet so quickly after that horrific injury". Bilal was happy and al-Lakhmi joined in.

"I feel better than ever. Luckily the arrow missed my brain, or at least I hope so." He tried to laugh but the pain shot into his head. "There is still some pain in my eye and I cannot make all the moves with my face", he seemed happy but could not smile or laugh, the arrow had cut some of the tendons of the facial muscles on one side and caused a stinging pain every time he moved his face.

"This is an amazing recovery, by the Grace of the Almighty, meet Wittiza, brother of Egilon, half-brother of Roderick. And you remember al-Lakhmi", Tariq embraced Bilal and then al-Lakhmi.

"Peace be on you!" Tariq welcomed Wittiza while kneeling down and grabbing a spoon of broth as he could not yet chew. "We have heard a lot. How did you get here?" He had to turn his body to be able to turn his view and look at everyone as he could not move his remaining eye yet, it was painful to even close it and he had to take it slowly.

"Peace on you. Well, first of all I never made it to Germany after I wrote the letter to your Sultan. Pelayo's troops captured me in the Pyrenees and Roderick broke his promise of offering my people freedom and justice, if I surrendered. Thinking about it I cannot believe I had been so naive. After that they took, my eyesight and locked me up here in Toledo. Anyway, what happened is that Egilon demanded my freedom from the dungeon from Ibn Musa as a wedding gift, my dear sister, bless her." He told them about the secret plan and an appointment with Egilon's sons in a few days.

Tariq and Bilal offered Wittiza their own camp and full hospitality and his sons and all were engaged in a debate with the Imams for a few days as Wittiza had asked curiously about this new religion, which he knew from the many delegations from Damascus, while Julian-Urban and Charles of Montril also were present but were helpless as the King showed much sympathy for the new religion, because he too had dreams since he had fallen blind, different from Julian's, but just as clear. Julian had recovered from his fever, but was still suffering from insomnia. With his wrinkled eyes and his tired face he spoke on the evening of the 3rd day:

"Well, there is not much difference between us, for as we worship our Lord Jesus Christ, the Saviour, you worship Mohammed as light and God." Julian said that with a pinch of salt as he knew fairly well that Muslims did not worship Mohammed (pbuh) and later generations of Christian scholars would use just this false argument to seduce the masses into the crusades, first and foremost Thomas Aquinas, ungrateful as he was for the teachings he stole from Muslims in order to introduced them to Christianity under the pretence of Trinity.

"Far from the truth, my friend Julian, I am shocked at your ignorance. You have learned nothing during your many years in Ceuta. Mohammed was but a man, it was revealed to him by inspiration that our God is one . . ." Tariq responded.

"He repeatedly said, especially during his last days, that we should specifically be aware not to do to him what others had done to Christ." Having said that Bilal recited:

"Say: "I am but a man like yourselves, (but) the inspiration has come to me, that your Deity is one Allah. Whoever expects to meet his Lord, let him work righteousness, and, in the worship of his Lord, admit no one as partner."
Surah 18 (the Cave) Verse 110

"We are very grateful for what you are doing here in Hispania certainly", replied Julian to Tariq, "and also how you have looked after our daughters, while Roderick impregnated my firstborn, that filthy swine, you saved her from his fangs at Reccopolis, we cherish her and my other two daughters you are looking after at Kairouan!"

Julian was from Gaulle nobility, his mother was an Arab Christian, and it was custom among Gaulles to enter Franciscan or Jesuit orders at mid life after leading a civilian life and having children. He had sent his first daughter to Roderick for education when he became king but he had seduced her. Then Julian had sent his two younger daughters to Tariq before the conquest as a guarantee for his loyalty since he was seen as siding with Roderick at the beginning. With his argument about worship he just wanted to provoke and he knew fairly well the teachings of Islam. Now Wittiza spoke with his wise thoughts and reasonable mind:

"I have now for a few days heard the arguments from both sides and pondered through the nights with my sons about the new religion you bring. Most of my life I had been a loyal Arianic Christian, with Rome I was at conflict. Then I converted to Catholicism as Arian's followers were deviating like Roderick into paganism. Now we see that Islam has the best of both worlds and brings back the original teachings of our Messengers, many of whom also came to Germany, such as Odin, Thor and Wotan in the old days before the time when elves and ferries roamed the forests, they were afterwards worshipped as Gods like we can see it is happening to Jesus, pbuh, now. We see the Jews and their messengers and we see the promise in the Bible to the firstborn, Ishmael, that a great nation will rise from his offspring and there is also the promise to the firstborn of Abraham, pbuh, that the Messiah will come from his firstborn's offspring. Clearly the firstborn is Ishmael and not Isaac. Islam brings it all together and we have always enjoyed the company of the Moors in our youth, they brought exotic smells and fascinating stories similar to those of Germanic legends. It has not been an easy decision, but as we can see how the Muslims are behaving in our land, as perfect gentlemen the noblest of the noblest, their clean tongue, eloquence in Latin and Greek, their actions at war and bravery at battle, their wisdom and knowledge, we have decided to join this what we used to call new cult and declare henceforth, that there is no God apart from Allah and that Mohammed is the Messenger of Allah!"

Immediately Tariq and Bilal stood up and embraced the King and his sons, who had echoed his declaration, with tears of joy in their eyes and the guards lined up to do the same, which was another miracle of Islam, nobility and footsoldiers as one and equal in an embrace, they then prostrated towards Mecca and sent to prepare the baptising bath at the nearby thermal stream for Wittiza and his sons. Julian and Charles were silent, although Charles had radically changed his stance and having seen the Muslims over the last few months, even stone-hard people like him became soft at heart. Julian stood up now:

"My dear friends, we are delighted at this event and shall review our position during coming debates and look forward to finishing the siege and monitoring your subsequent fulfilment of your promise, which you have made to us, namely handing back power to the monasteries of Hispania and restoring the spiritual rule of Rome."

Charles and Julian and their congregation of monks stood up, left the tent hastily and made their way back to their camp, which was set up next to the Jewish camp.

The coming day there were celebrations in the camp after breaking fast for the news of the conversion of a Gothic King was something special. Although many Goths had converted, none so senior and none so respected among the ranks. Many Goths came by from the local forces that had mobilised against Roderick and declared the Shahada that very day. It was established that perhaps one out of 4 Goths and one out of 3 Gaulles converted during these months of conquest with an increasing number during the siege. And the others were in any case sympathetic to the Muslim cause, many Arianic Christians did not see any difference between Islam and their form of Christianity and many saw the Muslims as people to aspire to. This was the state of the Muslims when they were still true to their teachings!

And the support of the Gothic royalty turned out to be essential during the coming days as the siege was entering a painful phase not only for the people in the valley, but especially the men stuck up on the hill, where tensions were rising by the day and a revolt against the leadership was immanent, so much so that ibn-Musa, or Filius Mosae as he was christened, ordered precautionary executions of those who failed in the assault on the Muslims to scare the masses and distract the attention from himself. Egilon did not approve of this at all and turned away from her new husband for many days, so he refrained from such practices at the end.

Another reason for the haste was the snow that had set in and it snowed for many days while the surrounding woods were diminished for fire-wood and the cold became unbearable. The men of Allah did not leave the tents easily apart from the early-morning exercises and the odd rider; the horses had to be kept in motion and Tariq had ordered for the majority of the horses to be withdrawn and locked into stables around the land for winter. They would not have survived the cold standing still for long. Some of the mastersmiths kept themselves busy by piling up coals to melt sand they brought from the beaches and blow glasses and pots, masterly mosaics of green, red and blue artwork of crystal-glass ware, pottery and tiles for trading in with local farmers and hunters. Iberian peasants had become art-lovers, established trade and maintained ties of friendship with the new masters of the land, learning from them about their skills and teaching them about their land. The Goths had merely imposed while these new people nurtured and cherished.

The land was now sunken in a deep winter-hibernation, snow-covered trees, fields and hills, scattered tents covered by snow and the frozen earth and streams left the men in a state of tranquillity most of them had never experienced apart from the Atlas elite-forces and they were alert and guarding the camp from all sides, but especially towards the fort and the slopes, the impenetrable city of Toledo. They would just have to hunger them out or wait for their next move.

It so happened that one of these winter days, just when Eid was expected anytime and the men stood awake late to have a look out for the New Moon cerscent, luckily before the melting would have set in and the valley would have been converted into a mudpool, the sons of Wittiza broke news to Tariq's camp that they had established communication with Egilon's sons. The Gothic royalty had invented a secret language of light, an early form of Morse-code in the deep darkness of the North that proved to be vital in this siege and for conquering the city-fort, they had seen the palace windows at night and Egilon had ordered her sons to prepare with Wittiza's sons for a secret opening of the inner gates at midday of the next day after that with the pretence of cleaning out the compartment between the walls, for which a troop of 100 men had been appointed by Ibn Musa.

During this period of the cleaning of the compartment between the two walls Egilon herself was suggesting a storming of the outer gate to invade the city rapidly. She had taken this measure seeing that there was no other way out of this misery and that her husband was becoming estranged, far from reality, sunken in the addiction of wine and in depression, not able to guide his men anywhere. And so she asked her sons to communicate that to Wittiza's sons. It was a big step for her and obviously she wanted something in exchange. But for the time being, Tariq thought it best to go along and so he appointed 1000 men to scatter around the hills and secretly make their way up the slopes at night, hide in the undergrowth along the walls unseen, snow-covered, in white camouflage. He had trained them in resisting the cold as they used to bathe in the cold streams even during winter days and take changing baths between hot thermal vents and cold streams, dive through the holes into the ice-covered rivers having to fight their way back up against the strong current underneath back up through the holes, while a security rope was tied around them and held by their comrades up on the ice. These men had become stone-hard, cold as ice and strong as steel. They were his best men and he didn't appoint them easily. They were his special-forces, his secret-weapon, who used to camp in the hills far away from the camp and live of nature itself as they had in the Atlas for many years, hidden, sworn into loyalty to Tariq for life and into death. Snow was their home and harshness was second nature to them. Now they would put it to good use.

And so it came that on the second day at midday when the sun was hidden behind the clouds and darkness was immanent, the day a permanent dawn, the forces managed to collect at the gate many vessels of dry black powder, their last reserves and, under a heavy shower of arrows, penetrate the outer gate while many men had climbed up the walls and slaughtered the front-guards to free the way and already made their way across the bridges to the second wall to hold the second gate open in order to avoid it being closed in time before more forces would invade.

The winter cool made the stench of the rotting corpses and excrement as bearable as possible and the interior between the two walls was filled with men engaged in heavy combat stepping on skulls and bones under an immanent hail-shower of burning arrows, ibn-Musa had stormed by and his commanders in panic to command full indiscriminate assault by burning arrows, regardless of the fact that most men in the enclave were his own. The thousand men from the Atlas-elite guard that Tariq had sent managed to keep them busy and the gates open while in the valley Tariq and Bilal and al-Lakhmi had collected 10,000 heads to storm up the main path and enter the gate, it took their frontal flank 30 minutes or so to get there. By the time they got there the outer gate was no more, burning, ashes, charred wood. It was imperative to keep the inner gate open so the elite-forces focussed entirely on that task and while engaged in heavy battle and slaughter, decimated, diminished by the many thousand men who were rushing by from all sides of the casern inside the city, who were hacking them to death, needless to say that many hundred men were martyred in this way immediately, sacrificing their lives for Allah. The task of bringing this siege to an end was the higher good that they were fighting for, not only to save valuable lives on both sides, but mainly to make it easier for the people inside.

The end of Ibn Musa had come near. In panic he ordered full assault on the gate but it was too late. The gate was broken, the men of Allah scattered through the streets in between the caserns and silos that were still half full of grain, it would have lasted all through winter and it had been essential to break these walls now before the thaw in spring would have made it unbearable. Ibn Musa withdrew into the palace and kneeled before the cross, Egilon stroking his hair as to console him in his moment of liberation from his own evil, her sons guarding the doors, but the city underneath engaged in heavy battle, all the streets scattered with troops from both sides all day, hacking, beating, slaughtering, fighting, clashing, slashing and pushing, to and fro, without mercy, both sides, exchanging arrows and dominance. The question was, was it worth it, as always, in war, the cause becomes ambiguous within each battle, the fight seems futile as many die and lie in their own blood, as lakes of red taint the streets, the roadsides collecting the stream from the wounds to the neck, gushing forth like a spring, nurturing the rivers, colouring them red, for days and days, the snow changing its substance to clot with the congealed organ from the bodies, the melting ice flowing dark and full. This is the colour of loss. The loss of life. An infinite loss for those who give it for the wrong reason and an eternal gain for those who are martyred, who see the light immediately. Over 10,000 men fell that day. What else was there to say?

The men of Allah and the men from the valley built an endless chain up the hill pressing into the city, those fighting inside realised that the fight was futile, laying down their weapons and putting their hands over their heads, tying white cloth to their spears and raising them, the Umayyad banner that also signified surrender. Within minutes after the surrender the palace was surrounded and those inside taken outside, brought to Tariq, who was busy guiding the process of arresting the troops of Ibn

Musa and his commanders, as he saw Ibn Musa again and Egilon for the first time with her sons, while Wittiza's sons immediately pointed out to him, who they were.

"I am delighted to meet you finally, Queen of Iberia, Ibn Musa, we meet again."

Bilal moved by and pulled his sword to strike ibn-Musa's head off, while Ibn Musa was looking at Egilon with fury, guessing at the truth of the betrayal by his wife, Tariq held Bilal back:

"We have to give him a fair trial. In front of Allah and also for the Sultan's sake, as he is under pressure from the Abbasids."

"I know, but my hand tells me otherwise . . ."

Bilal was not normally like that, it was treason that he could not stand. Ibn Musa had cost them many valuable lives and months they could have used to establish the reign and build up the country again from the ashes Roderick had left behind.

"You betrayed me, Egilon, what purpose do I have in life now?" Ibn Musa was crying with anger in his blood-red eyes and shouted at her, he would have killed her, if his hands had not been tied behind his back. She took a few steps back as she and her sons were untied and pulled to the side, guided out of the streets, back into the palace by Wittiza and his sons in happiness and joy, while Egilon reluctantly followed, shedding a tear for her dear but astray husband.

"You did not deserve any better than this, Ibn Musa, we will deal with you now." Bilal spit in his face and Tariq pushed Ibn Musa to the guards to capture him and put him under surveillance. He pointed to al-Lakhmi, who had joined them and it was clear he wanted him to deal with Ibn Musa as neither Tariq nor Bilal would have been in any way unprejudiced. Al-Lakhmi took hold of Ibn Musa's hands and pushed him through the streets with many words of anger from him at the repeated betrayal by his own blood and in laws. Thousands of commanders and men who had surrendered lining the streets were being tied up systematically and locked back into their caserns and the wounded attended to by the medics in the usual manner, the dead carried dripping with blood through the icy streets, down the hill to be buried, while the medics set camp inside the city. This was the scene all throughout the day and at night finally some peace came into the city, the fallen city, the liberated fort, the siege had ended, the conquest was completed.

Tariq and Bilal and al-Lakhmi were engaged in prayer and thanksgiving and conducted many voluntary prayers and thanked Allah throughout the night, a new scene in the snowfilled streets that were being washed with warm water to melt away the bloody ice, all through the night, to be shown as an immaculate jewel in this newly conquered land, with an open invitation to the people of the juvenile Emirate of Al-Andalus, cherished like a newly born child in a clan of Emperors.

And that very night news broke of the sighting of the new moon crescent, what an excellent timing, a brilliant Eid present Allah had given them and they would not need to fight on Eid day but celebrate victory. Hence the trial of ibn Musa was delayed until one week later. News was sent to Damascus and the Eid prayer was held in the main fortification on the hilltop, while the day was sunny and chilly, still the hearts warm and festive, while wood and charcoal was burnt for heating and to fire a barbecue in the palace yard and all around the valley sparkled with flames and excitement. A colourful display and also quite some exhaustion. The men rested and many travelled back home during the end of the Eid week. This first Eid was a legend for many centuries in Andalusia. A glorious and befitting beginning for a new Empire.

The following week they held court in the palace's main chamber. Subject was the betrayal by Ibn Musa and witnesses were Egilon, Alfred, Bilal Al-Din, Wittiza, Julian-Urban, prosecutor Tariq representing Sultan Alwalid and the judge was the Wezir of al-Lakhmi, while al-Lakhmi served the purpose of head of police. The generals and commanders were invited and it was other than that a closed circle, otherwise there would have been too many attendants. Ibn Musa's Arabic troops were tried with him, they were locked up in dungeons, not so the Goths who had sided with him. They were given a chance to convert and were being preached to in their caserns, albeit tied up, or inside the medical camps while their wounds were attended to, many limbs were amputated due to incurable damage, replaced by wooden limbs, skins sown together around the wood, before they would have started to rot after suffering heavy wounds.

The court's language was Arabic that now replaced the official language Latin, which was from now on secondary, and Egilon began with an appeal that was translated aloud:

"Whatever I did was for the sake of my family and my husband. I still love him very dearly, even if he thinks otherwise, but I feared for all our safety and for his own sensibility. Nobody can think alone under such pressure; even the biggest kings take advisors. Please forgive him for whatever he did. I know he cost you many lives and many months but he did it to be close to me. How can anyone stand being so close to his love and not be able to reach it? Surely it is a torture like a burning fire around the body. If it is any consolation, we suffered tremendously, all of us, as much as you did."

She looked at her beloved husband, who had heard and seen into her eyes, and understood, but how could that understanding help him? He sunk his head into his chest and the trial rushed by him without him paying much attention to it. He knew the end had come and he knew his own judgement against himself would have been harsh. Yet he treasured the love from his wife and her kind words. For some reason he was even glad now that she had freed him from the siege and freed the many men from his command. He was never much of a leader; he was more of a lover, too romantic and entirely devoted. Their short but intense love was manifested in these weeks up in the fort after a lifetime of waiting. To him it had been worth it. His love was unconditional, even after what she had done and vice-versa. And so it goes that after much hearing and witness-interrogations the time came for the verdict and the judge asked Ibn Musa for a last statement in his defence. He stood up as he had been sitting all the while:

"I know and I can understand that the judgement against me will not be very favourable. I am fine with that and I stand responsible for what I have done. Even my own judgement against myself would be harsh in any case. But know that I did what I did for love. A lifetime of unfulfilled love, unconditional and loyal love. This much I have proven and I want my life and downfall to be a symbol of that, a witness to a tragic and short marriage." He wept tears and was pushed back into his seat by the guards. Tears gushed out of Egilon's eyes and she fainted, while her sons held her and consoled her as far as possible. The judge declared his verdict:

"It is never easy to weigh out both sides and justice and truth requires seeing the relative perspective of all parties involved. The actions of Ibn Musa, the former Amir of Al-Afrique and the Maghreb might be in some ways lead by passion and love, in other ways, and clearly in the light of reason, despicable, and most certainly not defendable. It is therefore my unanimous decree that the defendant is guilty of treason and shall be put to death by the sword immediately! Guards, take him away!"

Egilon had fainted and Ibn Musa followed her into the realms of dreams, slipping away from reality to cope with the pain of the moment, only to awake with is head looking into the mud and falling, rolling, tumbling, slowly fading vision as the blood left his brain through the jugular vein. Silence, nothingness, then the realm of the grave and final judgement after the years ahead until we all are collected to witness the final fate and to learn the truth of all that we did, written in a clear record, played back to us and declared to mankind, apart from those who do righteous deeds and whose balance of good is heavier than the weight of their bad deeds. For the good deeds count 10-fold or even 10,000-fold in some instances, the special Mercy of Allah to mankind after His final Messenger (pbuh) has been sent. In case of Ibn Musa, his head was locked into a chest in essence of distilled liquor and shipped to Damascus to be displayed at the prison, right in front of the eyes of Musa as he was freed from captivity, who recognised the half disintegrated, perished flesh of his own blood, as he would have even in a state of decay far beyond this, and the proud man wept tears, endless chains of tears all day, the feeling he had given to many innocent people he now suffered himself for days. Ibn Musa had fulfilled his promise to his father that their eyes would meet again.

After this the head was shipped back to Andalusia to be buried in the same grave as the body and Musa was free to roam the streets and it was said he was seen begging at the Prophet's Mosque in Medina, last seen at the Kaaba, begging Allah for Mercy and conducting the Hadj pilgrimage. At one of these instances Mohammed II, the head of the Abbasid clan, found him, the son of Ali the 3rd Caliph, who in turn had been the nephew and son in law of the Prophet Mohammed (pbuh). Ironically this seems to be the way that Allah divides the believers so they may not become too powerful and not overtake the whole world, so that there is still place left for disbelief in order for man to be able to choose freely between both. Hence the direct descendents of Mohammed (pbuh), who were great Muslims no doubt, and on the other hand the ruling clan, the just Umayyads, who had spread Islam to distant regions, were both in constant conflict with eachother. Therefore Mohammed II spoke:

"Musa, where have you been? We have been looking for you. What are you doing here at the Hadj? I thought you returned to your Jewish ways?"

Musa clearly was a broken man and his mind had suffered as was his body, frail and weak, no longer the massive figure and posture that formed his voluminous chest, he was now walking with his head down to the ground and his back facing the sky with nothing but a dirty white cloth and a bag with some food in his possession, living of the streets and at the Mercy of the pilgrims.

"O, you, Mohammed. God is one; I am of the family of Salomon. You believe in him, don't you?"

"Yes in deed." Mohammed II was intrigued by the downfall of this once mighty figure and saw his own interests. Not many would have recognised him. If they had, perhaps they would have made him a leader, but he didn't seem to know that. Clearly he had a weak mind by now.

"How many men can you mobilise?"

"What?"

"I mean, do you not want to avenge your son?"

"My son was too soft. He is guilty of his own downfall. He was in love with a second-hand infidel Goth. She betrayed him and he deserved it. Marrying a Queen of another man . . ."

"What do you want to do?"

"I want to kill him."

"Who? Alwalid? Tariq? Bilal?"

"All of them!" His voice became harsh and his eyes sparkled as he leaned up on his rod and glazed into the eyes of Mohammed II, who was shocked at such immediate change of mood and took a step back.

He took the old man into his company as he could make good use of him. During the coming weeks he promoted him in his circles among the Abbasids and the Shiite in Mecca and Medina, took him back to Damascus and assembled in the streets groups of followers and let Musa lecture on his achievements in Al-Andalus and his bravery in battle and how he had been betrayed by Tariq and Alwalid and how his son was stripped of power in his absence. They were careful not to offend the Black population in Damascus as many of them were powerful traders and they did not mention Bilal. This kind of story mesmerised the masses in times of uncertainty, when entertainment was scarce as the artists and traders were more engaged in promoting the Empire abroad than keeping the local population smiling and distracted from every-day boredom and monotony. Damascus was wealthy, but is wealth enough to keep you busy? Or happy? Incitement was easily done in this case and loyalties had always been split. And all across the empire the Shiite had managed to corrupt Umayyad officials into treating the population unjustly.

And so they assembled, one day in spring when the new moon was full and the streets alight they marched from all sides, the Abbasid clans and the mob, towards the palace, filling the streets and waving spears and swords, banners of Mecca, black banners of the Shiite and the Jews under Musa. The palace-guard mobilised when they saw them coming, they had supporters too, but the supporters were intimidated, hidden away in the houses, far above street level, the palace guards were on their own when arrows showered from all sides.

Alwalid woke to the scream of thousands of people in the streets asking for his head. As he approached the window, it was too late for the guards to warn him and they had just entered his room to hold him back. He just stood there bleeding, the arrow had pierced his chest, breathing heavily, staring at the roof he fell to the ground, rolling to the side, motionless. As the medics came they examined him for hours while the uproar was crushed by the now mobilised elite-troops who poured into the streets from all sides. Surgeons opened up his wound to establish that the arrow was not to be pulled out, only cut into shape, as it had passed some sensitive blood vessels that were in danger of leaking, if it was removed. So he was laid to rest with the fragment of arrow inside his lung and breathed heavily for days, while the doctors were by his side, cleaning the wound, attending to every moment of pain and change in breathing. They figured out he had not long to live:

"Suleiman," he gasped for air, "I hand over Power to you. Please call my brothers from Al-Andalus, if they have time." He fell into a coma again after he had struggled to keep his eyes open while calling for his younger brothers.

Tariq had left as soon as news came from Damascus via pigeon and left Bilal in command at Toledo where reconstruction work had begun and the palace became a central command for coordinating the efforts nationwide and allocation of land and subdivision of the reign. He was on a vessel at the port of Kairouan, where he rested for a day to attend to the local Amir, whom he hadn't seen for over a year and the 2 daughters of Julian, whom he sent back to their father in company of the guards, unharmed and well-educated they had reached the age of marriage and he wanted them to be with their father when they would be wed to local gentry in Al-Andalus. He had fulfilled his promise to him and made his way to Alexandria and Damascus subsequently, praying for arrival before Alwalid would pass away.

The sea was safer these days than the land, Abbasid troops were known to massacre any delegations of the Umayyads and Suleiman, the new

Sultan, Alwalid's brother, had ordered shoot on sight for any rebellious group. Tariq could not afford to get caught up in the fighting in between them or being mistaken for one side or the other. The Empire was in turmoil and the tide was changing, it could be felt all the way home, from port to port a different welcome, never indifferent, at times welcoming, at times cold and short, open hostility was not possible under the eyes of the Umayyad guards who had heavily fortified the locations as these ports were the lifeline of the Empire.

After 3 weeks on sea Tariq finally saw the towers at port of Damascus near Beirut and was guided into the docks by escorting vessels from the Umayyads as all arrivals were checked thoroughly and protected for cargo, stripped of any Abbasid aide and revoltists. Tariq was well known to the guards and they had awaited his arrival at the port at which they cheered and informed the palace and the port and the streets of the city started to fill up with people, young and old to welcome the new Amir, the brave General, the hero of Al-Andalus. The region around Damascus all the way to Beirut port had multi-national population and all stood, friend or foe. Many cheered and all accompanied him through the land on the day long journey on horse-back into Damascus' heart city, covered by the shields of the guards, making space for him, pushing him through the narrow lanes towards the new mosque and the palace.

Tariq took a moment, amazed at the new mosque, the like he had not seen yet, it was the largest, and then hastily ran into the palace, which was heavily guarded and where he was split from the crowd, he ran up the stairs, the guards recognising him immediately and smiling at him, clapped and cheered.

He finally arrived at the chamber and saw his friend the Sultan who was leaning up and breathing heavily, half asleep and surrounded by the medics and his brothers. They all turned around at his entry and applauded, at which moment Alwalid opened his eyes, and said something inaudible.

"Peace and Blessing and Mercy of Allah be on you!" Tariq greeted the round.

In an echo all joined in loudly: "And the Peace, Blessings, Mercy and Grace of Allah be on you! Welcome back o Amir of Al-Andalus!"

The Sultan showed a smiling face although it was clearly difficult for him and he reached out for his hand, whispering:

"My dear Brother and friend, welcome back to Damascus," he rested for a few moments in between the speech, "how glad am I to see you before I die."

Tears started to roll down Tariq's face, again a stinging pain shot through his dead eye-socket, he held it tight as others supported him:

"I heard and rushed by immediately as I got the news, the sea is far and the winds blew against me, but your seamen did their best and left their trading for me. All the Empire is in mourning and praying for you and the ports are guarded and any revolt stricken down mercilessly. The perpetrators need to pay for this, I will personally grab Mohammed II and bring him here, this is not the way of his grandfather (pbuh)."

"You don't know who it was; it was a stray arrow from the mob, not his work." The Sultan was merciful to the Abbasids. He was too lenient towards them for Tariq's taste. It would cost him his life and the whole dynasty!

"As you wish, I will not leave your side as long as I am here."

"You will in deed not. You will join our family-circle, my sister has been asking a lot about you. Will you do us the honour and take her in marriage? We need you to be part of this family and you two have been secretly exchanging letters since long ago."

"You know?" Tariq looked down shyly.

"Why would I not? Leila always told me. She sent all admirers away and waited for you!"

"It would be an honour and a pleasure, Sultan!" Tariq's eye started shining as it hadn't for years, all the hard work in Al-Andalus had finally paid off and he was to be united with his love.

"You have to know that I had to marry in Al-Andalus as well."

"Do you think I would hold you back from that or Leila in deed? We know about that! Guards, where is my little sister?" Alwalid was gasping for air and the others tried to calm him down.

At the door she stood eavesdropping at first shy, with her far open shining eyes and her bright blue dress, a transparent scarf around her head and facial mask just below the eyes that she pulled down now and showed her full smile as she walked into the room. Everyone stepped aside to make space for the princess and the new couple to be. The Imams came and sprayed incense and recited the Koran, Tariq was sent for a bath to purify himself from the journey and they all waited as he returned within 15 minutes all in blue and they were wed there and then with the witnesses and family present, who had gathered across the chamber and the corridor down into the streets where the people lined up, stripped of their swords and searched before they were let past to congratulate the young couple in the palace hall. A day of festivities lasting long into the night and the jugglers and artists gathered in the palace yard. It was a moment of happiness for Alwalid who even recovered to the extent that he dared stepping to the window of his simple chamber that was covered in garments and mosaic of geometrical patterns, the window facing the new mosque that he had not been able to visit for weeks now. His pain was growing but his joy too at this union of his dear sister with his best friend and Amir of the new jewel in his Empire.

It was the happiest day for Tariq, whose tiredness from the journey faded away at the experience and the surroundings of his youth with his childhood sweetheart in his hands, marching through the palace, chamber to chamber, new scenes all over as the festivities unfolded, the couple being assigned their own room and there he stayed for a week after the feast had been completed that night, waiting for the recovery of Alwalid and permission to leave.

On the 3rd day Alwalid sent for him as he was in extreme pain and dictating his last will to his scribes, his Brothers already surrounded him and Suleiman had come, who was now Sultan, to pay his last respect to his brother, who was covered in blood, coughing it out like black liquor of poison:

" . . . equal amounts of vessels to Hisham and Umar, the stone-collection to . . ." He turned to the side as he saw Tariq and stopped for a while. Then he breathed heavily and said: "Tariq ibn Ziyad is to be Amir of Al-Andalus and distribute the Emirates in that new land to his wish."

"Thank you for this honour and if I may add that your family is welcome to live in that land and we will always have a place for you, any time, under any circumstance, you and your offspring."

The people in the chamber, the whole extended family, brothers and sisters, his in-laws appreciated this invitation: "Likewise you are always welcome here, our in-law!" Said Suleiman, the new Sultan. "We have always admired your bravery and skills as a leader, now you are our brother in law and we shall remain thankful for your service. We welcome you into the family and this is a strong bond of friendship for many generations to come, if Allah wills."

"Thank you, my Sultan!" Tariq was honoured and humbled.

During the coming days Suleiman and Tariq met repeatedly in the company of Alwalid and exchanged vows of friendship and guarantees of protection, while the wise and now frail Alwalid supervised the process, having dictated his will, he was more at ease with his conscience, seeing how his brethren got on well and how the young couple was in love and happy, while Leila did not leave Tariq'a side at any time.

"Take me with you, Tariq, to the new land they call Al-Andalus." She said in presence of her brothers.

"We shall gladly do so seeing the danger of rebellion here, but we shall leave you at Kairouan for the time being, until we have established the reign and subdivided the land into administrative Emirates. We also need to gain some control over the infrastructure."

Alwalid was recovering, he was a tough fellow, but it was clear the wound had punctured much of his lungs and he was not able to move or breathe much, leave alone speak or go about his duties, that he gradually handed over to Suleiman and withdrew into the inner compartments of the palace facing the backgarden and the springs and ponds, the flowers, the birds and the sunshine and benches became the resting place of his last days in this world, a slow but peaceful, albeit painful death over the coming years in 715 AD. Still he departed happily, content with his achievements, respected by those around him, the envy of his enemies, buried in the palace garden, the family cemetery.

The revolts became more intense over the years, the political climate became increasingly tense and many brothers and cousins and sons of Alwalid were killed while holding the position of Sultan. The mob was always stopped at the palace gates until 750 AD, when Sultan Marwan II, Alwalid's nephew, was murdered and his great-grandson Abd ar-Rahman I, later on to be the Magnificent, as the only surviving heir of the clan, fled to Hispania, in an epic journey via the Sahara with the help of Tariq's tribe, was welcomed at Granada by Tariq's grandson and declared Sultan of Cordoba, that became the capital of Muslim Al-Andalus.

The Reign

"*The Most Merciful!*
It is He Who has taught the Qur'an.
He has created man.
He has taught him speech (and intelligence).
The sun and the moon follow courses (exactly) computed;
And the herbs and the trees—both (alike) bow in adoration.
And the Firmament has He raised high, and He has set up the Balance
(of Justice),
In order that ye may not transgress (due) balance.
So establish weight with justice and fall not short in the balance!"
Surah 55 (The Merciful) Verses 1-9

Leila embraced her Brothers as she was escorted out of the palace and she kept turning her sight around to the place that she might not ever see again, where she had grown up and the city she had only once left for Mecca and Medina. She knew the Empire only from tales afar, Goths and Africans, Romans and Vikings; those were distant tribes she was going to meet, places she was going to see now. She had always dreamt of the journey with a warrior, who would take her away one day into the endless desert, across the infinite sea.

As they headed through the land into the port near Beirut where the sails were set with a mild breeze from the land, it was full speed ahead as soon as they had stepped onto the vessel for fear of attacks. The crowd waved good-bye and the boat left the piers, while the children were running along the strand as far as they could keep up with the gaining momentum of the lofty ship, the best of its Empire, a wedding gift from Alwalid, including crew and captain with years of experience and a hundred guards. Suleiman and the other brothers had loaded it with jewels and treasures, incense, spices, garments, clothes, perfumes, ivory, all the riches of the silk road, African goods were to be loaded on the way west, at Alexandria, where also goods from India arrived via the Red Sea canal. They would gradually progress towards Alexandria and Kairouan, a honey-moon journey they would never forget. Each day the sun rising in their back and setting mildly in their faces.

Slowly they made their way west against the winds and currents and reluctantly they approached Kairouan, where they were to stay for a few days before parting. Leila was still trying to convince Tariq to take him along and nearly succeeded, when news came of a rebellion in the North. Pelayo and his people had been raiding Barcelona and Saragossa in an attempt to reclaim the Northern kingdoms and establish their reign. Tariq had known that this problem was going to reoccur sooner or later, but he had hoped that that would be later rather than sooner. So the urgency to return was made clear to Tariq at the palace of the Amir of Kairouan and the honeymoon-period with Leila came to a sudden end. Tariq left his vessel at Kairouan and took a small army of riders West to Ceuta to sail across the straight once again towards the cliffs that now bore his name and proudly set foot on the coast of Al-Andalus for a second time. This time he was welcomed with flowers and not burning arrows by a delegation from Granada that had been placed there by al-Lakhmi especially for him and had awaited his arrival for many days, to escort him to the city he had conquered as the first on his way through this land and where he got the hero's welcome now. Buildings were rising on all sides and where once stood farms and fields, now the most formidable roads and buildings were completed, oil lamps glowing along the road in the mild spring-breeze as the sun was sinking behind the cliffs of the Sierra Nevada, flowers raining down from all sides, while he rode to the palace to spend a night in the chamber of honour inside these walls, where he was welcomed by his local wife with a newborn son. There he resided in a building that served as the organisational centre and casern of the region. The men they had left behind had done an excellent job in deed. They had lain the foundations for many generations to come.

Bilal had sent a delegation there to brief Tariq into the situation of the fresh campaigns and to escort him North to the newly opened front at Saragossa and Barcelona, where the Gothic hoards were plundering and making life hell for the local villages once again. Pelayo was a real pain in the neck and had inherited all the evil traits of Roderick, perhaps he was even worse because he was more sly and conniving, basically not willing to compromise in any way or lay the arms to rest. He was less of a coward. At the beginning they had hoped to achieve a truce with him by offering him Asturias and to tolerate his reign over the North, if he paid a special tax. But those hopes had been shattered by the frequent attacks on Muslim expeditions north. He also possessed better knowledge of the local mountain passes and highways, because most of the converts and local guides were from the South of the land.

Bilal had collected 1000 men from each city and sent them North. He and Alfred were the ones who knew that region best and Tariq could only push full steam ahead to rebuild the lines and reinforce the supplies. So during the coming week he was busy riding North along the paths of the old Roman roads that lead from now freshly settled and developing Cordoba to all corners of Al-Andalus and were now becoming stronger, trampled on by thousands of hooves every day, the melting snow and the rains of spring had seized and given way to the first spells of strong sunshine. The days were getting longer again. This gave Tariq the advantage of speed and before the week ended he passed the ruins of Reccopolis and arrived at Toledo, where the mastersmiths had established a strong guild, that was to produce the strongest steel known in Europe for at least 1000 years and where the valley had changed its face totally from a muddy camp to a new settlement. Architects and workers were busy planning and constructing, much like Granada the year before. Mines were being uncovered in the vicinity and they could extract building materials, metals and even precious jewels. This was definitely an excellent trading centre.

Now when Tariq arrived at Toledo, al-Lakhmi welcomed him with open arms and congratulated him to his marriage and lead him to his chamber at the palace. He then met with the leaders of the local mining projects and commissioned quarries and other projects to enhance the supply of building materials. The mastersmiths were already working overtime to train local peasants into their secrets and similar operations were commissioned throughout the land as they had sent delegations to each city they had passed. Equally the mining operations for weapon blades, shields, a central coinage system, agricultural instruments and road building work was progressing steadily concentrically from the cities into the deeper parts of the land. The old Roman roads and aqueducts were being repaired and reinstated as melting water from the snow-covered mountaintops was carried in a steady stream to the main centres to give them sufficient supply for washing and drinking. On top of that wells were being dug in places far from reach and irrigation systems were being introduced, watermills, water-lifts and pumps as well as canals and oxen-driven carts. Donkeys were circling pumps for well water to be driven to the fields throughout the land and windmills with cloth-sails began to scatter the landscape. These were entirely new introductions into European land and would spread across the continent within a few centuries.

As he had ridden from Cordoba to Toledo he had seen the full beauty of spring in the land unfolding itself, the many colourful flowers and fruit trees that had been hibernating for decades for the sun to break through again. The country was engulfed in a celebration of its richness that manifested itself after a long time in all its colours and splendour. Children were lining the streets playing their games and running about from village to village, young maidens bathing in the fresh springs and weddings and ceremonies taking place in the newly found liberty and relief from the Gothic hoards. An era of depression had come to an end and the first spring of this new episode in the Iberian country had established itself. It was too precious to be lost. The whole land was aware of the danger that the Northern kingdoms posed and they sent their best men towards the front. Some joined Tariq on the march, others would join him at Toledo, more and more coming from all sides, many had returned home after the fall of Roderick and Ibn Musa to tend to their land and families but were now available again.

In Cordoba Tariq had also seen the first observatory taking shape already, the first of many, to introduce astronomical observations and calculations, teachings of the movements of the celestial bodies. In Granada there was a guild that began producing brass pipes with glass-pieces for looking into the distance and in Seville some delegates began firing clay and producing pots and ceramic tiles with beautiful mosaics for the newly commissioned mosques throughout the Empire. Toledo now became a centre of learning and all guilds were represented there, especially the steel sector as weapons were now needed more than ever before due to the new fighting that broke out up North. News came to Tariq that Saragossa had been taken by Pelayo and Barcelona was subject to a Siege where the Muslim army under Alfred had been cut off from its supply routes. In Saragossa on the other hand the Muslims under Bilal were laying a Siege on Pelayo's army. It was to be the first time that Tariq would ride that far North and he was glad that winter was over.

At Toledo in the palace an assembly of elders had gathered in the presence of al-Lakhmi and Tariq. They consisted of the appointed leaders of the appeased gentry of the Goths from all across the land as well as Muslim leaders and commanders of the men of Allah. As they had been welcomed by the appointed Wezirs of the palace and given a home in the chambers, they were now called for an audience with the Amir and the large hall was prepared for a festive banquet for this purpose. Tariq was reluctant to attend due to the urgency at the Northern fronts but his Wezirs pointed out to him the strategic significance of this meeting and its potentially crucial role in the defence and future of the land. Also Suleiman, the new Sultan, had sent letters for him by pigeon to pass certain messages to them, that al-Lakhmi had safekept. Suleiman and al-Lakhmi were actually the ones who had initiated and encouraged such a gathering and the people were quick to follow. Al-Lakhmi had governed the administration of Toledo, Cordoba and Granada in the absence of Tariq, while Seville, Lisbon and Vallada, later to become Valencia again and only a suburban part called Vallada till today, were lagging behind slightly as Bilal and Alfred were up North and al-Lakhmi could not cope with it all alone. Now al-Lakhmi was chairing this conference that was held in Arabic with translators located at different points in the hall near their subsequent congregations, Latin, Gaulle, Germanic and Greek, Christians, Jews and Muslims. Al-Lakhmi began:

"Dear delegates of Iberia, Lords of the former provinces of Carthagensis, Reccopolis, Toledo and Cordoba, representants of Seville, exiles of Saragossa and Barcelona. Former generals of the Gothic armies of Roderick, Pelayo and Wittiza."

Wittiza of course was present in this round and looked up into the round with his fixated eyes, blind but content.

"We have come together today in the presence of your former King Wittiza, Tariq ibn Ziyad, the Amir of Al-Andalus, your land, my humble self and your congregation in order to plan an offensive against the forces of Pelayo and to commission tasks for the future of your beautiful country. Furthermore, we will talk about the status of the nobility, peasants and invading forces. Last but not least, a short timetable will be drawn up for the structuring and chronological prioritisation and scheduling of the points of action with a clear-cut allocation of tasks and duties as well as a system for evaluation and measurement of progress and success.

With this short introduction I would like to hand over to Tariq ibn Ziyad."

The round of elders, warriors and mastersmiths was knocking the heavy wooden table as was custom in those days, a thundering sound filled the hall, almost like a roaring hoard of Vandals mixing in with cheering and clapping from the lines behind, people were sitting, standing, leaning all throughout the long room, as Tariq approached the front of the long Gothic desk of his round of seniors from across the land with light shining through the tainted tall and pale stretched windows of the Gothic style castle.

"May the Peace and Blessings of Allah the Almighty be on you all. Let me reassure you that we will carefully collect everyone's concerns and find the most immediate and direct solution to all issues and that we will collate all ideas and plan a carefully structured approach. Let me outline a basic schedule. Restructuring and development has already commenced in a separate effort in each city-state in the South as I have been able to monitor and as it has been reported. So much for infrastructural work and we will appoint delegates to each region of the North after the battles seize there.

Furthermore, we have introduced a spectrum of activities to encourage trading, craft and agriculture, part of which is the regular traffic of vessels along the coasts of the Empire, the management of apprenticeship programmes for the local peasants which are conducted by the subsequent guilds, first and foremost the mastersmiths, then the medics, the distribution of seeds and digging of wells with pumps and canal-construction, aqueduct repair and last but not least, the employment of teachers to encourage literacy and learning.

Most immanently we have to come up with a plan for immediate action at the Northern front, these raids from the barbaric hoards who have messed up this land during the last decades cannot go on like this. We need to make an end to that once and for all and I ask you, people, representatives and rulers of Al-Andalus, are you in this with me?"

An unequivocal nodding and "Ita est (so it is)" in Latin, "Tayyab (pure, agreeable)" in Arabic and "Si" in Hispanic-Gaulle was heard in the round and spread throughout the congregation within seconds.

"You have seen our work that we have done under the guidance and permission of the Almighty Creator of the Universe, who begets not and is not begotten and there is none like Him. He has allowed us to repel the evil forces that ruled this country and spread the darkness over you and did nothing but harm you over the years, whether you were part of them or antagonistic towards them, lead you into a one way with a dead end. Now we have brought you a new way of life. So as we progress in this land, we would like to encourage you to understand and implement the benefits that this last revelation to mankind brings, the Message of Islam, which would be the ideal way ahead for you."

Some of the monks at the back end towards the doors left the hall in protest and Julian tried to hold them back while Charles lead them and there was some wrangling, but the majority of the congregation was amicable and kept the silence, even acted annoyed at the monks and ordered them to keep calm and refrain from such rebellion.

"My friends and fellow men. We are all Children of Adam and Eve. We all came from the same source, we all long for the same destination. Irresistibly. We need to unite. I declare from this day, henceforth, this Empire be ruled under this first and foremost principles of Islam, the new converts, the locals, the Whites, Black and Brown people, the born Muslims and the nobles as well as the peasants of this land embrace each other and the religion of Islam, it will be better for us all. Of course you are welcome to stay in your own religion, if you prefer, but it will not be as useful, although we will still support you. You have seen us lead by example as we have married locally and have children, who are to shape the future of this land, the Muwwalads. I want to encourage you to take wives from other tribes rather than your own alongside with wives from your own tribes and test your own justice by treating them all equally. As you know I have had the honour to be granted the hand of the sister of the Sultan. My policy will be to establish my offspring as Emirs of the cities alongside with their half-brothers from my local wives! My local wives are peasant women we met at Granada and Vallada when entering. Let this principle of love rule this country. I am telling you, as long as we adhere to this principle, Allah will grant us victory, when we deviate from it, we segregate into ethnicities and classes, we will be lost. I can promise you that!"

By now local lords had stood up and Tariq had feared they would walk out, but one of the lords raised his cup and was talking in Latin:

"My Lord and Amir," here he used the Arabic word, "Peace be on you! You have proven to be of my liking, you have fought like a true Gothic

Lord, better even and more brave than Roderick ever did. I ask you today, as a Gothic general who fought against you at Reccopolis and before that at Granada, where is she?"

He looked into the round and pointed at the other leaders and encouraged them to grab their cups too and waited for them. Others were a little baffled and pointed back at him asking what he meant.

"Where is she?" He raised his cup high so that the juice in it swapped over on to the table.

Again there was silence and people were confused while a smile escaped Tariq's lips and he thought he knew what this funny fellow meant. He had fierce eyebrows and long blond hair hung out behind his helmet, his arms were bare and well toned, massive muscles all over his body although he had already achieved quite some age and his beard reached down to the table as he said louder and louder each time raising his voice, hammering, pounding on the table . . .

"Where is she? Where are they?"

The others were amused and started joining him in a frenzy and swing of the mood from passive to active enjoyment, they all now shouted out together:

"Where is she, where are they?" The whole hall was echoing in the rhythmic chant of these ecstatic Gothic warlords, who were not even drunk and then all of a sudden, at a sign from the tall fellow, there was complete deafening silence. This style of the Goths needed getting used to, but Tariq was actually quite amused at their enthusiasm. These people had character and courage, and so he played along, laughed and looked down, then raised his head towards this mighty man, who stood perhaps twice his own height easily and asked in Latin:

"Do you mean what I think you do, Sire?"

"Where is my Arabic-Princess? Where is my African-Queen? Where is my Asian Empress?" All the round burst out in laughs and some of the Goths started falling to the floor and rolling around in laughter, but they tried to control themselves, as the guards got a bit nervous and reached for the swords, but Tariq made signs to them to restrain themselves while he joined in the laughing mood. When the round had calmed down he spoke:

"I will send you in a delegation to Damascus and you are free to ask for the hands of the noblest maidens of the Empire, Sire, what is your name?"

"They call me Alaric, after my ancestor, who shook and took Rome and brought the Empire to its knees!" Said the proud and tall blond warrior with a bronze tan, who had thoroughly enjoyed the sun since it had broken through and shook his head at the same time, swung his hair, with a smile as bright as the summer sun and eyes as blue as the bright sky. The charismatic leader stared into the round and dared the others to resist him in what he was about to do. Tariq, al-Lakhmi and the guards listened very carefully as if they could not hear well, was this true?

"I have seen these Arabs and Africans, what they did in this land. I have heard what they told me during the weeks after they broke the walls and captured me. I have understood what is wanted of us by them and by the One and Only. I declare this very day, at this exact hour, in this my own land that my ancestors from Germany, the plains of the Ukraine and the Northway (Norway) once conquered, and I ask anyone who wants to challenge me, to do so in public and with his naked blade in the palace-yard, that there is no God apart from Allah and that Mohammed is Messenger of Allah! Dare anyone say anything else and return to that religion that brought us three Gods with a dead corpse on the Cross and a mother holding a baby to be worshiped and the other cheek to be turned and I personally will separate his head from his chest, right now!"

This was what he really said and the Muslim guards and Tariq immediately fell on their faces towards the South-East and praised Allah in a loud and clear:

"Allah-hu-Akbar", ascending with tears of joy filling their eyes, lining up to embrace Alaric and immediately the other Goths in the round joined in:

"No God apart from Allah, Mohammed Messenger of Allah!" The hall was filled by a cascade of conversions and ecstatic chanting again, and Julian slowly made his way out at the back, while Tariq stood there smiling at this moment, which was perhaps the most victorious moment of his life. He was enjoying it and he was delighted and well pleased, while Alaric held Tariq's arm grabbing the elbow and vice-versa, they stood together, Tariq with his turban reaching Alaric's chest. Alaric grabbed his neck and squeezed him against his heart, while observing the conversion of his men, smiling and proud. This was the Gothic style that added a whole new dimension to the Muslim conquest. The guards brought them presents of clothes, because the Goths used to show nearly the whole body at formal gatherings, only the genital area covered and long boots up to the knees with capes reaching down behind the neck, exposing their strong thighs, which was a part of the body to be covered by a Muslim. While Alaric was wrapping his new gown around his legs, he stated:

"But now I will not rest until I get that bastard Pelayo and his stupid hoards. I always despised him trying to order me around. He always hit the weakest and never had any honour, Roderick's dog! First I thought with this ibn-Musa or Filius Mosae or whatever he called himself trying to push us around that you Arabs were not any different. But now I know better!"

"Let us leave tomorrow morning, by the will of Allah." Said Tariq to his new friend and brother.

"By the will of Allah!" Replied Alaric.

The conversion of the Gothic nobility was celebrated by an evening of festivities as the new religion was announced by the very people who had fought the siege and were locked up in the caserns for weeks after the siege had been broken. This new development introduced a change in the tide. Where there had been fierce resistance from the side of the majority of the Gothic gentry, now there was complete openness and friendliness towards the Muslims. Wittiza was also pleased since his whole clan had basically converted to Islam and adopted the surname Al-Quti (the Goths) and Alaric, which means the all rich, proudly announced his new Arabic name Al-Ghanie Ul-Quti, The Rich of the Goths, and grabbed everyone by the neck who dared calling him by his previous name, while he was observing and testing the new armour the mastersmiths tailor-made for him as they had taken measurements and the new emblems and gowns. The sword seemed to be his favourite, he was practicing eagerly at the yard, while his cousins surrounded him. He was the tallest among them and the strongest. Still this latest contribution to the Islamic conquest had to learn a lot about how to restrict himself and behave like a Muslim, but for now he was excused and was free to follow his old ways under the pretext of Islam, as long as he knew his limits. Towards the new arrivals he behaved like a perfect gentleman, only with his own cousins he behaved in a vehement and tough manner. Perhaps such a ruling was essential to keep them at bay. In any case, the men of Allah had won a powerful and charismatic new leader and he was to prove essential during the final phase of the conquest.

For now there was a preliminary festival for the second Eid Day, the end of the Hadj-period, a taste of what was to come after the final victory when the whole peninsula was to be finally integrated into the Empire and the feeling was in general that that day was not too far away anymore. The masters of the guilds had put together a wagon load of their most precious achievements, armour, tools, garments, glassware, ceramics, medical equipment and dresses, musical instruments, crops, fruit and vegetables were lining the streets and being pulled through the lanes by oxen, donkeys and buffalo, accompanied with drums and flutes.

It was more a fare to promote the guilds and attract local apprentices and the masters from the smiths, medics, tailors and merchants as well as the farmers were walking along in shining suits and hats reaching tall into the air with feathery displays and beautiful colours. It was to become later on what the Europeans, especially the Iberians and their colonies in the Caribbean's and South America, but also the Germans would know as the Carnival or Fasching. Calls of "Alla-hu" and "Allah-hu-Akbar", later changed by locals to "Allah-hu-weh" as carried to Germany by the Goths and the Habsburgs who later reined over Spain and Mexico. Calls of "Hellau" and "Hellawe" that till today mark the Fasching-festival in the Rhine and Hesse-regions, Cologne, Mainz and Frankfurt during the spring new-moons when people dress up in shining costumes and mount huge wagons to display their achievements of the previous year. Of course the meaning of what they are saying is entirely alien to the people today, when they say the very same words, "Hellau" and "Hellawe". In Brasil and the Carribeans and also in Germany the implication of the festival would of course be entirely lost since very often naked flesh is exposed rather than the achievements and music, dance and alcohol take over rather than praises of the Lord. Typical for deviation.

But that day in AD 712 in Toledo was a true delight to the eyes of the Believer as people had packed out their most colourful and decent dresses and were standing alongside, clapping and cheering while the armies had assembled and were riding behind the guilds and displaying their strength throughout the valley before leaving the next morning to fight Pelayo and his hoards up North. Tariq had put Al-Ghanie in charge of 10 garrisons, albeit under strict observation by his elite-troops as he could not risk it with Al-Ghanie yet. He might have been a spy. And Tariq took 10 garrisons himself. Al-Ghanie was to join Bilal at Saragossa and Tariq himself would march towards Barcelona to fight the Siege that locked Alfred into the city walls. Till late into the night one could hear the praises of the Lord and marching in the streets, until the men of Allah had withdrawn into their camps and caserns to rest for the hard task that lay ahead the next day, because they wished to make quick progress and save their energy.

And the morning came. Al-Ghanie could be seen taking a bath in the streams with his cousins, covered in linen. These people were used to doing that anyway and he enjoyed the newly won freedom since they had been locked up for many months as captives. Tariq had seen the bravery he and his troops had fought with, albeit reluctantly, when they stormed out of the city, down the slopes when al-Lakhmi had saved them by deserting ibn-Musa. Who knows, Al-Ghanie could have overwhelmed them that day when he was on the wrong side of the battle. It was a good feeling to have an ally from the former opposite side, who knew the ways of the Goths better than anyone else, and who had ridden this land up and down while in charge of the armies of the previous rulers.

"Will you do us the honour and lead the morning prayer, Al-Ghanie?" Tariq shouted through the powerful current along the waterfall that they had chosen to bathe in, the melting ice-water was too much to bare for the average soldier and the guards began to tremble at the mere sight.

"I merely know the Opening Chaper (Al-Fatiha) and I am still struggling with the sequence of the movements, but I can give it a shot, if you stand by me and rectify any possible mistakes."

"It will be an honour. You will have to lead your men during the travel and you can shorten the prayers and put them together so you can focus on the tasks. We do that when we travel, the 5 prayers become 3 essentially, morning, afternoon and evening after sunset. We do 2 periods (Rakat) in the morning, 2 + 2 in the afternoon and 3 + 2 in the evening."

"You have to appoint an Imam for my journey, otherwise I will get lost."

"Of course, we will send along a few of our learned men who will guide and instruct you and I also suggest that we mix some of our troops up so we can get them to know each other's ways."

"That is an excellent idea. I want to learn some of the sword techniques of your men and I saw your magic at Granada. I wish to implement some of that."

"Magic?"

"You said some words and swung the sword faster and faster until thunder-bolts and lighting gathered and the sunlight broke through the clouds and your sword lit up and blinded all my men. We had to flee through a tunnel."

"Ah, that was not magic. It was a prayer we use and it is only permissible in life and death situations. We can only use it in such extreme situations and it is only as a last resort that it works. It also takes many years of practice and experience in the mystical martial arts and the verses of the Koran."

"It was most impressive and amazing. I wish to achieve that level one day, either me or my offspring."

"You will, by the Grace of the Almighty."

"Our ancestors knew the secrets of the universe and Thor and Odin had possession over the powers that you command, they sent thunder and lightning towards their enemies. Not in vain did they call upon paradise as literally the Walhalla, nearness to Allah, the resting place of the warrior. Later the Romans rewrote the books calling them our gods and stating we worshiped them alongside other gods, while they were mere mortals subservient to the Almighty God Allah. Till today we call the universe, das All, and everything is, all is from Allah!"

"Yes, it is typical for deviated Empires to rewrite history books. Similarly the Greek with Homer wrote about Hercules or Achilles and the Romans about Zeus like before the Greek about Apollo, all of whom were merely ancient warrior lords who were worshiping one God and were granted the control over certain elements of nature and later on they were called sons of God and half-Gods, even lifted to the stars as Mars and Jupiter, while they were mere Messengers or errands, just like the Hindu Shiva and Rama. This is also what happened to Buddah in India and Isis and Osiris, the ancient Egyptians, similar to what happened to Mary and Jesus, peace be upon them, as there too was a virgin birth, healing of the lepers and wakening of the dead. Also the Pharaohs who even asked the people to worship them, while the Pharaoh at the time of Abraham (pbuh) accepted Islam and the Brahmans in India even descend from Abraham, as they even call themselves by his name. And they all know fairly well that there is only one God."

"We knew that even when the missionaries came from Rome and Byzantine and asked us to pray to statues of mortals, we preferred Arius of Alexandria's teachings in which Jesus is created and not one with the eternal being, who is light."

"Yes, that is exactly the picture in the Koran, Jesus (pbuh) being created and not son or begotten son. Son of God was an expression for any believer in the Old Testament. God in the Koran is light, an eternally bright and strong, dense light, as if there was a niche . . ."

"Allah is the Light of the heavens and the earth. The Parable of His Light is as if there were a Niche and within it a Lamp: the Lamp enclosed in Glass: the Glass as it were a brilliant star: Lit from a blessed Tree, an Olive, neither of the East nor of the West, whose oil is well-nigh luminous, though fire scarcely touches it: Light upon Light! Allah doth guide whom He will to His Light: Allah sets forth Parables for men: and Allah knows all things."
Surah 27 (Light) Verse 35

"The similitude of Jesus before Allah is as that of Adam; He created him from dust, then said to him: "Be". And he was."
Surah 3 (The Family Of 'Imran) Verse 59

"I like it more day by day. We shall learn more during the march from your appointed scholars and we shall progress as Allah pleases." Al-Ghani was adement and enthusiastic. "We shall inflict a malicious damage on the enemy and we know the enemy better than it knows itself, for we once lead their troops and know about their cunning and treacherous ways. Now we can put that knowledge to good use and it was meant to be like that. By the will of the Almighty, inshallah, Ameen!"

"These are mighty words, my dear Brother, may Allah keep you and preserve your stance. May he make you victorious in this life and in the hereafter and may he always make you smile and rejoice as you rejoice now!" Tariq was amazed at this fellow, while he was glancing at his congregation with his only eye and wished they would have joined forces much earlier. A feeling of bliss and happiness overcame him.

As they joined for Morning Prayer Al-Ghanie was able to complete it without many flaws and he was a born leader. One could tell from the way his every command was followed. He knew the right tone and Allah was guiding him perfectly. One could tell that he was being set on the right path as he had dramatically changed his expression, there was much more focus and earnestness behind his words:

"But Allah doth call to the Home of Peace: He doth guide whom He pleases to a way that is straight."
Surah 10 (Jonah) Verse 25

Al-Ghanie was reciting wonderfully the few verses he had learned. In the local Roman tradition it was commonplace and fashionable to compete in character by making people feel special and smile at them with a few lines of small talk that was relevant to their area of interest. In this culture one had to know the limits of these superficial conversations and if one exploited the patience of the other person, one was very quickly repelled by the reaction. The Goths did not have this type of hypocrisy. If they asked you about your wellbeing they really meant it and were ready for a long conversation. Otherwise they would not ask and would not put up a bright smile, if they didn't feel like it.

Until today this marks the fundamental difference between the Germanic and Anglican cultures, the Anglican being more diplomatic within limits and the Germanic more open and straight-forward, in good or bad. Britain was fully conquered by the Romans and held for many centuries, Germany only conquered up to the Teutoburger forest and only held for 100-200 years maximum under the Pacem Augustinum, a treaty that defined the approximate line of the Main-river as the northern boundary of the Roman Empire.

In Britain the Hadrian's Wall was more of a trading and custom's check-point rather than a real border and later on the Romans even conquered the whole of Scotland. Britain was also given to the Anglo-Saxons as soon as the Romans left as a promise for converting to Christianity. In any case, the Germanic culture lacks the sort of Roman diplomatic style that can be found among the gentry in Britain.

Therefore any word from Al-Ghanie could be taken for granted. If he was in a bad mood, he would let you know very quickly. If he was in a good mood, everyone would notice and follow. Such were the Goths, the new Muslim clans who would become the leaders of many of the emirates and form the backbone and founding fathers of the mixed society called the Muwwalad. They had stepped down from their thrones and given up their supremacist stance to embrace the new religion while neither submitting to the foreign culture nor asking others to be subservient to theirs. And they were keen learners. This was an entirely novel approach in which a multitude of cultures would coexist under the rules and regulations of Islam that was at that time directly based on everyone's understanding of the Koran. There had simply not been much time since the Prophet's (pbuh) death for secondary literature to be produced, interpretations from scholars and law books that would during later centuries replace this very direct and untainted approach. And the Koran merely confirmed in writing what the pure heart longed for and guided it to a straight way.

After the prayer within the palace yard that attracted a huge amount of people who prayed for blessings for the mission, Egilon stepped down from the palace where she had been granted Asylum with her sons, who were involved with Wittiza's sons in learning about Islam intensively over the last few weeks since Tariq had left for Damascus. Bilal had lead the teaching of new converts at Toledo and in his absence he had appointed Hafiz of the Koran to attend to new converts and to teach literacy to the population, most of whom had been illiterate. Such schools sprung up across the land. But in Cordoba and Toledo most of the elders had found a home and made a living on the basis of teaching. Many men from Musa's former veterinary army had decided to stay and teach what they knew in this new part of the Empire, in exchange for food, shelter and clothing. Keen farmers had provided them a home and even the nobility that was beginning to grasp the basics of Islam and the Arabic language tried to grab one of these knowledgeable teachers as well.

Wittiza's and Egilon's sons had been well protected princes who never went out to battle or dared taking up a physical challenge. During these recent weeks however they had undergone a dramatic change of nature and the Islamic teaching inspired them a lot and so did their role as the protagonists of the breaching of the city walls of Toledo. It was made clear to them repeatedly by their teachers and parents that they had been key to ending the siege and by most men they were seen as heroes rather than traitors with their secret light-code now being taught to a selected few in the ranks they also enjoyed somewhat of a special status of teachers and military trainers. All those who saw them as traitors and who had tried to get rid of them were gone, namely Roderick and Pelayo, while Al-Ghanie saw them as his own sons. He was their second uncle and was now stepping towards them to embrace them and they merely reached his neck:

"If it is not my dear nephews, my Kings to be." Al-Ghanie was smiling brightly.

"Uncle, we seek your permission to march along, we wish to engage in battle . . ."

"Most definitely, why not!? But have you had any training?"

"We have experience in archery and we will use our skills in planning assault and leadership." They pointed towards their parents and Wittiza was slowly making his way down the stairs, his helpers holding him by the arm, but he pulled it away not wanting his blindness to be an obstacle.

"What is the objection?" asked Al-Ghanie turning towards Egilon and Wittiza, as if he knew what to expect for an answer.

"Well, for once, they have never been to battle and secondly we wish to allocate more essential tasks in the land to them." Egilon was confident and adamant with her long white dress waving behind her, dragging along the stairs. Her face was marked by sorrow and grief for her late husband Ibn Musa and she had yet to recover from what had happened. Any person would have been overburdened with such a huge sacrifice, but now she knew that it had been for the higher good and her sons confirmed that to her. They were extremely precious to her and she had learned much about this new religion along with them and was very sympathetic towards it. Naturally she was concerned about the wellbeing of her sons and did not want to loose them as well now. She had taken the name Umm-Asim, mother of Asim, which was the Muslim name her elder son Erwin had taken.

Wittiza added: "We are not keen to loose our blood after loosing our sight."

"How would it be, if we only took the firstborn with us?" Al-Ghanie suggested, his long gown waving in the summer breeze and his turban hanging down at one end, a sight all of them still needed to get used to.

"We all wish to go!" All 4 cousins were adamant and did not bow down.

Now Tariq interfered: "It is a question of lineage and we will not allow families to be wiped out, just one son goes from each parent and you make up your minds."

"I have one more thing to say", Umm-Asim interrupted him. She joined hands with her sons and the sons of Wittiza, who was now called Al-Wariz (Alvarez, *Spanish*) and Al-Wariz himself. They all stood in a circle with Al-Ghanie joining hands and stated:

"There is no God apart from Allah, alone, without associates. To Him belongs all sovereignty and Praise and He is over all things, fully capable. How perfect Allah is, and all Praise is for Allah, and there is no other God but Allah. Allah is the Greatest and there is not Power nor Might except with Allah the Most High, the Supreme."

What they said together was the manifestation of Belief, the 3rd Shahada, the absolute eppicle of truth and certainty, in fact the only certainty in the universe and therewith they not only declared the faith and embraced Islam as their religion but catapulted themselves into the league of Mumins, the elite of Believers who lead the Ummah, the collective of the Muslims. They form the groups of the wisest of the Wise. Tears came into Tariq's eyes and his right eye hurt tremendously, everytime that happened and he had to hold back, while cramps shot through the right half of his face he held his eye and sunk down into his knees. His one-eyed face would earn him the name "Al-Tuerto" among some evil tongues of Hispania, meaning the one-eyed. In history however he was to go down as the mightiest General undoubtedly.

After a few minutes while the others were concerned and the guards started to gather from all sides he stood up again:

"Today you have made me the happiest man alive. My brothers and sister, welcome to the leadership of this Ummah. We offer you the leadership over the city state Reccopolis and those to be conquered back in the North. We welcome you into our family and wish our offspring to choose each other for marriage. Also, we would like to add to your statement the most beautiful essence of the declaration of Faith from the Koran constituting the last few Surahs:

"I seek refuge with Allah from Satan the accursed.
In the Name of Allah, Most Gracious, Most Merciful."

. . .

Shariq Ali Khan

"Say : O ye that reject Faith!
I worship not that which ye worship,
Nor will ye worship that which I worship.
And I will not worship that which ye have been wont to worship,
Nor will ye worship that which I worship.
To you be your Way, and to me mine."
Surah 109 (the Unbelievers)

"Say, He is Allah the One and Only
Allah, the Eternal, Absolute,
He begets not, nor is he begotten
And there is none like Him"
Surah 112 (Purity)

"Say I seek refuge with the Lord of Mankind
The King of Mankind
The Judge of Mankind
From the Mischief of the whisperer of evil
Who withdraws after he has whispered
The same one who whispers into the Hearts of Mankind
Among Jinns and among Men"
Surah 114 (Mankind)

Epilogue

"Verily We have granted thee a manifest Victory:
That Allah may forgive thee thy faults of the past and those to follow;
fulfil His favour to thee; and guide thee on the Straight Way;
And that Allah may help thee with powerful help.
It is He Who sent down tranquillity into the hearts of the Believers, that
they may add faith to their faith;—for to Allah belong the Forces of the
heavens and the earth; and Allah is Full of Knowledge and Wisdom;-
That He may admit the men and women who believe, to Gardens beneath
which rivers flow, to dwell therein for aye, and remove their ills from
them;—and that is, in the sight of Allah, the highest achievement (for
man),-
And that He may punish the Hypocrites, men and women, and the
Polytheists men and women, who imagine an evil opinion of Allah. On
them is a round of Evil: the Wrath of Allah is on them: He has cursed
them and got Hell ready for them: and evil is it for a destination.
For to Allah belong the Forces of the heavens and the earth; and Allah is
Exalted in Power, Full of Wisdom."
Surah 48 (Conquest) Verses 1-7

In a lengthy military campaign the North of the land was conquered up to the Pyrenees and later Muslims pushed even further into Gaulle (France) but in 715 AD the last resistance of the Goths in Iberia was crushed. The reconquered areas of Barcus (Barcelona), Sarakusta (Aragon, Saragossa) and Valladolid (Eid-ul-Alwalid/Alwalid-ul-Eid), were governed by Gothic gentry, many of whom converted to Islam. But the Northern regions were to stay in a constant wrangling between Moors and Muslim Goths on one side and Christian and pagan Goths on the other for the coming century or two until the Christian Goths and Franks would eventually take them back entirely, because they would never abide by the truce and always breach the terms of peace and they would never pay their taxes. Upon the Shiite/Abbasid revolt in 750 AD Muslims started fighting amongst each other as well and there were changing loyalties within the population.

They named the big region in the North Eid-ul-Alwalid (celebration of Alwalid), later changed to Alwalid-ul-Eid and eventually to the present day Valladolid. They chose this name because Alwalid died on the very day in 715 AD that Pelayo's troops surrendered and his commanders handed over power to Tariq while Pelayo fled back North to Asturias. The victory was somewhat tainted by Alwalid's death but they decided to celebrate his life and his achievements rather than mourn for his death. At the funeral prayer the new name for the region, Eid-ul-Alwalid or in a twist of the tongue Alwalid-ul-Eid was announced, which was later on amended by locals to Valladolid. In any case Sultan Alwalid was a keen celebrator and his people loved to celebrate with him. He was a just ruler, one of the last of his kind.

Pelayo, who after a decisive battle in Asturias signed a truce with Tariq, kept Asturias, Galicia and Basque as long as he would pay the tax, equal to the compulsory charity that Muslims have to give, 2.5-5% or in case of landlords up to 10% of the harvest from irrigated fields. It was passed to the poor and needy, not the government. The administration earned its money for paying the army, civil workers and infrastructural projects from the trading activities of the Sultanate. The gilds also traded and spent their funds on educational and developmental projects as did the Emirates for building, irrigation systems and roadwork by trading with the local population and farmers to fund their activities in mining and training. Much of the land was left for the peasants. A significant chunk of the land of the Gothic gentry was repossessed and turned from hunting ground into farmland for small farmers or as nature reserves and reservoirs for wildlife and waterways. Land-repossession did not take place in Europe again until the French Revolution! In England the Norman gentry still owns 75% of the land! Nature reserves and waterways were not planned in Europe again until the 19th century.

Based on the tax from the Christians and Jews and the obligatory alms from the Muslims, a social system was introduced that guaranteed education and minimum wages as well as housing, food and clothing. Such an elaborate system was not found in Europe again until the 20th century. In Muslim Spain it lasted for centuries as long as the barbaric hoards from the North and the pressure from the Abbasids would allow it to.

Furthermore, according to many Koranic verses about David and Salomon (peace be upon them) and the Hadith of the last and final Messenger Mohammed (pbuh), who ordered kindness to animals, a strict legal code was formulated that observed the right of animals of all kinds. Apart from domestic animals, also the wild animals were to be treated as equal partners and Muslims. An example was the strict relocation of ant populations from buildings or soils that were to be demolished or restructured. A prison sentence was ordered for neglect of animals or torture, especially vertebrate animals and in particular mammals, other than for hunting in case of threat from predators or slaughter for food. This was the blueprint for animal protection laws of the 20th century in Europe, which much of the Muslim world has forgotten alongside most other original applications of Sharia law, which is now mainly seen as cruel and obsolete not only by non-Muslims. Sharia has been amended to prioritise physical torture and punishment rather than sound legislation and implementation by means of reason and encouragement.

Women's right to inherit, divorce, witness, own businesses and equality in many ways was introduced for the first time anywhere in the world based on the Koran and Hadith!

Agriculture was intensified and the right types of crops chosen for each location, diversity, stereo culture and bi-annual harvests were introduced, while the irrigation system that the Muslims built was essential during the climate change from damp to predominantly sunny after a century of darkness. A thorough infrastructure was established, roads, grain chambers, water tanks, windmills, renovated aqueducts, etc. Administration was decentralised with local self-rule and public voting, debate and inclusion of the common public in decision making was new to mankind and practiced in Iberia. Slavery was abolished not reintroduced until many centuries later and only through deviation.

A fully comprehensive justice-system based entirely on the Koran and the teachings of the Prophet (pbuh) was introduced, in which witnessing, evidence, jury and mercy was dominant and any criminal could plead for it based on permission by the victim of the crime. He could then in case of a first-time offence serve a sentence in form of compensation or labour for the victim of the crime, i.e. the criminal would have to serve the family of someone he has murdered for a period of time or until death, if they wish so and forgive him. In case of repeat offence this was not an option. In case of adultery or fornication stoning was abolished and only in case of 4 witnesses and a strict chronology of oaths as given in the Koran (Surah 24, Light, verses 1-15+) a penalty was given in form of 100 light lashes at the market meant to embarrass rather than physically hurt anyone or in serious cases of repeat offence exile into another land or the wilderness.

Stoning was never ordered as it was in effect only ordered by the Prophet (pbuh) before the appropriate verses in the Koran were revealed that order lashes rather than stoning. The Prophet's (pbuh) order to stone 2 people during his lifetime was on demand of the Jews in Medina who asked him to judge about one of their adulterers based on the Torah and in another instance where a woman kept coming back to him over many years repeatedly asking him to punish her in this cruel way. He very reluctantly granted her this wish after she had reared her child that was not from her husband. Afterwards the verses referred to above were revealed and stoning abolished. This knowledge of the way the Prophet (pbuh) judged was preserved at that time. Today it is even known that one is labelled an extremist by some Muslim "schools of thought", if one refers to the Mercy of the Prophet (pbuh) in this way. In Iberian Islam however limb amputation for example was only recommended in case of major repeated-theft, which exceeded the value of a house. In no case was anybody punished for stealing food if hungry. In this light the penalty was always proportional to the offence.

The right priorities were still intact among Muslims back then and the emphasis was on science, arts, culture, industry, technology and learning that flourished during the coming 7 centuries in Spain and attracted scholars from across the Empire and Europe likewise. Astronomy, algebra, physics, mathematics, geography, zoology, botany, medicine, chemistry as well as social sciences were practiced, developed, innovated and passed on carefully. Literacy and numeracy were never as high as in Muslim Spain. It needs to be re-emphasised that slavery was abolished during the first few centuries and not until much later it was reintroduced, unfortunately, due to deviation, as the Koran encourages the freeing of slaves.

The lengthy Muslim rule over Iberia, to its disadvantage, enabled travellers from all parts of Europe to access higher education, strengthened the European fundament and enabled not only the Spanish and Portuguese Empires, but also other European superpowers as well as English universities, European imperial seatravel. Gallilei's, Kepler's, Kopernikus', Newton's, Leibniz's, Descartes', Bacon's, Einstein's and Heisenberg's theories would not be possible at all without Muslim Spanish translations of Arabic books into Latin. These were not a mere copy of ancient manuscripts from China, India, Persia, Egypt, Greece and Rome, but in essence an improved and entirely new, more modern and practicable, experimental approach to science including 60-70 entirely novel ideas! Ironically Christopher Columbus was at the forefront when Ferdinand and Isabella conquered back the last Muslim stronghold of Granada at the end of the 15th century. There he snatched the Muslim sea captains as slaves who would show him the way to the New World. Word of their ability had naturally spread across Europe during the seven centuries before and reached Florence, Venice, Rome, Pisa as well as Byzantine. Even city-walls far North (Vilnus, Estonia), fortifications (Luxembourg, etc.) and churches (Chartres) were built by Muslim architects taken as slaves from Spain. The flame of culture and the spirit of civilisation were passed on to Europe in Muslim Spain.

Naturally the arts too were in the foreground of Spanish Muslim rule. Mosaic patterns as never seen before in history, the most complex geometric forms, fractals, honeycomb-patterns, three-dimensional patterns that entirely dazzle the senses evolved, arithmetic fractals in patterns and architectural wonders of handicraft exceeded one another as well as material sciences in the healthy competitive mode that the cities' guilds set up and which they showed off in annual competitions and fares, trade shows and merchant caravans that spanned the land from North to South. Trade shows and annual festivals, carnivals and markets were introduces in regular intervals and this tradition spread across Europe. Enlightenment lasted as long as there was relative peace and calm and the eppicle of this civilisation is until today manifested in the only surviving building of the 7 wonders of the world, the Alhambra in Granada, the Qilat Al-falama (red castle, flamed-brick), whose Hispanic name was derived from Al-falama and Alhamdulillah (Praise be to Allah). It is until today the most frequented place and tourism hotspot in modern Spain.

In any case, for many centuries the land was governed by people who longed for justice and cooperated with one another for at least 100 years until Franks from the North, Goths from the North-West and Abbassid delegations from the East and South started to invade.

Egilon was granted governorship of Reccopolis upon conversion to Islam. Al-Lakhmi was offered Toledo (Tulaytulah) and took over as Amir of Al-Afrique and the Maghreb. Tariq resided in Granada after returning from battle in Asturias and his sons from a local wife later took Seville. Bilal stayed in Seville until his return to Hammamet and Kairouan and then went to Mali leaving his sons behind. Bilal's sons with local wives took Ollisius (Isbunah, *Arabic*, Lisbon) and Porto/Braga. Alfred took charge of Vallada. Saragossa was given to Al-Ghanie. Barcelona to Asim, son of Egilon. Valladolid to Wittiza's first son. Reccopolis to Egilon's and Wittiza's second sons.

Julian Urban died soon afterwards of cancer as he coughed blood constantly and shortly before his death, at his bed in Toledo before the congregation of monks and in front of Charles he called for Tariq and Bilal and in presence of the clergy and the Muslim nobility he confessed:

"There is no God apart from Allah and Mohammed is Messenger of Allah", these were his last words and that was his last breath. Muslims supported the reconstruction of monasteries, churches and synagogues, much of the clergy converted to Islam; Charles headed the churches of Hispania and maintained a controversial stance towards the Muslims and a strong bond with Rome.

They all decided to leave Asturias to Pelayo's commanders as long as they paid the substitute-tax, which was equal to the compulsive charity of the Muslims. The Al-Quti noble clan (the Goths) ruled much of the North as long as Hispania was under Ummayad rule. Cordoba (Qartubah) was taken by Tariq's sons with Alwalid's sister Leila and later, around 755 A.D. by Abd ar-Rahman I, Alwalid's brother and Hisham's grandson, who established a Sultanate and later on his offspring a Caliphate there with the help and support of Tariq's sons and grandsons, who still held the friendship between their great-uncle Alwalid and their father and grandfather Tariq in honour.

Tariq built major fortifications at Gibraltar (see cover photo), Isbiliyah (Seville), Vallada (Valencia) and repaired numerous old Roman castles at Tulaytulah (Toledo), Qartubah (Cordoba) and Sarakusta (Aaragon, Saragossa) before he left Iberia in 730 AD with his wives and side by side with Bilal and his wives and was martyred around 750 AD in Damascus while defending the Umayyad palace from Abbasid attacks (read the second book of the Andalusian Quintology, Cordoba, the Rise of Magnificence). They both left behind their sons and daughters to rule the land and would return regularly to Iberia and meet in Mecca.

Henceforth the Muwwalad or Mulati , who were the mixed descendents of Muslims and locals became the ruling class of the country. In later centuries some Arab descendents would claim superiority over them, cause discord, revolts and civil war in this manner. And inevitably also the attacks from all sides left this new Empire crumbling steadily over the centuries, gradually, but very slowly and reluctantly. Let us not forget that ancient Rome lasted a maximum of 5 centuries and the modern day European Empires, and they are still Empires, nothing different or better than that, have only lasted a maximum of 4 centuries so far, the USA only 2!

Moorish Iberia lasted for 7 centuries and side by side with the Abbasid Baghdad, Cordoba was to be the competing centre of the Muslim world until the 14th century. As already mentioned, Granada fell in the 15th century when Muslims were enslaved by Conquistadors and forced to serve as architects, scientists and captains to the imperial fleets and even teachers, much similar to the Greeks around 300-200 B.C., who were enslaved by the Romans at that time. The last outpost of Muslim civilisation in Iberia was a small cave on Majorca, where Muslims dwelt in hiding until the 16th century.

When Tariq returned to Kairouan at the Sultan's summer palace in 740 A.D. after nearly 30 years of establishing reign in Spain with Bilal, the Shiite revolts were omnipresent. Bilal and Tariq parted ways there, Bilal joined a caravan to Mali and brought Islam to his home country, founded a new dynasty from which later Manka Musa the Mighty would spring off, the Great explorer of the Americas who sent a thousand ships across the Atlantic into the Amazon. Europeans such as Columbus were to follow his footsteps, but of course never admit that it was Black Muslims who took them to the Americas first. A movement among Muslims in North America today represents this fact stating that the first rulers of the Americas were a mixed Muslim tribe of Native Americans and Black Africans and that the USA is built on the fundament of that civilisation.

Tariq, as already mentioned, went back to Damascus and grew old happily in Damascus where he died in 750 A.D., just at the beginning of the Shiite revolt while fighting the mob. He instructed the Umayyads to follow a path West in case of emergency and left his outposts at Alexandria, Tripoli and Kairouan near Tunis, the former Carthage, and Ceuta. This was to the convenience of Abd ar-Rahman I (read the second book if the Andalusian Quintology, Cordoba, the Rise of Magnificence), who subsequently fled under cover through the Empire that was under the command of the Abbasids by then, who were hunting him everywhere, before he crossed to Iberia escorted by Tariq's sons in an epic journey of many years that later on inspired the stories of 1001 nights like Aladdin and Sindbad.

It took the life of many martyrs over many centuries to establish and uphold the relative peace and prosperity that Iberia enjoyed during the Muslim rule. Many say today that Islam was spread by the sword. They fail to consider that Muslims came to save the native populations from suppressive ruling and violent exploitation following the invitation of the clergy, bringing justice and freedom. This story was an attempt to project a balanced view from a Muslim perspective.

Europe and America play the role of colonial judges and a world-police today trying to implement their view of peace and justice on the world with far more massive weapons in their armoury than the Muslims of Iberia ever had. One should not forget that the 1st and 2nd World Wars in the last century cost around 200 Million innocent lives or maybe more, a huge sacrifice in order to attain a state of relative peace and a balanced Status Quo in the Western World.

Islam is still omnipresent in Western and Eastern libraries to be learnt as the last message from the Creator to His created and ready to be grasped by any individual in person, although collectively Muslims today are a mere shadow of their past.

One shall not dwell in the past, but one shall learn from it.

A teaching is a scripture and not the people who practice it.

Reform means to build something up again and not to change it.

"Indeed I've sent a source of endless supply,
So give to your Lord in sacrifice.
In deed who hates you is torn (from paradise)."
Surah 108 (Endless Supply)

Prologue

The Four Empires:

Between 632 and 700AD[4] (11-81 AH[5]), within 70 years after the death of the Prophet Mohammed (peace be upon Him, pbuh) Islam spreads fast. Traders carry it via the silk-routes, the Sahara and the Indian Ocean out of the desert of Arabia to Morocco in the West and Indonesia in the East. In the North they reach as far as Tartarstan and the Baltic. In the South to Mozambique and Tanzania. Islam rules Arabia, Egypt, North-West Africa, Persia and much of Asia. Under the Umayyad Caliphate (see table below) it is the super-power number one of the early Middle Ages and it is growing and spreading fast, even reaching China.

Rome in the meantime is crushed between the Mongols from the East and the Gothic occupation from the North while Byzantine[6] lies in ruins. After the death of its Emperor Justinian, Constantinople[7] it to compromise with the Vikings and appoints them as its guards to roam the Mediterranean and inflict damage on any potential invaders with Greek fire. During this epoch in the 6th century Europe has been crippled by a huge plague that has decimated its population in half. It is called

---

[4]   Annum Deum, year of the Lord (Jesus Christ) by the Gregorian calendar introduced in the 10th century.

[5]   Annum Hijrah, year of the Hijrah (migration of Mohammed, pbuh, from Mecca to Medina).

[6]   Eastern Rome, ruling over the Balkans, Eastern Europe and Turkey.

[7]   Capital of Byzantine, what is today Istanbul.

the Plague of Justinian and his dynasty ends followed by the Heraclian dynasty.

Heraclius, the next Emperor of Byzantine, whose dynasty ends with the beginning of the Conquest of Iberia, has reluctantly rejected the Prophet Mohammed (pbuh) due to pressure from his congregation and thereupon a possible comet shower and perhaps a synchronously occurring large volcanic eruption have both devastated Europe. These have darkened the skies for decades and lead to failed crops over many generations** (see excerpt from a website at the end of this prologue on the "Dark Ages"). This is literally a dark period and it has gone down in history as the Dark Ages. The Goths, Vandals from the North, have taken over much of what was once the mighty Roman Empire.

Other Empires are not in much better shape. The once mighty Egypt, Persia and Abyssinia are long gone and now mainly Islamic. India and China are too distant and engulfed in their own conflicts. Ancient Greco-Roman and Babylonian culture has been inherited and assimilated by the Muslims, who conquered the library of Alexandria and in this way saved it from Constantinople that declared Greek philosophy other than perhaps Plato's as heresy while burning the scrolls of Aristotle and Socrates that were eagerly adapted by Muslim scholars under the attribute of Islam. In Christianity only Plato's philosophy survived as the favourite of the church. In the meantime Roman infrastructure throughout Europe is crumbling under the rule of the Goths.

By contrast, at that time at least, the strength of Islam consists of its multi-tribalism and its embracing of the strengths of the cultures it meets. Hence there is an eager exchange of goods and know-how as well as brides and soldiers in Mecca, where all the tribes meet regularly. The Chinese coming along the silk-route bring along gunpowder and telescopes as well as compasses and paper with maps, Indians bring algebra, astronomy and medicine, Africans alloys, gold, diamonds and minerals, Hussars of the North their horses, military tactics and weapons. There is an annual festival after the Hajj-pilgrimage to celebrate this mixture and richness with exhibitions, markets and theatres.

Arianic[8] Christian Visigoths[9] from Germany rule Iberia, much of France, Italy and the Balkans all the way back into Germany after Rome has fallen victim to the Great Plague named after Justinian I, the Emperor of Byzantine, who has managed to briefly unite Rome and Byzantine during the early 5th century. Afterwards Rome has succumbed to Alaric, the Gothic King.

A Frank called Clovis, the founder of the Merovingian dynasty has united the Franks and lain the foundations for the Carolingian dynasty from which Charles Mattel and Charlemagne would spring off. He has managed to save Rome by building a union between it and the Northern-Gaulle Empires, but Visigoths have managed to hammer a gap between Rome and its Western provinces.

As the strongest of the big tribes that roam Europe at that time, such as Vikings, Bretons, Saxons, Gaulles or Franks, the Vandals, also known as Goths, are contrary to Catholic Christianity as they do not believe in the Trinity but follow Arius of Alexandria's teaching of one God and Christ being a divine part of that God rather than a Trinitarian element. This interpretation might in itself be a convenient misconception among scholars and the original teachings of Arius' might have been entirely different, pointing to one God and Jesus (pbuh) being his messenger.

---

8   Following non-Trinitarian teachings of Arius of Alexandria, contrary to Catholicism.

9   Western Goths, as in opposed to Ostrigoths, Eastern Goths.

Why the conquest?:

Therefore the Muslims, who have a similar concept of God and Jesus (pbuh), are initially neutral in the conflict between that Vatican and the Goths, especially as the Goths rule much of Italy, Germany, Spain and France already. The Umayyads, the ruling Muslim emperors, have a truce with the Goths. But Arianism is dwindling and many Goths after converting to Catholicism, leave Christianity altogether.

The neutral stance of the Muslims is disturbed when the trade routes of the Mediterranean and Eastern-Atlantic are intercepted by Visigoth pirates at Gibraltar, who make no difference between Byzantine and Arab merchant ships. The King of the Visigoths, Roderick, whose father Ergica and grandfather Wamba, descendents of Alaric, conqueror of Rome, have been close friends of the Sultan Abdulmalik, refuses to act against the piracy of his men despite of the request by the current Muslim Sultan of Damascus, Alwalid, son of Abdulmalik. Roderick is too busy seizing power from his half-brother Wittiza, who flees North after sending a letter to the Sultan with a call for help for his people.

Hence the truce is broken and when the Muslims receive several letters from Catholics as well about the cruel rule of the Visigoths under Roderick over the Catholic Gaulle tribes of Iberia, which is more reminiscent of their potential pagan-Germanic roots rather than their Christian faith, the Muslims are urged to act. This urge is underlined by a delegation from the monasteries of Iberia to Alwalid, the Sultan of Damascus. The delegation is lead by Charles of Montril, who quickly returns to his year-long fight with the Goths and Julian-Urban of Ceuta, Catholic Consul of a province of Hispanic Goths at the tip of North-Africa. They have hit on deaf ears in Rome and Byzantine since the pope himself is too busy coping with the humiliating Gothic rule and Constantine is not only crippled by Hun attacks but also in subtle confrontation with Rome and the Goths.

What kind of Conquest and by whom?

The subsequent Muslim Conquest of Iberia weakens the Visigoths so much that Central-Gaulle (today's France) is taken over by the Franks, a Northern Gaulle Catholic tribe from what is today Belgium. A complex relationship between Catholics on one side and Arianic Gothic tribes that are partly being assimilated into Catholicism on the other with Muslims taking over rapidly is the climate that Europe and the Mediterranean are engulfed in during the 7th century until Tariq ibn Ziyad crosses Gibraltar and makes an end to Visigoth rule in 711 AD (91 AH). Tariq is a delegate vice-General from Alwalid, son of Abdulmalik under the initial command of General ibn-Musa, Consul of North-Africa and the Maghreb.

The tumultuous story of the origins of the Umayyad Caliphate is a very complex one as well. Abdulmalik ibn Marwan comes from the Umayyad dynasty that stems from Mecca. His father's second cousin, Muawiyah I, Abu Sufiyan's second son, nephew of Usman the second Caliph, is the great Sultan who has conquered and established Damascus, the ancient Phoenician homeland, in 650 AD as the capital of the Muslim Empire. Abdulmalik is a wise and gentle man. Although he stems from a fraction of the Koreshite clan that has been in rivalry with Prophet's family, he lives by the tradition of the Prophet Mohammed (pbuh). He puts mercy above punishment and is among the last few rulers who follow the unadulterated habits of the Last Prophet (pbuh) of Allah to mankind. This is in line with the well-known promise of the Prophet (pbuh) that the Best of People would be his generation and the subsequent 3 generations, after which they would gradually decline. Abdulmalik is the 2nd and Alwalid is the 3rd generation after the Prophet (pbuh).

Abdulmalik builds a gigantic palace, the size of a city and frees thousands of slaves, brought to Cairo and Damascus from the North, East, West and South. Inside the palace they live side by side with his own families (from his 4 wives) as equals. He is respected by the tribes of the distant regions, Azerbaijan to Sindh to Tartarstan, Mali to Carthage to Guinea, but his closest cousins, the Abbasid Arabs, plan and plot against him under pressure of the Shiite. His son Alwalid continues his tradition alongside with his accomplices, the sons of the families from abroad, who are much more loyal to him than his own cousins. Especially Tariq,

219

a Berber, and Bilal, a Malian, who have both been brought up in the palace.

In this way Islam spreads to those distant regions very quickly, propelled by the Umayyad Sultans' adaptation of refugees from distant places and the subsequent envy of the Shiite, who support the Abbasid cousins of the Umayyads. Shiites believe in the direct lineage of the Prophet Mohammed (pbuh). While the Umayyads are ruling, the Abbasids are more directly descended from the Prophet (pbuh). Later on after coming to power the Abbasids abandon the Shiite. In any case Alwalid manages to conquer much of India, Persia, Azerbaijan and, with Tariq's support, also Spain before he dies around 714-715 AD.

The Umayyads

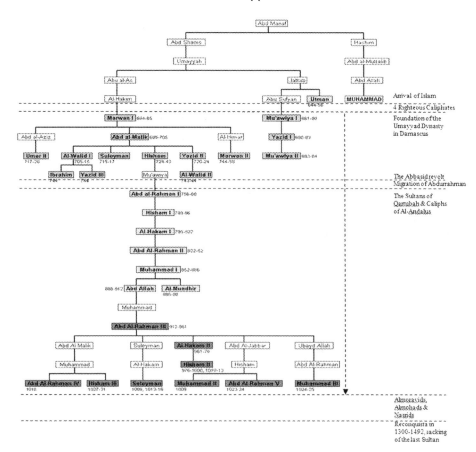

Who are the conquered?

Let us take a closer look at the Goths again. Since the Gothic occupation of Rome under Alaric in the early 5th century AD, the Goths have been divided into Western and Eastern-Gothic tribes, the Visigoths and the Ostrigoths, the former being occupants of Gaulle and Iberia, the latter Byzantine and Rome. Both tribes still have their common link in Germany.

Visigoth history is somewhat shrouded in mystery. Very little is known apart from the names of the Kings and vice-Kings and their partly hereditary and partly electoral crowning, the steady adaptation of Roman laws and even monastic Catholicism in written form known as the "Gothorum Legum Hispaniae" (the only copy available is a latter version published in 1600 called the "Liber Judiciorum"), the constant wrangling for power in the 5 or so provinces of former Romanic Hispania and their complete assimilation by mixture into Romanic, Gaulle, Greek and other tribes as well as eventually the Moors, a potpourri which today's Spanish people consist of.

Wamba and Ergica are the main Visigoth figures of the 7th century AD whose legends are manifold such as their strict ruling, declaration of heredities, alternate persecution and appeasing of Jews, governance by monasteries and even Roman assistance, etc. Ergica's sons Wittiza and Roderick however are clearly engulfed in an intense power-struggle, the former having to give up his land and the latter somewhat violently either loved or hated by the people, conquering the land very quickly and vehemently, only to lose it to the Muslims very soon. There is a vacuum that is filled by the Moors and it is well-known from even monastery accounts of that time that they are welcomed with open arms in most of the city-states of Iberia. They acted as liberators from a long grip of repression and exploitation by the Goths under Roderick either by strict legislation and amendment, decree of addendum or even breach of that in its root Romanic law, which they have developed out of adaptation to the Roman past of Iberia. Tulaytulah (Toldeo, *Spanish*, Toletum, *Latin*) has also seen a Jewish revolt against Roderick crushed brutally by the Gothic gentry.

All the while the threat of Roderick crossing the sea and conquering North-Africa is very real, since he is very conveniently not acting against his own pirating hoards, to make room on the waters for his potential crossing and the Vandals already occupy the stronghold of Ceuta in North-Africa. But Tariq and Bilal manage to unite with Julian of Ceuta, the Catholic-clerical consul and cross the Straight before Roderick, as Roderick is still busy subjugating Southern-Spain, where he has seized power from his half-brother Wittiza.

What kind of change?

The Iberian Visigoths are effectively eradicated by the Muslims and the Franks. Catholicism and Islam are the only dominant religions left in Gaulle after 711 AD. 50-70 years later Franks and Muslims clash at Tours/Poitiers in France but not until Muslim rule has been firmly established for the coming 7 centuries in Iberian Europe. This is the rule of justice that forms science, medicine, technology, legislation, arts, architecture, literature and the society of modern Europe more than any other culture ever has, casting a bright light on the Dark Ages, teaching Charlemagne his wisdom, inspiring the founding fathers of Oxford and Cambridge the likes of Adelard of Bath[10], who studied in Tulaytulah (later Toledo, *Spanish*, previously Toletum, *Latin*) under Muslim teachers before returning to England and bringing together a clerical team to pioneer the English centres of learning. Similar learners come from all over Europe. The Moors, as they go down in history, eradicate the gruesome shadow of Rome and Greece by extracting the essence of these ancient civilisations. They wipe out the deviations of the late Roman emperors from the truth and justice which left the Dark Ages behind it and trigger a European Renaissance, the Reformation, Age of Enlightenment and even the Age of Reason, whose fundaments are rooted in Muslim theology, philosophy and science.

The term "the Dark Ages" is actually rooted in a natural disaster. Europe has literally been enveloped in a cloud of ash** between 650-711AD after an overwhelming comet-strike followed by a volcanic eruption** in Germany, the legend of the golden light-horse that wakes the mighty howling Beast which then blows out (or swallows) the sun. Generations of Europeans have not seen the stars or the moon, the sun only as a silver lining in the deep-grey cloudy skies, crops have failed**, plague has decimated the population in half** and wildlife and cattle have given room to scavenging lions, hyenas and coyotes, who are native to Europe at that time side by side with foxes, wolves, bears and wild boar, feeding on human corpses like the knowingly cannibalistic Vandals. Rome,

---

10 "Adelard of Bath: an English scientist and Arabist of the early twelfth century", By Charles Burnett, published by Warburg Institute, University of London, 1987 Original from the University of California, SBN 0854810706, 9780854810703

Byzantine and the Goths have a hard time holding their populations back from an exodus to Africa and Arabia.

The dark cloud of smoke vanishes precisely at the moment when the Muslims cross the Mediterranean**, defeat the Vandals and bring with them Light and Enlightenment, banishing the Dark Ages far away. They establish a thorough infrastructure based on the old Roman tracts, irrigation based on the ruins of the Roman aqueducts, medicine progressed from Greek, Chinese and Indian tradition, science and innovative technologies such as windmills, irrigation channels and water lifts, Astronomical observatories as well as centres of multi-disciplinary learning across the Iberian Peninsula.

This is the Conquest of Iberia.

The Umayyad Empire in 711 AD

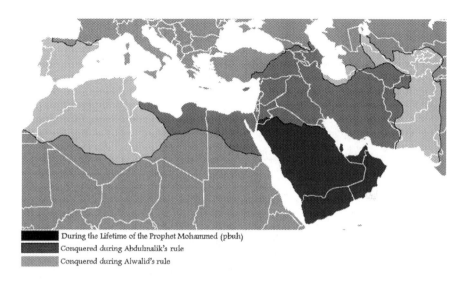

During the Lifetime of the Prophet Mohammed (pbuh)
Conquered during Abdulmalik's rule
Conquered during Alwalid's rule

**>>>(*Citations here are from a BBC magazine article, 8 September 2000, by Jonathan Amos citing Prof. Mike Baillie, paelaeo-ecologist, Queen's University, Belfast.*)

"*. . . Perhaps, comet fragments flew into the atmosphere, a kind of nuclear winter occurred, resulting in crop failures, famine, even plague, as peoples were weakened.*

David Keys, Catastrophe. Arrow, 2000. ISBN: 0099409844. Keys outlines a scenario where from 536AD, a volcanic eruption meant the Earth was enveloped by a cloak of lethal dust which changed the climate for decades. The sun's rays grew dim and total darkness reigned for days, it was a catastrophe of unparalleled proportions. Tens of millions of people died around the globe as a bubonic plague epidemic broke out. There followed waves of migration and the military, political and religious changes which the disaster set in motion re-ordered societies throughout the world, the collapse of the Roman Empire, the invasion of the barbarian hordes and the rise of xxx Islam. "It was the nearest humankind has ever come to Doomsday and it marked the real beginning of the modern era . . . Keys attempts to set the record straight by placing this pivotal point in world history as the mid-6th-century Dark Ages and shows how our fragile civilisation almost ended." And if Keys is right, it was the series of disasters he outlines which also gave rise to the concept of "Europe" as possessing a way of life and a religion—Christianity—which distinguished it from Africa and the Near and Middle East, in fact from the rest of the world.

By about 700AD, plagues had halved the European population . . . we can find that from about 400 A.D. to around 900, the climate became much colder. The winters of 763-764 and 859-860 were extraordinarily cold, with the ice so thick in the Adriatic near Venice that it could hold up heavily-loaded wagons. There was ice even on the Nile in Egypt . . ."

-http://www.danbyrnes.com.au/lostworlds/features/vikings1.htm

(Also look in, "Catastrophe: An Investigation into the Origin" by David Keys and "Climate, History and the Modern World" by Hubert H. Lamb)

The Andalusian Quintology:

1. Gibraltar, the Conquest of Iberia
2. Cordoba, the Rise of Magnificence
3. Alhambra, the Ruling of Reason
4. Reconquista, the Downfall of Glory
5. Inquisition, the Persecution of Truth

Other Books by Shariq Ali Khan:

1. The Koran, Clear, Concise, Contemporary, Every Line Poetry.
   - A new, precise translation of the Holy Koran fully in rhyme-form.
2. Koran in the Age of Science, Islam in the Age of Terror-
   - A detailed treaty of the scientific signs of the Koran.
3. Islam and Science for Starters. - A small compilation in 7 books.
4. Gog and Magog (Sci-Fi).
5. Adam, the Cycle (Sci-Fi).
6. Poetry Emotion.—A collection of Lyrics, 1989 to 2009.
7. Karachi, London, Frankfurt.—A Biography.

About the Author

Shariq Ali Khan has been lecturing Science and Religion and reading History for over 15 years. He holds an MSc., speaks 5 languages, 3 European ones, and has lived in Europe since his early childhood. With a passion for Science, History and comparative Theology he is now working on many books including the Andalusian Quintology, which this book is a part of. Currently he lives in Central London, has 2 children and works for an international organisation . . . He enjoys travelling, reading and sports.